FALSE REPORT

Further Titles by Veronica Heley from Severn House

The Ellie Quicke Mysteries

MURDER AT THE ALTAR
MURDER BY SUICIDE
MURDER OF INNOCENCE
MURDER BY ACCIDENT
MURDER IN THE GARDEN
MURDER BY COMMITTEE
MURDER BY BICYCLE
MURDER OF IDENTITY
MURDER IN HOUSE
MURDER BY MISTAKE
MURDER MY NEIGHBOUR

The Bea Abbot Agency mystery series

FALSE CHARITY
FALSE PICTURE
FALSE STEP
FALSE PRETENCES
FALSE MONEY
FALSE REPORT

FALSE REPORT

An Abbot Agency Mystery

Veronica Heley

This first world edition published 2012
in Great Britain and in the USA by
SEVERN HOUSE PUBLISHERS LTD of
9–15 High Street, Sutton, Surrey, England, SM1 1DF.
Trade paperback edition first published
in Great Britain and the USA 2012 by
SEVERN HOUSE PUBLISHERS LTD.

British Library Cataloguing in Publication Data

Heley, Veronica.
 False report. – (An Abbot Agency mystery)
 1. Abbot, Bea (Fictitious character)–Fiction. 2. Widows–
 England–London–Fiction. 3. Women private
 investigators–England–London–Fiction. 4. Detective
 and mystery stories.
 I. Title II. Series
 823.9´14-dc22

ISBN-13: 978-0-7278-8117-5 (cased)
ISBN-13: 978-1-84751-408-0 (trade paper)

Typeset by Palimpsest Book Production Ltd.,
Falkirk, Stirlingshire, Scotland.
Printed and bound in Great Britain by
MPG Books Ltd., Bodmin, Cornwall.

ONE

As a successful business woman and owner of a thriving domestic agency, Bea Abbot knew perfectly well that there was no such thing as a free lunch . . . or tea. And if she'd realized the offered treat was a bribe to get her to investigate a murder, she would have said, 'Certainly not!'

Wednesday, late evening

'Nance, where are you?' A man's voice, hoarse.

'At the conference. Where did you think I was?' A woman's voice, middle-aged, educated. Bored.

'Josie's dead! Flat on her face. In the bushes behind the church.'

'What? No, she can't be. What do you mean, dead?'

'Strangled, I think.'

'But . . . who would . . .? Are you sure? I know she was upset but—'

'That phone call from him spooked her out of her mind.'

'You shouldn't have let her out of your sight.'

'I couldn't lock her up, could I? If you'd been around—'

'You knew I was going to be away this week. Surely, between you and Jonno, you could have taken better care of her. How did he get hold of her mobile number, anyway?'

'She gave it to him while she was baiting the trap. Yes, I know she should have thrown the mobile away after we'd got him on film, but she went on using it. This evening he said he knew where she lived, which he couldn't know, but she believed him. She was wild with fright, wanted to go back home for a while. I told her punters never carry through their threats, but she wouldn't listen. She said if I didn't give her the cash for a ticket, she'd get it from someone who would. Then she ran out on to the street, right through the traffic, on the phone to the music man—'

'The music man? But he's history! He wouldn't help her, would he?'

'So I ran after her. She went down the alley and I could hear her begging him to meet her. Then a crowd of drunken yobs came storming through, and I lost her. I looked everywhere, into all the pubs, round to the little man's flat. There were no lights on there, though it was getting dark. I rang his doorbell, no reply. Came back through the alley, and saw something . . . You know where the path widens out at the back of the church, and there's seats and a bed of flowers under the wall? I got in among the bushes and made sure. She's dead, all right.'

A heavy silence.

'Look, no one saw me, and I kept my head. I couldn't see her mobile, but I took that purse she hangs round her neck and her watch, so it'll look like a robbery gone wrong. I don't think she had any other ID on her, had she? No one can connect her with us.'

'Let me think.'

'What do you want me to do? Someone's going to spot her soon, there's always people walking their dogs through the alley.'

'Well, if the little music man killed her, why don't we point the police in his direction? Use a public phone; say you're Joe Public, reporting a body. Tell them you overheard a young girl pleading with a man on her mobile, and later saw her body in the bushes. Give the police his name. That should do it.'

Thursday afternoon

Bea knew there was no such thing as a free lunch, but an invitation for tea at the Ritz was different, wasn't it? Even if it was at the last minute? Apart from anything else, it meant getting away from the problems at the office for a while.

The Abbot Agency had a reputation for providing reliable domestic staff, but – although she couldn't quite put her finger on it – Bea felt something was amiss. True, she'd recently taken time off for a long overdue holiday, but . . . No, she couldn't really say that the agency had done badly in her absence because business was booming. Turnover was increasing. Every month there was more money in the bank, and almost every month they were having to take on extra staff.

What could possibly be wrong with that? Well, nothing. Except that since her return Bea had had an uneasy feeling that she'd lost control of the business which had provided her with enjoyable work and an income since her husband died.

She laughed at herself, but the suspicion persisted. It was as if she were no longer in the driving seat of the car, but had been relegated to passenger status – back seat passenger status, at that.

Bea Abbot was not the sort of person who blamed other people for her mistakes. Somewhere along the line she was beginning to think that she'd made a bad decision at the agency . . . but exactly what had it been?

She argued with herself. Was she uneasy because all her hand-picked, tried and trusted staff, recruited over many years, had left for one reason or another? Well, but staff did move on, get better offers, or decide to retire.

The old-timers had been replaced by a competent team who were making the place buzz. Bea might not feel so comfortable, with the newcomers, but she couldn't fault their performance.

So why this dragging suspicion that all was not as it should be? Everything at the agency was operating like clockwork, tick tock, ting! as yet another payment fell into the bank account.

She wondered if she were getting old and losing her grip. Perhaps it was the very efficiency of the new staff that made her feel redundant?

Or perhaps her important son Max – who was a member of parliament and liked to tell people what to do – was right in saying that she was not up to running the agency any longer and should retire. He'd never thought she would be capable of running the business in the first place, so over the years she'd taken some pleasure in proving him wrong . . . until now.

Had the time really come when she should sell the agency and her beautiful house in a prestigious part of London and retire to a small bungalow on the South Coast? Was she to end her life playing bridge with other senior citizens . . . even though she didn't know how to play? The prospect appalled.

She needed advice. So when she received an invitation to tea from an old friend, she jumped at the chance – and only later realized she'd made another bad decision, because there really was no such thing as a free meal, was there?

In honour of the occasion Bea took the afternoon off work, brushed her ash-blonde hair so that her fringe lay slantwise across her forehead, renewed her make-up – paying careful attention to what her dear husband had always called her 'eagle's eyes' – and was ready on time.

She had decided that tea at the Ritz justified the wearing of a new outfit and picked out one which her clients at the domestic agency might have considered unsuitable for a business woman. Bea was well aware that a sleeveless silk sheath in crème caramel was a trifle daring for a woman in her early sixties, but she believed she was tall and slim enough to do it justice. And, for those who wondered whether an older woman's upper arms might still be her best feature, there was a matching gauzy jacket edged with satin ribbon of the same shade as the dress. She'd selected a shift dress not only because it echoed the colour of her ash-blonde hair, but also because it was loose enough round the waist to accommodate an intake of the delicious sandwiches, pastries and cakes which would be on offer at the Ritz.

She'd been acquainted with CJ for some time, as he was something of a guru to her adopted son, Oliver. CJ was a mandarin used by the police as an expert in various matters too complicated, he said, for the ordinary man or woman to understand. But no one talked of such things while having tea at the Ritz, did they?

Perhaps, then, she could be forgiven for not suspecting an ulterior motive when CJ called for her in a taxi and whisked her off to the Ritz; that prestigious, if slightly stolid hotel beside Green Park. The trees were looking lushly green after a recent shower, the clients in the world-famous hotel were dressed in their garden party best, the decor was well over the top with gilding on all the baroque twirls, there were stands of orchids everywhere, the waiters wore tail coats, and a pianist tinkled the ivories at the grand piano.

Bea relaxed. What a treat! Just fancy, there was a whole menu devoted to the different types of tea available: six different kinds of sandwiches; two of cake; and three different pastries. And would madam like a refill of tea, or perhaps another sandwich or two? Is there anything else madam fancies?

Bea did full justice to the tea, telling herself that she wouldn't need to think about getting any supper that evening. When she couldn't eat any more, she leaned back in her chair and gave a deep sigh of appreciation. What bliss!

'That was just wonderful, CJ. I'd been letting things get on top of me at the agency, and now I feel insulated against whatever happens next. Is *insulated* the right word? Possibly not. But you get the idea.'

'Ah. Hmm.' He steepled his long fingers and gave her a sideways glance.

She felt the first intimation of disquiet. She wanted to say, 'Whatever it is, I don't want to know.' Instead she frowned, remembering that he'd helped her clear up one or two nasty criminal cases in which her agency had become involved over the past few years. She owed it to him at least to listen to what he had to say. She supposed. 'More tea?'

He shook his head. She poured herself another half cup. The temperature had dropped around him, and it was nothing to do with the air conditioning, which was perfect.

He said, 'I don't suppose you ever doubt yourself, do you, Bea?'

'As a matter of fact, I was going to ask you about—'

'I need a second opinion. My ability to judge my fellow men has been called into question. I was visited this morning by the police, asking if I'd spent last evening with a man called Jeremy Waite. Which I had. The detective inspector pressed me for time and place. He tried to make me admit that Jeremy might have been out of my sight for ten minutes here or there. I said he hadn't.' CJ stopped, looked vaguely around, picked up his empty cup to sip from it, put it down.

'The inspector was not amused to find that I could give Jeremy an alibi, since he was suspected of killing an under-age girl with whom he'd been having sexual relations.'

Bea stared at CJ, hoping against hope that he wasn't going to involve her in another murder.

'The inspector believed I'd provided Jeremy with an alibi out of a misguided sense of friendship. I must admit I was shocked, but it didn't alter the fact that I'd been with the man the whole of the previous evening. And I said so. However, after the inspector had removed himself, I began to wonder if I had, in fact, been set up to provide Jeremy with an alibi, while he arranged for someone else to kill the girl.'

At this point the head waiter intervened with the bill. Around them tables were being cleared and relaid. The Ritz allowed you only so much time to have tea, and then shot you out so that they could prepare for the next sitting.

CJ laid his card on the bill. 'Have you seen the latest exhibition at the Royal Academy? It's only just down the road.'

'Not my scene,' said Bea. 'And—'

'A stroll around the pictures is just what we need after that tea, don't you think?' It wasn't a question.

'And even if I didn't, you intend to prolong this conversation?'

'Certainly,' he said, returning his card to his wallet. 'He blushed, you see.'

Bea frowned. What had that got to do with it? Part of her wanted to tell CJ to get lost – but the other half was telling her that another hour away from the agency might help to clear her mind and enable her to think constructively about the mess she'd got herself into there. If, indeed, there was any such mess, which was a moot point.

She got to her feet, wondering if wearing a new pair of high-heeled shoes had been a good idea if they were going to walk the streets. They seemed comfortable enough so far. She was almost as tall as CJ when he stepped to her side. A grey man, well brushed, well tailored. A man who could melt into the background or take control of a gathering at will.

He held the door open for her. 'Do you ever go to concerts at our parish church in Kensington?'

She gave him an old-fashioned look. 'This is relevant?'

He nodded.

She shrugged. 'Occasionally, when my dear husband was alive.'

'I hadn't intended to go last night, but there was nothing on the telly, it was a fine evening, and I thought I might stroll round to the church, see if there was anything on . . . which there was. A man was reading the poster outside. He moved away, hesitated, came back to read it again. I thought I recognized his back view from somewhere but couldn't place him. I followed him in, checking my watch, wondering how long the concert was likely to last because I hadn't eaten yet. It was half seven. I found a seat at the back, saw him some way in front of me. Saw one or two other people I knew by sight. Nodded, that sort of thing.'

He gave a little cough. 'I have made a study of physiognomy, as you might expect. In idle moments I often catch myself studying the man across from me in the tube, or restaurant. Is he a fool or a villain, a saint or a sinner? Does he belong in the dock, or on the judge's bench? This particular man was an oddity. I seemed to recall seeing him in an academic setting, something to do with music.'

CJ steered Bea across the road, as if she were incapable of judging for herself when the traffic lights had turned green. He raised his voice to be heard over the noise of traffic.

'A middle-aged woman whom I knew slightly – we're both members of the local History Society – came to sit next to me. She was excited because her daughter was playing second violin in the chamber group for the first time. All young players, you know. Some on the way up. The oboist was particularly good. I made a note of the name. Afterwards, my neighbour introduced me to her daughter. Nice girl. Needs to lose a few pounds, but pretty enough if you like that sort of thing. I said the usual.

'The man I'd noticed, but couldn't place, was hovering, waiting to speak to one of the cellists. I'd noticed he'd been watching her throughout. She, on the other hand, didn't seem keen to be spoken to.

'My neighbour's daughter sent him such a look. "How dare he!" she said. She told us – alleged – that he'd seduced an under-age girl, been thrown out of the house by his wife, sacked from his teaching job, and quite right, too!'

Bea shrugged. 'It happens.'

'Yes, of course. Some girls look eighteen at twelve. I remembered where I'd seen him before. My old college had held a fund-raising event for a new music laboratory and he'd been on the same table at dinner, keeping us all amused. Someone told me that though he was a music teacher at a school in Kensington, he was beginning to develop another career under a different name, writing music for films and television programmes. I had to leave early so we were not formally introduced.'

CJ steered Bea through the archway into the comparative quiet of the Royal Academy's courtyard. There were seats in the sun and also under an awning where cups of tea and coffee were being served. CJ ushered Bea to a pair of isolated chairs near the water feature. She noticed he'd chosen their seats well, because the burbling of the fountains made it unlikely anyone could overhear them.

'Shall we sit awhile?' Again, it was not a request.

They sat. Bea tilted her head back and closed her eyes as a

sign that she was not particularly interested in what he had to say. What was she going to do about the agency? And why hadn't she thought to bring her dark glasses with her?

He said, 'Have you noticed that even young girls fail to blush, nowadays? Is it a lost art, do you think? Older women rarely blush, but they're usually wearing so much make-up that I probably wouldn't notice if they did. As a woman, do you have an opinion on this?'

He was serious? Incredible.

She said, lightly, 'Modern society holds that there's nothing we can do that we need to be ashamed of, that every kind of behaviour is acceptable. I suppose I might blush from embarrassment if I'd made a really stupid remark and hurt someone's feelings.'

'Precisely my point. You might blush out of embarrassment but that's not the same thing as blushing for shame. My question was: did he blush from shame, or from embarrassment? I'd watched him psyche himself up to go to the concert. He sat by himself, talked to no one. He had gone there to watch the cellist perform. When she played a wrong note in her solo, he reddened out of embarrassment. He was concerned for her.

'Afterwards, he waited till she was free to speak to him. He congratulated her on her performance, and she rebuffed him. He overheard what my friend's daughter said. There was a general drawing back of skirts. And he blushed.

'He caught my eye. He recognized me and saw that I'd recognized him. There was no shame in his eyes. Defiance and embarrassment, yes. But no shame. At that moment I decided that he didn't belong in the dock, and that if he had done what they said, there must be extenuating circumstances. So, as we left the church together, I introduced myself and asked if he'd like to join me for a spot of supper. He agreed.'

'Even though he'd been accused of abusing an under-age girl?'

'In my time I've observed some young girls who were more predator than prey. I wondered who was the victim in this case. His name is Jeremy Waite, by the way. His wife is Eunice, twice married, a barrister who is so absorbed by her career that she's never had any time to be a housewife and has handed over the upbringing of her only child to paid help. Her daughter is the cellist Jeremy spoke to at the concert. No children by him.'

'Is she the girl he seduced?'

'That's why I need a second opinion . . . yours. I'd be surprised if he seduced anyone . . . but maybe I'm wrong. You see, we went to an Italian restaurant where the young and pretty waitress failed to stir his pulse, as did the young and pretty wine waiter. I was watching for a reaction from him to either, and there was none. We moved on to have coffee at my place, where he received a phone call from a girl – I could hear her high, clear voice – on his mobile. He told her that no, he was not going to meet her under any circumstances, and shut her off.

'He explained to me in what seemed genuine bemusement that a young girl he'd befriended had been causing him no end of trouble. He said that being accused of misconduct with an under-age pupil was one of the professional hazards of being a teacher but he'd never thought he'd be a victim. She'd lost him his job teaching, but fortunately he had plenty of other work on, and he wasn't going to let it get him down.'

'Didn't you say his wife had kicked him out because of his liaison with a girl?'

'From the little he said, I gather,' said CJ smoothly, 'that that might have been a relief to him, but he didn't comment, so I didn't enquire. I got out the brandy. A pleasant evening. Apparently the girl in question was killed soon after we went into the church for the concert.'

'And he wasn't out of your sight all evening?'

'He went to the loo upstairs at my place when it was time for him to go, just before midnight. I was going to ring for a cab for him. He said he'd walk, as it was a fine night, but as I was letting him out, a taxi drew up outside to let off a fare, and he took it on. He's renting a flat in one of the roads at the back of Church Street. It's small but convenient. Only, he admits he's not very domesticated. I told him you might be able to find him someone to come in several times a week to look after him.'

'What?' Bea gave him an old-fashioned look. 'Do I take it that you aren't sure he's as squeaky clean as you imagined, and that you want me to spy on him?'

CJ got to his feet with a smile for a man approaching them across the courtyard. 'Judge for yourself. Jeremy, this is my good friend Bea Abbot, who runs a domestic agency and may be able to help you out.'

TWO

Bea shot CJ a glance of pure cyanide as a small but well-made man, bearing a distinct likeness to a garden gnome, trotted over to them. He wasn't a dwarf, but he was vertically challenged. He must have been in his fifties, with a mop of greying hair which curled up into two 'horns' on top of his head, and a short, curly goatee that curved upwards, too. His eyes were a bright blue, and his cheeks shone as if they'd been polished.

Unlike a genuine garden gnome, he wasn't wearing a red jacket and green trousers, but Bea did note he was wearing odd socks and brown sandals. The rest of him was clad in a Canadian-style lumberjacket in some designer's fanciful idea of a tartan, over a white T-shirt and jeans. The jeans looked new; everything else looked well worn.

The gnome twinkled at her. 'My saviour, Mrs Abbot. Did my friend tell you I'm in need of rescuing, house-wise?' His nose twitched. 'Why aren't you eating? Do I smell good coffee and sandwiches? I'm afraid CJ hasn't been looking after you properly. Do let me treat you to something to eat. I haven't eaten all day; quite forgot, you know. Been taking pains, har har, as the king said about his visit to the dentist . . .'

Bea rolled her eyes at CJ, who hid a grin behind his hand as he backed away, explaining that he was late for another appointment.

The little man said, 'Come on inside, this way, are you a Friend of the RA? Very useful place for meetings, and the food is tasty. I sometimes come here when I'm working; when I remember, that is. I've often thought I ought to bring a doggy bag with me, in case there are any leftovers, but sadly there never are. Now what would you like, dear lady?'

Bea tried to take control of the situation. 'Frankly, Mr Waite, I've just been treated to a good tea and I'm not hungry.'

'What a pity.' He had the innocent look of a hungry child denied a treat.

'But I'd be happy to have another cup of tea while you eat, if we can do it straight away. I mustn't be too long, though.' Looking at her watch.

'Delightful,' he said, bouncing along at her side into the restaurant. The top of his head just about came up to her shoulder. 'Now, if you take a slice of that tart and some cheese and biscuits, I'll have the salmon en croute and finish up anything you can't eat, right?'

He laughed, and the sound was agreeable. 'I'm so pleased to meet you. My housekeeping skills are not – you know? We had a weekly order from Waitrose that I could dip into whenever I wished, and I'm hopeless with a computer, the last time I tried to order something it turned out I'd pressed the wrong button several times by mistake and we had a mountain of frozen peas delivered and they lasted for months. I desperately need someone who'll organize putting some decent frozen meals in the freezer for me every week. I never really bother about food when I'm working, but when I stop I feel ravenous and have to make up for lost time. And I'm not particularly good at keeping the bathroom clean. So, do you think you could help me?'

'I might, yes,' said Bea, amused.

He carried a loaded tray to the cashier, paid for his and her meals with a gold card, and ushered her to a table near the windows. 'Perhaps it ought to be a woman of a certain age, preferably married? What do you think? If she could also manage a few bits of admin for me, paying bills and so on, that would be wonderful but perhaps too much to ask for? CJ has told you about the little problem I've been having? Just a cup of tea for you? Is that all? Are you sure you can't manage some of that tart? It looks good.'

'CJ softened me up by treating me to tea at the Ritz.'

'Do they still have a pianist? The last time I went, I got the impression that the soft pedal had been wired down so that she didn't make too much noise.'

Bea spurted into laughter, and he smiled. He was not – as CJ had noted – agonizing over past sins of omission or commission. Rather against her better judgement, Bea found herself liking the little man. She found it difficult to imagine anyone less likely to start pawing young girls. He hadn't even looked at her legs, which were worth a look, though she said so herself. Neither had his eyes lingered on the cleavage to be glimpsed under her gauzy top. CJ had been right; this man was not particularly interested in sex.

'I need someone to come in perhaps twice a week to keep me straight. Can you arrange that? I'm currently in a furnished one-bedroom flat which is also my studio for the time being, though I'm looking for a place where I can have my grand piano and where it won't matter if I play music all hours of the day and night.'

'Two hours, for two mornings a week?'

'You would know best. Do I have to sign a contract or something?'

'I'll send you one, if you'll let me have your current address.'

He extracted a business card, crossed out one address and wrote in another. 'The mobile number is the same. I haven't been able to fix up a landline yet.'

'Lots of people don't bother with a landline, nowadays.' She gave him her card, too.

'I see you live very near my new place.' He smiled, relaxed. 'Thank you, Mrs Abbot. I don't know why CJ had to drag you out here. We could have done this over the phone.'

She was terse. 'You know perfectly well that he's staged this meeting in this public place so that we can talk without being overheard. He wants me to find out if you are a saint or a sinner.'

'Neither, I'm afraid.'

'Who is? Would it help to talk?'

'Not really. I'm sorry about the girl dying. She didn't deserve that. But –' an expressive shrug – 'I have an alibi for the time of her death, which is rather extraordinary when you come to think of it, because I had intended to work late by myself last night, only I got stuck and went out for a walk. That's when I remembered Clarissa was playing in a concert locally. And then I met CJ. If I hadn't, I suppose I might even have gone to meet Josie when she asked . . . and then I'd have been in the soup, wouldn't I?'

Thursday afternoon

Nance, on the phone. 'I'm on the train, just coming into Kings Cross station. Have the police arrested him yet?'

'They took him away for questioning all right – but he's back, free as air.'

'You must have messed up, telling them about him.'

'I told the police, just as you said, then I went round to watch his flat from across the road for a bit, but there's no cover there and I didn't half get some odd looks. Anyway, he came back in a taxi about midnight, went upstairs, put the lights on for a few minutes, then turned them off. Didn't come out again. Some busybody said I was up to no good, lurking in the shadows, and she was going to ring the police if I didn't scarper, so I did. But I went back this morning to check.

'His flat's above a corner café, all the locals use it. The chap who runs it is quite a character, a great gossip. Someone said he'd been inside for drugs once, but has been clean for years. Anyway, Josie's murder was front page news, as you can imagine. Everyone was talking about it, and they were only too happy to include me in the gossip. Apparently the police turned up this morning and took my laddo away with them. So everyone added two and two, and connected him with it.

'I relaxed, ordered a panini, but blow me down, he was back an hour later, just as I was about to leave! The only thing I can think of is that he'd arranged for himself to have an alibi and got someone else to knock her off.'

'True, his wife's got contacts through her work in the courts, but she threw him out so—'

'There's more. I told the man at the café that I earned my living feeding news items to the newspapers and would pay good money to find out what was happening. So he phoned me a while back to say the little man had come down from his flat and was walking along the road towards Church Street. Well, I'd just settled in with a pint up the road so I scrambled back only to see him getting on a bus into town. I was lucky enough to get a taxi to follow him. And, would you believe, he got off in Piccadilly and walked along to where all the toffee-nobs hang out, the Royal Academy, you know, private courtyard with all those weird sculptures in it?

'He went straight up to a woman, not young, well-preserved fifties, looks the sort you wouldn't want to mess with, and took her through into the café at the back. He's sitting in there now, chatting away to her like they were old friends. Could this be his wife?'

'*What? I don't believe this!*'
'*I'm having a sandwich myself, but keeping them in sight. Don't worry, he's no idea he's being followed.*'

Thursday afternoon

Bea said, 'Jeremy, do you really think that if it hadn't been for the coincidence of meeting CJ, you'd have been arrested for murder?'

'I suppose so.' He eyed the cheese and biscuits. 'Aren't you going to eat those? No?' He transferred them to his side of the table and tucked in. She was amazed at his ability to put away so much food so quickly. And him without an ounce of fat on him. She remembered her mother saying, of a healthy, hungry, teenager, 'He's got hollow legs.' She stifled a grin. 'What was the girl like?'

'Josie? Nice kid, I thought. Well, I wasn't thinking, was I? I was wafting around on the wings of song, on a deadline, should have delivered the day before but fortunately they'd let me have an extension till the end of the week . . . just like this week, come to think of it, when I've had it up to here, my brains made of mushy peas, and I'm taking the day off, hoping that I think of a way to lead back into the theme song without . . . but you don't know anything about music, do you? I can see from your face that I'm boring you. I'm afraid I do tend to bore people about it so I usually don't start but . . .' He tapped a rhythm out on her teapot, shook his head, and said, 'No, no. That won't do, either. I have to finish in the key of A major, which probably sounds like Esperanto, or as near as, to you.'

'Josie,' she said, trying not to laugh. 'A nice kid, you thought. But . . .?'

He shook his head at himself. 'You know, I taught music in that school for twenty-odd years and I still didn't see it coming. I mean, I'm not exactly the sort to attract kids, am I? What's more, I'm married, though I suppose . . .' Again he shook his head at himself. He seized the last piece of cheese, lathered a biscuit with the last of the butter, and popped the whole into his mouth. 'Yum, yum, bubble gum. You don't fancy some more tea, do you? That cup must be cold by now.'

'You say you were married,' said Bea. 'Not any longer?'

'She threw me out. Is divorcing me.' He looked around with a vague expression on his face. 'I don't know why I was surprised when it happened, because we hadn't had much to say to one another for a long time, and I'm not exactly love's young dream, am I?'

Bea shook her head, smiling. Indeed he wasn't.

'It suited us both to stay married, I suppose. I was proud of her, and we both love the house. It was my parents' house, you know. Both dead. I suppose I'll have to sell up and give her half the proceeds. Clarissa's eighteen, almost grown-up. I love having a stepdaughter. I probably saw more of her when she was in her teens than Eunice ever did. I'm sorry that she believes . . .' His voice trailed away.

Bea said, 'CJ said you were a teacher?'

'From Eunice's point of view, mine was never much of a job; teaching the rudiments of music to adolescents, no great kudos or money or anything. Looking back, I suspect she'd begun to get bored with me, what with her being such a high flyer and getting more and more highly paid briefs. Understandable, don't you think? I know that when I tried to tell her about writing music for television, she wasn't at all interested. I suppose the writing was on the wall then, only I didn't see it coming.'

'Couldn't you have kept your house?'

'To tell the truth, I was so shocked that I . . . I couldn't think straight. She told me to pack some things and go to a hotel. So I did. Then I went down the road to the estate agents and asked them to find me a flat, and they did. Ideally, I'd like to find somewhere with a bit more space. I've got this small flat over a café at the back of Church Street at the moment. It's a bit shabby, but there is an upright piano there, iron frame, wonder of wonders, and it's reasonably in tune, too, which you can never be sure about in rented accommodation.'

'Might I be correct in saying that Eunice married you, rather than that you courted her?'

'Mm? Oh yes, I suppose so. She'd had a bad time with her first, you know, and there I was, managing to push Clarissa through her exams and I was a good listener in those days because I've never had anything to do with the law courts, and I did find her work fascinating. Could you manage a coffee by any chance? Keep me company?'

'In a minute.'

'She's brilliant, you know. Quite brilliant. A divorce lawyer, top class. I admire her tremendously. How she manages the house and her job and her daughter, and me . . . I have to take my hat off to her, I really do. But when she's on a high-profile case we don't see much of one another, and of course when she is free she likes to party, and that's not really my scene, you know, which was a bit of a disappointment to her. Though I did try to fit in at first. Later she got someone from her chambers to squire her around. Nice man. Younger. He's going through a divorce, too.'

A marriage heading towards the rocks? What had Eunice seen in this gentle, talented man? A house in a good location. A biddable partner, who wouldn't create waves if she had someone else to party with her? 'What about your stepdaughter?'

'Clarissa? Oh, she's well on her way, doesn't need me any more, which is as it should be, don't you think?'

'Would you have called yourself a house husband, then?'

Another laugh, genuine. 'Heavens, no. I'd have forgotten to pay the paper bill, run out of toilet paper. We had a woman who came in two hours a day and I suppose she really ran the house for us. Eunice usually ordered the food online because I made such a mess of it when I tried and caterers dealt with all the important social occasions.'

'And then Josie came along? How did that happen?'

'She rang the bell after I got back from school one day. Said she'd just arrived in London and was looking for a Mrs Shackleton who was supposed to be letting her a room. She was on the verge of hysterics, said she'd been mugged when she'd asked a man for directions. She was in a terrible state, mud all over her legs and coat. She practically fell into my arms. Eunice and Clarissa were out. I sat her down in the hall, looked up Mrs Shackleton in the phone book; she lived in the next road. I gave the girl a cup of tea and sent her on her way with a fiver. I told Eunice about it, I think. She says I didn't. But I . . . I suppose she's right and I forgot.

'Anyway, the girl came back a couple of days later with a bunch of flowers for me, saying how everything was turning up right for her, that she'd been promised a good job to start the following week and would pay me back the fiver then. I congratulated her. She was a pretty little thing, appealing. She asked if I were any good at arranging the flowers she'd brought me, and I said I wasn't, so she came in to do it for me. Then she made me a cup of tea and chatted for a little while. There wasn't anything in it, you know.'

Except that he hadn't been getting much attention from the other women in his life, by the sound of it. He'd been lonely. He'd been set up.

'What was her full name?'

He looked blank. 'Kelly? O'Reilly? Something Irish. I really can't remember.'

'How many times did she return?'

'I wasn't counting. Four or five? Over a couple of weeks. Looking back, it seems more, but I don't think it can have been more than five. And then the sky fell on me. I'd got into the habit of going to bed early and working there when Eunice was away, as she was that night. Clarissa was out, partying. The bedroom door opened, and there was Josie, stripping off a coat to reveal herself in the altogether and jumping on top of me in bed. And me without me dentures in! Then there's camera flashes all over the place, with her pressed close to me. Screaming, "Oh, no!" And me shouting, "Get off me!"'

He gave a sad little laugh. 'Do you know, I still can't believe it? We used to call it "the Badger Game". Do they still call it that nowadays?'

'Entrapment? The girl gets the man into a compromising position, her partner takes photos, and then demands money for the negatives. How did she get in?'

'I've no idea. I suppose she must have taken an impression of a front door key on one of her visits. We used to keep a spare key hanging up above a table at the back of the hall, for emergencies. Maybe she even took that one. I didn't think to look, after. I certainly didn't watch her all the time she was in the house. I thought we were friends.'

His mouth turned down into a clown's grimace of misery. Yes, her betrayal had hurt. 'They must have looked at the house – which my parents bought fifty years ago and which is worth a mint – and worked out how much my wife earned and thought I was worth a shakedown.'

'Who's "they"?'

'The man with the camera, I don't know his name, he said to call him John. John and Josie. They were a team. He was dressed all in black and he wore a Mickey Mouse mask. Frightening, you know?' he added, thinking about it. 'Rough voice. As soon as he'd got enough pictures, she put her coat back on and said she'd wait outside till he'd finished. It was like a bad dream. I got out of bed and put on my dressing gown over my pyjamas—'

'You were wearing pyjamas?'

'The central heating goes off at ten and the house can be chilly even in May. I always have cold feet, which is one of the reasons Eunice didn't like me in her bed.'

'So the snapshots showed her naked and you in pyjamas? Not exactly an erotic scene.'

'She's erotic enough in her bare skin, I can tell you. I was very nearly aroused and it takes something for me . . . Well, you won't be interested in my health problems, will you? He had one of those cameras where you can see what pictures have been taken, and he showed them to me. The head shots didn't show my pyjamas, but they showed a lot of her. He sat down on the end of my bed, and he patted my hand and said that I'd been having it off with an under-age girl and these photos could get me into a lot of trouble. He said that he knew a way out. That's when he asked for money. Not all that much. Five thousand pounds. He said he knew I owned the house and that my wife was a top earner, and I could easily afford to pay. I simply couldn't believe it was happening, and I laughed out loud.

'He didn't like that. He said . . . Oh, he said a lot of things, most of which I can't remember. But the gist of it was that he'd give me twenty-four hours to pay up, before sending the photos to my wife and to the school where I taught, so that they could see what I'd been up to. He said it was my choice, to pay up or be destroyed.

'Then he left. He just walked out of the house. I was trembling. Shock, I suppose. I got myself a large brandy – I don't usually drink, but that was . . . Then I tried to ring Eunice, but she was out of town and had turned off her mobile to get a good night's sleep, so I left her a message and I got myself something to eat and then – I just waited for her to ring me back. There was nothing else I could do. Copies of the photos were pushed through the letter box before eight next morning. That Josie could . . .'

He shook his head at himself. 'I'm a right mug, aren't I? At first I told myself that no one would believe that I'd interfered with a young girl. I told myself Eunice would laugh when I told her. But she didn't. Ugh! Bad time, that. She was furious with me. She warned me not to tell the police because she didn't want her husband to go to jail, which I suppose I might have done. She said she didn't want me to tell Clarissa, either, but then she told Clarissa herself. She told me to get out of the house and go to a hotel that night. She said she never wanted to see me again, that she would divorce me. I took the photos into school and told the head what had happened. He was fair enough, I suppose, suspended me rather than gave me the sack. I had to leave my pupils almost ready to take their exams . . . Oh well. Perhaps they'll be all right.

'Looking on the bright side,' he said, attempting a smile, 'I'd been working night and day to do my daytime job while trying to keep up with a commission to provide background music for some docudramas: television, cutting edge, fascinating stuff. And there's more work to come provided they don't hear about what I'm supposed to have done with Josie and make me persona non grata. Should I tell the television people about it? I think not.' His brow furrowed. 'A pity you don't know anything about music. I'm having trouble with the coda. I can't quite see how to . . . It'll come to me in the middle of the night, I expect.'

He sounded committed to his music-making. He'd moved on. Good. Bea hoped the television people would be understanding if his connection with Josie ever came out, but there was one troubling point. 'I'm told the girl was under-age.'

'I thought she was Clarissa's age, eighteen. Maybe a spot older. She told me she was eighteen, and I never doubted that it was so. In very young girls, there's a certain look about the neck; unlined, slender. I can see that if Josie were under-age, it would make everything look worse, but . . . You know, I've seen other men – and women teachers, too – destroyed by false allegations from pupils. Usually there are warning signs: a pupil who's always wanting to be counselled, or feels hard done by a particular teacher, or is so consumed by hate or disgust with their family that they go around flying flags of anger at the world in general. Those are all danger signals to an experienced teacher. But I didn't see any of these things. What sort of idiot does that make me?'

'Didn't Josie's minder threaten to go to the police if you didn't pay up?'

'Blackmailers don't, do they? They want money, not publicity.'

'Did they not know about the work for television? I'd have thought they'd have threatened to expose you there, as well.'

'I don't think I ever talked to Josie about it. I write music under another name, you know.'

CJ had told her that, hadn't he? So what had CJ been after, when he'd arranged this meeting? Was it really to confirm CJ's conviction that Jeremy Waite was innocent of murder? Bea snorted. The little man's innocence was shiningly obvious. So what had CJ really been after?

Jeremy polished off the last crumb of food, looking at his watch, playing five-finger exercises on the table. 'Do you know, I rather think I've solved it? I can bridge into a different rhythm while shifting into the next key. Do you mind if I get on with it now? You'll send me a contract in the morning, right? Lovely to have met you. CJ really has been my guardian angel, last night and now today.'

He got to his feet, and bustled away, leaving Bea to stare at her untouched pot of tea.

Her phone rang. 'CJ here. Just checking how your meeting went. What did you make of Jeremy?'

'Genuine. Innocent. I'm going to fix him up with some domestic help.'

'Good. I'd like you to keep an eye on him, all right?'

The phone went dead. Bea looked at it, disillusioned. What did CJ expect? A round the clock supervision of an eccentric genius? No way. He didn't want her to investigate Josie's murder, did he? No way in spades.

At the back of her mind, she heard her mother say, 'No good deed goes unpunished.'

Nonsense. She shook the thought away and turned her mind to more pressing matters, such as what was wrong at the agency.

Thursday afternoon

'Nance, are you there? I'm still in the restaurant. I don't think she's his wife. It's more like a business meeting. Could she be his solicitor?'

'His wife's a redhead in her late forties.'
'This one's ash blonde and older. So it's not her. He's leaving.
And she's still here. Shall I follow him – or her?'

THREE

Thursday late afternoon

The moment Bea stopped puzzling over the little man, her own problems flooded back into her mind and it seemed that the few hours away from the agency had given her a new perspective on things.

The thought popped into her head that the agency had perhaps expanded too fast. The words 'a runaway success' presented themselves to her. Mm, yes. But a runaway car might be a hazard to other road users. Was it, perhaps, time to apply the brakes?

She gathered herself together and set off for home. Should she take the bus? No, a taxi presented itself as she left the Academy. She settled herself into the seat and immediately another problem surfaced in her mind.

Bea had caught her sort-of-adopted daughter Maggie in tears last night, but when Bea asked what was the matter, the girl had rebuffed all enquiries, saying she was going down with a cold. True? Hm. But if not true, what had upset her? Had her almost-boyfriend urged her to marry him? No, he was too sensible to do so before Maggie was ready for it. So what could be troubling her now?

Maggie had been spectacularly unsuccessful as a member of the domestic agency, since her skills had never lain with either the telephone or the computer. But she'd discovered a flair for working as a project manager for various building jobs in the neighbourhood. And Maggie loved to cook . . . which reminded Bea that she wouldn't need to eat again that night.

She ought, perhaps, to ring Maggie and warn her not to provide a big supper. She got out her mobile phone and tried Maggie's number. Engaged. Of course. The girl spent most of her life with her phone attached to her ear.

Frustrated, Bea made a mental note to try again in a minute. She wondered if the last of the new furniture had arrived for the flat she'd created for her second family at the top of the house. Wasn't there still a bed missing? She must check.

Maggie and Oliver – Bea's adopted son currently away at university – were very close to her heart and she cared deeply for both of them. She believed they cared for her, too, but . . .

Bea frowned. Oliver hadn't been in touch since she'd returned from her holiday; he must be busy. He'd made new friends, had been invited into some new line of research which was bringing him kudos in his chosen field of Higher Mathematics, but he usually emailed her several times a week. And hadn't.

It was a something and a nothing.

For heaven's sake, he was a grown man now, wasn't he? She must stop being such a mother hen and pay the taxi driver, who'd drawn up on the opposite side of the road to her house.

On a bright summer's day the early Victorian buildings in her street were a sight for sore eyes. She admired the freshly-painted cream facade of her own mid-terrace house and the neat, paved forecourt with its matching bay trees in pots. A discreet sign indicated that the Abbot Agency could be found by descending the steps to the basement area, while four wider steps led up to the front door under its imposing portico.

Ranks of tall sash windows glistened in the afternoon sun, reducing in size as they marked the positions of the large reception room and hall, and the bedrooms in the upper storeys.

The sky was blue overhead. A jet crossed the sky in the distance, humming to itself.

Bea got out her keys, thinking of Jeremy Waite, thrown out of his family house and confined to a small, rented flat, where he couldn't even have his grand piano. She couldn't be that sorry for him. He might have lost his wife, his job and his home, but she had to admire the way he was forging ahead with his new life.

Bea still had her family, her home and her job. So what was she complaining about? If something was amiss at the agency, it was up to her not to whinge, but to do something about it. And if there wasn't anything wrong at the agency, then . . . Oh well, retirement couldn't be that dreadful, could it?

There was permit parking only in the street. As she crossed

the road, she checked that her own car was safe and undamaged from brushes with passing vehicles, which it was, and spotted another familiar car. Her important – in his own estimation at least – member of parliament son's car. A Jaguar. She'd given him a book of visitor's tickets some time ago and he'd stuck one in the window, just as he ought to do if he wished to avoid a fine for parking in that road.

What was Max doing here? Waiting for her, obviously. She felt a familiar tightening of nerves, because a visit from Max usually meant he wanted something. But . . . a nasty thought. Was all well with her darling grandson? She usually saw him twice a week but for some reason it hadn't been convenient the other day. Perhaps he was ill?

She had planned to go down into the agency, but instead she mounted the stairs to the front door and let herself into the house.

Thursday late afternoon

'Nance? The bird's let herself into a big house on the far side of Kensington Church Street, not a hundred yards from where I found Josie. It looks as if she's running some kind of business from the basement. The Abbot Agency, whatever that might be. Escort agency? She'd make a fine madam. It doesn't sound like a solicitor's office, does it, but it's only a hop, skip and a jump from the music man's new flat.'

'She's not a totty?'

'Far from it.'

'We'll know where to find her if we need to. Meanwhile, we've got to think of the future. I've done all the groundwork for a new project, and I'm not giving up, especially after we lost out so badly on the last one. Someone's sending round a girl who might be a suitable replacement for Josie, and I'd like you to see her.'

'It's too soon. Josie's not even buried yet.'

'It's never too soon to earn some more money. Be there.'

Thursday late afternoon

'Max, my dear! How nice to see you. And how is my beautiful grandson? I was so sorry to miss him earlier this week.'

'Now, Mother. Don't be obtuse. You know perfectly well that

Nicole has taken him up to our house in the constituency for the summer break. I hope to join them soon. Our flat here in London is not pleasant in this heat.'

'I'd forgotten you were going so soon.'

Bea's drawing room was pleasantly cool as she'd had the forethought to lower the blinds over the windows at the back of the house before she left. She raised them now and threw open the French windows so that, just for a minute, she could step out on to the wrought iron staircase which curled down into the garden. A breath of fresher air stirred the curtains behind her, and she thought how pleasant it would be to go down and sit in the shade of the sycamore tree, perhaps with a glass of iced water. But not yet.

Max had taken up his stand with his back to the fireplace – which held a display of ferns at this time of year. Bea loved him dearly. He was the only child of her first marriage to a tom-catting portrait painter who had wooed her as an eighteen-year-old but, finding marriage and responsibility not to his taste, had abandoned her to bring up their son alone. Piers was in the money nowadays, and he and Bea were now good friends. He'd even managed to re-establish some sort of relationship with his son. Piers had never been handsome but had all the charm in the world.

Max, on the other hand, was tall, dark and handsome . . . if carrying a little too much weight. Bea held back a sigh. Max was wearing his 'official' face. Max was on the warpath about something.

Would a diversion help? 'Can I fetch you a cup of iced tea? Some home-made lemonade? I think there's some in the fridge.'

'You should have told me you were going to be out this afternoon. I've been waiting for over half an hour for you to return.'

She subsided on to a high-backed chair. 'Well, I'm here now.' No point in telling him why she'd gone out, because he disliked CJ – perhaps was a little jealous of his influence? – and he'd be horrified to hear she'd been in conversation with a man accused of having under-age sex. She ironed out a smile. 'Max, dear; do sit down. You're looming over me.'

'Now you're being frivolous, Mother.'

'I'm sorry, Max. What can I do for you?'

'It's not what you can do for me, but what I can do for you. Everyone agrees that you've done wonderfully well to keep the agency going since Hamilton died. As I've often observed to Nicole, he was more like a father to me than my own father ever was, and I still miss him.'

Was Max implying that Bea didn't miss him? She did, every day and in every way. Her eyes flicked to Hamilton's portrait by the window. A round-faced, wise man of middle age, who had run the agency till cancer took hold of him – and he died. Max had had a go at running the agency himself for a little while, but since then Bea had taken over and done pretty well, she thought. On the whole.

'Yes, dear. I miss him, too.'

His eyebrows snapped. He didn't care to be interrupted. 'The world of commerce marches on, and changes are afoot which even I have difficulty assimilating into—'

What on earth was he talking about? Yet another new system from Microsoft to bewilder the computer operator? And why did he always have to get his metaphors in a twist?

'So I realize how desperately hard it must be for you to keep up to date. It is nothing to be ashamed of. No. Far from it. Better brains than yours have been brought low by the technical revolution which is flooding the microwaves—'

Bea suppressed a giggle. He'd be terribly hurt if she showed amusement at his verbal slip.

And then she felt acid rise at the back of her throat. He was going to say she had lost her touch and should retire. He was going to put all her vague worries into words, and make them real. It hurt.

'I do worry about you, Mother. You know that I do. I talked to Nicole about it, and she agreed with me.'

Naturally. Nicole had no ideas of her own, which made her the perfect wife for Max, who had plenty of opinions – even if they were mostly second-hand.

He sat down beside her and patted her hand. Patronizing. But he meant well. 'Mother, it's time to face facts. You're not getting any younger—'

She had a shocking impulse to box his ears, but controlled herself.

'—and as you know, nothing ever stands still in this world. The agency is continuing to grow, thanks to the new blood you've brought in—'

That reference to 'new blood' rang an alarm bell. He meant the new manageress, Ianthe – pronounced Eye-An-Thee – didn't he?

'—and it's no longer an exclusive little affair which you can run part-time, but has the potential to expand. It needs more staff, more investment. It needs to become a limited company with a suite of offices, perhaps in the High Street. If you sold out now, you'd be a very rich woman. You could retain shares in the new company, and you wouldn't have to worry about a thing, except how to spend your dividends.'

She eyed him with suspicion. 'How long have you been thinking about this?'

The faintest of reddening in his cheeks. 'Oh, for a long time, but I didn't like to say anything, knowing how you've clung on to the business to keep you going since Hamilton died. And then someone said . . . in the House, was it? No, no. At the club. Admiring the gallant way you've been carrying on, and saying that other people of your age hang on too long and then . . . they can't keep up with the way the world is going. You see?'

'Who, precisely, have you been discussing this with?'

'Nobody you know. At least, I wouldn't think so. But he does say he'd be interested in talking to you, if I sounded you out first.'

'I see.' But she didn't, not really. Who would want to buy her out? She couldn't think of anybody who'd be interested. Ah-ha. What about Jackson's, who were her chief competitors in the agency world?

'There's more.' He shifted on the seat and pressed her hand harder. 'If the agency goes elsewhere, as I'm sure it should, then this house . . . Well, it's rather on the large side for one older woman living by herself, isn't it? You've been wonderful, taking in Oliver and Maggie, but, well, Oliver's at university now, and Maggie . . . a delightful girl, of course, but she's no kin of ours and will be moving on eventually . . .'

Max had been brought up in this house. After she married Hamilton, he'd adopted the boy. It was a prestigious address and a beautiful house. Max had always wanted to live here. Something inside her cried out that it wasn't his home; it was hers!

Again he shifted on his seat. 'I thought we – Nicole and I – could get a mortgage to buy this house off you on generous terms, and if you were to buy a smaller place somewhere, you could give Oliver and Maggie some thousands each to start them off on the housing market. What's more – and I know this will appeal to you – your grandson wouldn't have to be brought up in a flat, and he'd have a garden to play in.'

She stood up, trying not to show how much he had shaken her. The prospect of making a lot of money didn't particularly appeal to her, but if selling out meant her grandson and extended family would benefit, then she supposed she ought to think seriously about it.

He stood, too, and put his arm around her. 'There, now. That wasn't so terrible, was it? You have a good think about what I've said. You've always been a sensible woman, and you'll soon come to see that I'm right.' He looked at his watch. 'Now, I'd better get going, I suppose. Busy, busy. Committee meetings, correspondence, people to see. Nothing for you to worry your head about. I'll call round again soon, shall I? And then we can talk ways and means.'

She saw him out and returned to the living room, crossing her arms, hugging herself. If she did as he suggested, life would still go on. It wouldn't be the end of the world.

She straightened the photographs on the mantelpiece, picking up the silver-framed one of her grandson. He was smiling at the camera, chubby-cheeked and bright-eyed. Seeing him twice a week was one of the joys of her life. She was going to miss seeing him grow over the long summer holiday, although he would have lots of love and attention from his other grandparents. She mustn't begrudge them their time with him. After all, she saw more of him than they did.

But still; it hurt.

And what Max had said hurt, too. He wanted to tidy her away into a bungalow in some retirement haven, where she would lose all contact with her friends and family. A living death to someone who'd worked hard all her life.

Max had always been jealous of Oliver and Maggie, though he'd no need to be for she had more than enough love to go round. She loved him and knew him well. She understood that he was afraid she might divert part of what he saw as his inheritance their way.

He was afraid of many things, wasn't he? Of being found

inadequate as a husband and father, as a member of parliament, and of losing status in the eyes of the world . . . unlike Oliver and Maggie who'd both been knocked out by things that had happened to them in their teens, and who were only now beginning to rebuild their lives.

Yet Oliver and Maggie were rebuilding on a firm foundation. Bad things might still happen to them in the future; they knew that, but they'd also learned that it was possible to survive.

Did Max know that? Possibly not, because up to now, someone else had always picked him up if he fell down. Hamilton had adopted the fatherless boy and put him through university. When other jobs had faded out, Max had run the agency during Hamilton's illness . . . and then he'd met and married Nicole, whose parents were only too keen to help him establish himself as a Member of Parliament. He was painstaking and thorough and a loyal party member. He worked hard for his constituents. With luck, he now had a job for life. But if that failed him . . .?

She sighed. Who could foresee the future? Who would want to?

A fly blundered into the room. She shooed it out and stood, looking out over the quiet, shady garden which was enclosed – as all the houses in this terrace were – by high brick walls.

Maggie had filled the great urns with summer bedding plants, and various shrubs and small trees around the perimeter were doing well. The sycamore was in two tones of green with the flowers showing lighter splotches against the leaves. The leaves trembled in the breeze, and through them she could glimpse the spire of St Mary Abbot's at the bottom of the hill.

Hamilton had worshipped in that church, and so had she for a while though it was a trifle too ornate and high for her. Hamilton had said God was everywhere, not just in church, and sometimes she could believe that. And sometimes not.

Dear Lord, I am in your hands. You know everything. You know my weaknesses and my strengths. If my work here is done, help me to retire with a good grace. If you still have work for me to do here, then . . . do you think you could give me a sign of some kind? Faithfully yours, Bea Abbot.

She was alone in the house. She listened for the comforting noises which would tell her that there were other human beings around, but there were none.

There was no clashing of pans or sound of radio and television coming from the kitchen next door, which meant that Maggie had not yet returned from whatever job she'd been doing. Maggie didn't seem able to function without a lot of noise around her.

Oliver's year at university had finished but he'd told Maggie he was staying on for another week or two to finish up some research project or other. So he wouldn't be popping in and out, or playing jazz on his saxophone at the top of the house.

Bea was not hungry after eating that big tea, so she went down the inside stairs to the agency rooms. Her office lay at the back of the house. More French windows there would let her out on to the garden, since the house was built on a slope, and what was a semi-basement at the front of the house was level with the paved garden at the back.

Everything looked neat and tidy.

In the old days she would have expected to see a pile of papers on her desk for her to peruse, sign, or mark up for discussion. Now there was nothing except a folder containing an up-to-date report on the agency finances, broken down into different categories.

Once it had been Bea's job to oversee the accounts and make whatever decisions might be necessary. All that was in the past. With the advent of Ianthe, her new manageress, the agency was going from strength to strength, and surely they would soon iron out any bumps in the road. If, indeed, there were any bumps. Probably not. It was all in her mind.

The agency was a success story, as Max had said.

How had he known it? Through Ianthe? Though how the two of them might have met was something of a puzzle.

Bea tried to switch on her computer, but there was no power. Ianthe liked to turn off the power to all the computers on her way out every night. It was a sensible step to take, but it grated on Bea to have to go into the main office and unlock the cupboard to access the big new switch-box and turn the power on again. Fortunately, she'd insisted on having a key to that cupboard.

Back in her office, she switched on her computer. She wasn't completely redundant. At least she could find a suitable housekeeper for the little music man. A name had leaped into her mind: someone who had worked for her for a long time but recently decided to leave. Celia had said she wanted something less stressful now, though in the darkest hours of the night, Bea suspected this was simply another example of Ianthe managing to ease out anyone who'd worked for the agency before she arrived. There could be no other explanation for such a complete turnover of staff, could there?

It was understandable that Ianthe would feel more comfortable working with a team that she'd selected herself. Bea's people had all been with her for so long that it must have been irritating for the newcomer to be referred back to the way things had been done in the past.

Bea felt nostalgic for the old days. But when dear Miss Brook, the indefatigable, long-time mainstay of the Abbot Agency, had finally conceded that she was no longer able to keep track of every job that came to the agency, Bea had been forced to interview for someone to help out. And Ianthe – bleached to honey blonde, scented and perhaps slightly too well upholstered – had arrived with the highest of recommendations, to take over the interviewing and allocation of new clients and staff.

Within twenty-four hours of Ianthe's tripping lightly into the agency, Bea had thanked heaven for her efficiency, while at the same time becoming aware that the advent of Wonder Woman might not altogether suit Miss Brook. The two women had taken an instant dislike to one another. A well-disguised dislike, of course. Voices were never raised, though eyebrows went up and down like yo-yos. Smiles were pinned to faces throughout the most wounding exchanges. Offers were made of tea-biscuits from cherished tins normally kept in bottom drawers of desks, and declined with barbed remarks about not wanting to put on weight, or of butter creams being bad for the complexion.

Bea had told herself that things would settle down. Ianthe assured Bea that she had the deepest respect for Miss Brook and would take every opportunity to learn whatever gems of wisdom the older woman might care to impart to her. But soon even this attempt at harmony ceased. Allegations of ineptitude were offered to Bea from both sides in tones of deep apology. 'I wouldn't dream of troubling you, Mrs Abbot, but . . .'

The worst of it was that Miss Brook couldn't substantiate her contention that Ianthe was not the right person for the agency, whereas Ianthe was able to point to instances of Miss Brook mislaying paperwork and not returning phone calls.

Miss Brook represented the best of the Old Style of doing business. She had managed the transition from card indexes to computers as if fingers had been invented for tapping keyboards, and she could sense a false reference at fifty paces. But perhaps, Ianthe hinted with sorrow, Miss Brook was beginning to let things slip, which, though understandable at her age, was not doing the agency any good.

Ianthe had a university degree and a delightfully warm manner, setting clients at ease from the moment they spoke to her on the phone or entered the office rooms.

Miss Brook had broken down and wept when she tendered her resignation. Bea had wept, too. They'd been through so much together over the years, but it was undeniably true that Miss Brook had been eligible to draw her state pension for a good number of years, and therefore ought perhaps to make room for a younger person.

Bea sighed. Oh dear. Happy days.

She wondered if it would be a good idea to telephone Celia about Jeremy, rather than email her. Yes, it would be good to have a chat with her, find out what she was doing nowadays. Bea delved into the right-hand drawer of her desk for her address book. It wasn't there. That was odd. She always kept it there.

Well, she could access Celia's address on her personnel files.

Except that the computer screen was asking for her password.

Bother. What was it today?

It was Ianthe's idea to change the password every day, and of course that was good business practice. The only problem was that Ianthe always seemed to come into Bea's office, to tell her what the new password was to be, when she was on the phone. It would be a mixture of upper and lower-case letters, with some numerals thrown in. Quite brilliant, ensuring no one from outside could hack into their system.

Only, Bea's visual memory was better than her aural, and it was beyond her to memorize something she'd been told but not seen written down.

In other words, she wasn't able to get into the office system. It wasn't the first time this had happened, or the second. She seized a piece of paper and wrote on it, 'Ianthe; please give me the password in written form every day. This is my third time of asking. Bea Abbot.'

She considered the note a trifle harsh, but . . . no, it was fair.

She switched on her photocopier, copied the memo, and took it through to tuck under Ianthe's keyboard.

Looking around, she had to concede that the big front room had become rather crowded of late. Once upon a time Miss Brook had run the agency with the aid of two part-timers – and for a short time with Maggie, who'd never been much help in that area. Then Oliver had come to update them in every way, and after that dear Celia had arrived and been a tower of strength. All gone now. Bea hardly knew the names of the new girls who Ianthe had imported. All very bright and literate, with good telephone manners.

But somehow . . . the fun had gone out of the business.

Fun? Yes, it had been fun in the old days, matching difficult clients with the right personnel, solving problems that would have tested the imaginations of agony aunts, fielding requests to avert last minute tragedies; yes, it had been fun. And they'd felt they were fulfilling a need, smoothing their clients' path through life.

Now it was a business, run on strictly practical lines. There were time limits for everything. No phone call should last more than so many minutes, as time costs money. No private phone calls or emails were allowed. Other agencies should be called upon to supply hard-to-fill vacancies, even if the personnel had not been vetted by them.

It all made for efficiency, an improved turnover. And a small regret – which was most unbusinesslike – for everything they'd lost in transit.

Perhaps it *was* time for Bea to sell up and move out. She would find Celia's address, put her in touch with the little music man and . . .

Bother! She couldn't even do that! In her own agency! This was ridiculous.

She swept back into her office and went through every drawer in her own desk, looking for her personal address book. If it wasn't in the top right-hand drawer, then where was it? Might she have put it in her handbag? No.

Had she left it out somewhere? Most unlikely . . . but she looked, anyway. No.

There was one place she hadn't looked, and that was the small office which had once been Oliver's and had subsequently been taken over by Maggie. Her paperwork was always in confusion, but her jobs were almost always completed on time and within budget.

And there – ta-da! – was her address book, poking out from under some architect's plans.

Bea picked it up. It felt different. Grainy. And discoloured. She opened it at random and found much of the information inside was illegible. Had someone spilt a cup of coffee over her book?

A nasty, suspicious thought wormed its way up from the back of Bea's mind. She imagined she could hear Ianthe fluting, 'Oh, poor Mrs Abbot, such an important little book, I know how much you rely on it. I suppose Maggie took it by mistake. Such a sweet girl, but perhaps . . . I hardly dare say it, as I know she's a special favourite of yours . . . but perhaps a little clumsy at times?'

Everything Bea touched seemed to go wrong.

FOUR

B ea could well imagine Maggie borrowing the book for some reason and, yes, she might well have upset her coffee over it.

What she couldn't imagine was Maggie failing to own up. Maggie wasn't like that. Or was she? Was this trivial accident the cause of her tears the other evening?

Bea sat down in the chair at the desk with a bump. Was the open-hearted, vulnerable, feisty girl she had taken into her heart a reality? If not, then why should Bea worry about the girl's future?

Silence grew around her. The light faded fast down here, though it couldn't be very late. She looked about her, with an uncomfortable feeling that something was amiss. The chair she was sitting on, for instance. Maggie was tall, as tall as Bea, yet as Bea sat in the chair, her knees were pressed to the underside of the desk.

Which meant that someone had recently been sitting at this desk who was shorter than Maggie, and who had raised the seat to compensate for her loss of inches. Had someone else been using this office?

This room was something of a battleground, as Ianthe coveted it for herself, saying they were uncomfortably crowded in the main office. Which was true. But this was where Maggie kept all her paperwork: estimates, bills to be paid, enquiries, samples of tiles, books of wallpapers, catalogues. Maggie did use a computer, but she also kept hard copies of everything that passed through her hands, storing them in a fashion only she could understand, in various boxes parked in piles around her desk. On the notice board above the desk, yellow Post-it notes vied for space with postcards, reminders from the library and the dentist; evidence of a life lived at speed.

Something was missing.

There was no computer or telephone.

Dimly, Bea recalled Ianthe apologizing for removing Maggie's computer for a few days while another was being repaired or updated. But that had been some time ago, surely? Maggie had a laptop. She would have that with her. Ianthe had suggested they install a hub in the house so that all the computers could be used in any room at any time. Did that mean Maggie's laptop was subject to the same password routine as Bea's? Surely not! Maggie would have an even greater struggle than Bea to remember an intricate password.

And the telephone? Maggie lived on her mobile phone, which meant she wasn't always available to take other people's calls. Ah, but Celia had always taken messages for Maggie.

Celia had resigned. Who was taking messages for Maggie now?

Bea rubbed her forehead. Ianthe had been arguing that Maggie's side of the business should be completely divorced from the agency. Maggie should have separate insurance, said Ianthe, and submit her own accounts to her own accountant.

Bea had agreed with Ianthe in principle and said that she would discuss separating the two sides of the business at the end of the financial year, by which time Maggie might be able to employ a part-timer to keep her straight. Bea had suggested that Celia might be able to do this . . .

Bea did not like unanswered questions. No doubt Ianthe would be able to sort everything out on the morrow.

The house was quiet. Too quiet. Maggie couldn't have returned yet. She hadn't said she'd be out late that evening, had she?

Maggie's last job had been to organize the loft conversion at the top of the house. The attic rooms had been gutted and the space opened up at the back of the house, creating two bedrooms, a sitting room, a newly-fitted bathroom and small galley kitchen. One reason for Bea's recent holiday had been to avoid the disruption to water and electricity supplies to the house caused by the building works.

Bea made her way up the stairs, and as she did so, her mobile phone rang. She dived into the sitting room to disinter it from her handbag.

It was CJ. 'I tried ringing your landline but it went through to answerphone.'

'Sorry about that. I was down in the agency rooms and didn't hear it.'

'Finding a housekeeper for Jeremy?'

'I will, when I can get into the system. I seem to be locked out at present.' She tried out a laugh. It didn't work very well.

'Mm. I heard about that.'

'Did you?' Now how had he heard about it? Ah, through Oliver, no doubt. It made her wince to think that Oliver was still in close contact with CJ, but hadn't troubled himself to contact Bea for a while.

How had Oliver heard? Through Maggie, of course. Bea sighed. The clues went round and round and came out . . . where?

CJ said, 'If you've got a bit of time on your hands, would you care to have dinner with me tomorrow night?'

'Delighted.'

He switched off, and so did she. She wondered why she'd agreed so readily to dine with him. He'd not asked her out for dinner before. Ah well, he couldn't complicate her life any more, could he?

Thursday evening

'Nance; this new girl. She's pretty enough, I'll grant you that, but there's nothing between the ears. Josie seemed to know by instinct how to get a man interested in her, but this one . . .!'

'I'm not wasting all the research I did at the conference. The girl will be all right.'

'I'm not so sure. Another thing; did you have to throw all Josie's things out so soon? It seems a bit, well, callous.'

'I was fond of her too, but we can't risk the police linking her to our flat. If they can't find any connection to us, they'll put her death down as just another prostitute coming to a bad end. Life goes on.'

'I'm not letting the little man get away with what he did to Josie. I'm going to pay him a visit, remind him of the realities of life.'

'We can't afford to draw the attention of the police to us.'

'I promise I won't lay a finger on him. But he's got to pay for what he's done!'

Thursday late evening

Bea inhaled the scent of new paint. Maggie had made a good job of the loft conversion. The rooms were light and airy, painted in white tinged with the palest of pastels, with matching blinds at the windows. The original furniture had been moved back into the bedrooms, and yes, the new sofa-bed had been delivered. Good.

But, there were no books on the shelves, no pictures on the walls; no attempt had been made to personalize the space.

Bea reminded herself that Maggie had camped out in the guest room downstairs while the builders had been in, and that Oliver was still away at university. Now the boxes containing Oliver's belongings stood squarely in his bedroom awaiting his return, and Maggie seemed to be living out of suitcases in her bedroom. As if she didn't expect to be here for long?

The living room should have been a cool and restful place. A white leather three-piece suite, a television and an occasional table had been delivered, half denuded of their packaging and left in a huddle.

A fine new wooden floor had been laid there, but it was currently hard to spot as it looked as if someone had emptied a filing cabinet over it – and stirred it around. Bea recognized some of Maggie's drawings, blueprints, estimates. Her familiar Post-it notes had been scattered liberally around. Her laptop was there, too – plugged into the mains.

Bea received various messages from what she saw, none of which gave her a happy feeling. The new rooms looked unlived in. She had a horrid suspicion that Oliver was never going to return home, but would be asking her to send his boxes on to . . . wherever.

And Maggie? Was she thinking of leaving, too? They had every right to live their own lives wherever they wished, but . . . Bea hugged herself, though the evening was warm enough.

Think positively, Bea. These rooms on the top floor would make an excellent self-contained flat to rent out if she sold the house to Max. He'd probably employ a nanny for his son, and she could live up here or in the basement rooms. Lucky Max.

From the back window of the sitting room she looked down into the garden, thrown into shadow by the sycamore tree at the far end. The evening sunlight was fading into twilight. Was that a star in the sky above the tree? No, an aeroplane.

Before her rose the pale spire of the church, one side lit to glory by the setting sun.

Dear Lord, I don't understand what's going on. I feel so lost. Everything I took for granted – my work, my family – is shifting from under my feet.

All right, I know in my head that life moves on, that people move away. I can't expect Oliver and Maggie to live with me for ever, but I thought . . . no, I hoped . . . no, I really believed that they were happy to have me in the background of their lives for some time to come.

I mustn't be selfish if they want to move on, even if I don't think they're ready to do so.

Again, I must not be selfish and keep this big house all to myself if they want to leave. I must be grateful that my grandson will be brought up in a house with a garden, even though he's hardly old enough yet to enjoy it.

She began to pace the shadowy room, arms folded around herself.

Dear Lord, you gave up so much to show us the Way and the Truth and the Light, when you came down to earth. I wonder how much and how often you regretted leaving your home to help others. And here am I, crying inside because I may have to leave my safe little niche so that other people can have a better life.

*I ought to be ashamed of myself, but I'm not. I'm resenting it
like mad.*

She stood at the window, trying to understand what was
happening, trying to resign herself to leaving all that she loved,
her work, her extended family, the house which had been hers
and Hamilton's for so many years . . . good years, filled with
hard work and loving kindness.

Finally, she ran out of words to hurl at God and just stood.

In the end, she prayed again. For patience. For guidance. For
the knowledge that she was still His much-loved child, however
much she railed at Him.

In the stillness she remembered someone else's tears.

So what if Maggie had been crying? Maggie had ruined Bea's
address book. Maggie was going to leave her. Maggie's tears
were nothing to Bea, who must accept what was happening,
pretend she didn't care. Move on with her life.

Max had said Bea would be a very rich woman when she sold
up. Well, she wouldn't be that rich if she gave a decent sum away
to Oliver and Maggie . . . on top of which she had guaranteed to
see Oliver through university, which was going to cost an arm and
a leg. She supposed that she could let Max buy the house on easy
terms – which is no doubt what he intended – but then she'd have
to buy herself somewhere else to live in a less fashionable neighbourhood and try to find something to do with the rest of her life.

In the silence came the sound of the front door closing, not
with a bang, but a quiet thunk. Was that Maggie returning?
Maggie usually rushed in, letting the door bang to behind her
and yelling that she was back – 'Hello, it's me!' She would then
thunder into the kitchen, turning on the television and the radio
as she went, talking on the phone to one of her friends or a
workman, and then there would come the clatter of pans and the
burble of the electric kettle.

Silence, except for quiet, slow footsteps mounting the stairs.
Burglars? Or Maggie in unusually pensive mood?

An unshaded light bulb was switched on above Bea, and both
she and Maggie jumped.

'Sorry about the mess! I meant to clear it up, but . . . I didn't
realize you were up here. This light's awful. There's some
uplighters been delivered somewhere, but I haven't got round to
unpacking them yet.'

'I suppose I should have waited for an invitation to visit your new rooms. You've done a really good job up here, Maggie.'

'Yes.' Maggie usually dressed in strident colours and coloured her hair in whatever shade took her fancy that week. Bea was concerned to see the girl was all in black today, and that her hair approximated to its original mid-brown. But so what if the girl was down in the mouth? Was that any concern of Bea's?

Well, yes. It was. 'What's the matter, Maggie?'

'Oh, nothing.' The girl looked around her as if she'd never seen the room before. 'This overhead lighting's all wrong, don't you think?' She threw down her large tote bag. 'It's quite all right, you don't have to say anything. I know it's time I moved on. I've been to look at a place today, but . . .' She moved her shoulders. 'It wasn't very nice. I've got my name down for a rented flat at the estate agency in Church Street.'

Bea's tongue tied itself into knots. It wanted to say, 'Do you really have to go?' and, 'Why are you deserting me?' Instead, she managed, 'How about a cuppa?'

Maggie made as if to move to the kitchen area, and stopped. 'I don't think I've got any fresh milk up here.'

'Come downstairs where it's cosy, and then you can tell me all about it.' Now why had she said that? Maggie's defection had wounded her. She felt raw. And here she was, offering to listen to the girl's troubles. Well, the offer had been extended, and Maggie followed her down the stairs, switching on the lights as they went.

The kitchen was warm, and their huge black furry cat Winston was lying on the central work surface, waiting for them. Maggie picked him up and buried her face in his fur. Bea filled the kettle and switched it on. She busied herself getting out mugs, fresh milk, tea bags and biscuits.

'Tell me all about it.'

'Oh, it's nothing, really. I didn't get the Thomason job, and I'm in a muddle with my paperwork as usual.'

'What a shame. Did they say why not?' Bea had been consulted when Maggie had been preparing the estimates and thought Maggie's scheme had been sound and her quote well within the client's budget.

'It was all my fault. I should have checked, and it's no good saying that I'd never needed to check before when Celia typed quotes up for me, and I know I ought to do my own typing, but . . . there's always been so much to do, and Celia was brilliant at fielding messages for me, and she always managed somehow to fit my work in with hers, and I know you were worried that I was taking up so much of her time, but you never mentioned it to me.

'No, I ought to have realized. I feel so stupid. Ianthe said she'd have to find someone else to do my work for me after Celia left, and she did get one of the girls to type up the estimate for me, but it was all such a rush at the last minute that I didn't check, and the girl put it in the post for me. I've no one but myself to blame.' She shrugged. 'The total was five thousand over budget. A simple typing error, and I didn't spot it.'

Bea poured boiling water on to the tea bags. 'Ianthe said I thought you were taking up too much of Celia's time?'

Another shrug. A dip into the biscuit tin. 'They're so busy down there. I ought to have realized they haven't time for my bits and pieces any more. You should have said something, though I can see why you didn't, not wanting to hurt my feelings and all that. As if! Maggie the Thicko, what? Anyway, I've got the message now.'

'I'm not sure that I have. Maggie, have you seen my little address book recently?'

No blush, no embarrassment. No sigh of shame. 'The one Oliver gave you at Christmas? Have you lost it? Do you want me to have a good hunt round for it? Where did you see it last?'

'In your office downstairs.'

A frown. 'What? But . . . why should . . .? I don't understand.'

'Neither do I. Maggie, I'm wondering if perhaps Ianthe has been a little too businesslike—'

'One can't be businesslike enough, she says.'

'Oh yes, one can. It seems to me that in her care for one side of the business, she's let *you* down.'

'Yes, but I'm not really part of the agency nowadays, am I? And she's so busy. And the girl who's replaced Celia is . . . Well, she doesn't know me, does she? She doesn't see why she should do any work for me, and she's right.'

Bea thought about that. And followed on with, 'Have you any other jobs which you've asked Ianthe to see to?'

'Well, yes; and she's trying hard to fit them in. I'm a bit worried about one estimate which needs to be in next week. Ianthe keeps putting me off, so I'm thinking of taking it to a typing agency I've heard about. It's not your problem.'

'I think it is. Maggie; I want to help.'

'Bless you, but I can manage.' Maggie looked at the clock, checked her watch, and gave a little scream. 'I promised to ring someone back tonight. Do you mind if I . . .?'

'Go ahead.'

'Oh, but what about supper? I ate something earlier, but—'

'I've eaten already. Go on. Get on with your life. I'll clear up here.'

Maggie vanished, already talking into her mobile. Feeling better now she'd talked to Bea.

Bea felt worse. Ianthe was right in thinking that Maggie ought to outsource her own typing. Or was she? The fact was that the agency was changing. Most people would say it was for the better. Bea wasn't so sure.

She made a phone call of her own. Her first husband Piers, who had tom-catted himself out of their marriage, had become a good friend over the last few years, and he could always be relied upon for some cool-headed advice . . . that is, if he weren't totally absorbed in whatever subject it was that he was painting at the moment. He might have been the stereotypical painter who starved in a garret when he was younger – except that Bea had gone out to work to keep him going in those years – but nowadays he was a much sought-after portrait painter, wooed by all the great and sometimes not so good.

'Piers, can you spare me a minute or two tomorrow?'

'Ah. Yes. Been expecting this. Got a sitting at ten, early bird. Half eleven do you?'

Yes, indeed.

Someone was leaning on the front doorbell. What? At this time of night? After ten. Whoever it was had no intention of giving up.

Maggie was returning back down the stairs, still with her mobile to her ear. 'Who . . .?'

Bea went to open the door, and the garden gnome tripped over the doorstep and fell into the hallway. Slap, bang, down he went, falling sideways, landing flat on his back. There was blood on his forehead, which he was trying to cover with one hand, while clutching a handful of manuscript paper to him with the other.

'So sorry,' he said, not making any attempt to rise. 'Shock. You know?'

He closed his eyes.

'Who on earth . . .?' Maggie switched off her mobile.

'Jeremy Waite,' said Bea. 'Musician. Murder suspect, though I don't think he did it. It looks as if he's been duffed up.'

'Not so.' Jeremy opened his eyes but made no attempt to rise. 'Shock. If I might just rest for a bit . . .' His eyes went up to the ceiling and followed the plaster frieze around. 'Nice bit of moulding, that. Early Victorian? Black and white tiled floor, probably. I do hope I'm not bleeding on to it.'

'Er, no,' said Bea, seized with an inappropriate desire to laugh. 'Do we call the police or an ambulance?'

He jerked to a sitting position, still holding on to his head. 'Neither. It was my flat they did in, not me. Fortunately, I was out when they arrived.'

'When who arrived?'

A shrug. 'Josie's dead, so it can't be her. Her photographer, I suppose. I'd popped out for ten minutes. Came back to find the front door downstairs open. Thought I must have neglected to pull it to behind me when I left, but when I got upstairs, I could see I'd been burgled. Or not burgled, probably, because what do I have that's worth stealing?'

'Nothing missing?' Bea helped him to his feet and deposited him in a chair.

'A random act of burglary?'

'I might have thought that, if they hadn't massacred the piano.' He dabbed at his forehead. 'Am I still bleeding? I'd gone out to fetch a pizza, was feeling peckish, and I still had the carton in my hands when I got upstairs and saw the mess. I thought that whoever it was might still be there, so I grabbed some paperwork and ran for it, but I must have caught my foot on the carpet, and what with holding on to the pizza and all . . . I took a tumble down the stairs.'

'Yes, yes. Let's get you cleaned up.'

Maggie and Bea lifted him up between them and carried him through into the kitchen, with him still talking.

'So I got out my mobile and rang the police. And they said they'd log the incident and try to get back to me tomorrow and I looked at the front door and saw the lock had been smashed and I realized they could come back and get me at any minute so I couldn't stay there. Only, I couldn't think where to go, and I started walking up the road and suppose I must have dropped my mobile somewhere because I couldn't find it to ring anyone else, and I remembered you lived nearby, and that's why I'm here. Ouch!'

Maggie applied a dressing to his grazed temple. 'Hold still, now.'

He took a deep breath, looking around him. They'd put him on one of the kitchen stools. His legs dangled way off the floor. 'You haven't got a biscuit or two handy, have you?'

'And a cup of tea,' said Maggie, refilling the kettle. Maggie was good with children of all ages. 'I'm Maggie, by the way.'

Bea was thinking. 'I agree you can't go back to your flat, Jeremy. I suppose – just for tonight – you could sleep here, and then look for something better in the morning?'

Maggie chucked mugs on to the table. 'The bed in Oliver's room is already made up. I'll put out some towels for him.'

Jeremy had already worked out that Maggie was going to be more sympathetic to his need for food than Bea. 'You haven't by any chance got a cheese sandwich, or perhaps something a little more substantial?'

'An omelette?' Maggie went into production. 'Spanish: tomatoes, mushrooms, onions and potatoes. Right? With a baked apple and custard to follow?'

'Bliss,' he said. Then shivered. 'It wasn't a random burglary, was it? Not if they used an axe on the piano. The rest of the furniture didn't amount to much, and they just tossed my papers around so I can easily catch up on my work, but the piano . . . what am I going to do without a piano?'

'Rent one,' said Maggie. 'I can arrange that for you. No, wait a minute; it would be almost impossible to get a piano up to the third floor here. How about a good electronic keyboard? Would that do you?'

He turned his glowing, innocent smile upon her. 'You are an angel.'

Bea escaped into the living room, where she doubled over, giving vent to a bout of painful laughter. The little man reminded her of Rumpelstiltskin, the dwarf in the fairy tale who came to an unfortunate end, but this modern-day gnome always fell on his feet, didn't he? He was like one of those toys that, no matter how often you laid them down, bounced back to an upright position as soon as you took your hand away.

She got out her mobile and keyed in CJ's number. 'Yes, I know it's late, but you'll never guess what's just happened. I appear to be sheltering a suspect from a murder enquiry. Do the police need to know I've got him?'

FIVE

Thursday evening

'**N**ance, he's slippery as an eel. We got in, no problem, the cafe downstairs had closed for the night, no one around, forced his front door open. He wasn't there. We roughed the place up but couldn't wait for him, because Jonno had double-parked the van outside and a car came up behind us, honking his horn and shouting, so we left and drove off before they called the police.

'We hadn't got to the end of the road before I spotted him returning to his flat, but there was this car right up to our bumper and no room to turn round. We had to circle right round the block to get back to his place. I left Jonno in the van with the engine running and went back up the stairs, but he'd only been and gone again, hadn't he!'

'How do you know he'd been and gone?'

'Dropped his pizza on the stairs. Mushroom and pepperoni. No sense it going to waste, so we brought it away with us. I'm thinking I might pay him another visit if you don't want me for anything, right?'

Friday morning

Bea stumbled downstairs, yawning. The first person down – usually Maggie – turned off the house alarm. Bea, groggily, checked, because if it wasn't turned off, the agency staff would be ringing their doorbell, trying to get in. Ianthe knew how to turn it off, of course, but she wasn't always the first to arrive.

It was off. Good.

There was no sign of Rumpelstiltskin at breakfast. Maggie said the little man was still snoring, and she'd thought it best to leave him be. Bea agreed. Not even someone as resilient as Jeremy could have his flat trashed, his piano chopped up and survive a fall down the stairs, without suffering some degree of trauma.

Maggie said she'd keep an eye out for him and accompany him back to his flat if the police arrived to inspect the damage. Besides which, he had only the clothes he stood up in, and it might be possible to rescue the rest of his belongings if someone held his hand while he did so.

Maggie seemed to understand Jeremy, and Bea was happy to let the girl play at being nanny. Bea certainly didn't feel like looking after him herself.

'Now, Maggie; about that estimate you wanted typed up. Give me the name of the client. I'll get the paperwork from Ianthe and deal with it myself.'

'Would you really have the time?'

'I'll make time,' said Bea, and she marched down to her office. Her staff were already there and hard at work. Telephone lines were buzzing, computers were flickering, all was muted efficiency. Splendid.

Ianthe smiled and bobbed her head at Bea as she passed through the main office. Ianthe was on the phone.

Bea tried to boot up her computer, and it failed to respond. She unplugged it, put the plug back, tried again. It gulped at her and produced a blue screen. Bea stared at it in horror. Blue screens meant sudden death. Rest in Peace. Finis.

'Oh no, you don't!' Switch off. Unplug. Switch on again. This time the screen produced the usual start up . . . and then asked for the day's password. Which of course she didn't have.

She left her desk to stand at the French windows, looking out into the garden. It was going to be another hot day. Her phone rang. She had an idle thought: would Ianthe pop in to give her the password, the moment Bea answered the phone?

Of course not. That would mean that Ianthe was working against, and not for, Bea.

She lifted the phone to find it was a complaint. Bea often dealt with complaints herself. Sometimes the client had been mismatched with the customer. Sometimes the customer had asked too much. Bea was always anxious to soothe ruffled feelings and make recompense if by any chance the agency had not been able to fulfil their brief to everyone's satisfaction. As seemed to be the case this time. Didn't there seem to be rather a lot of complaints recently?

Bea let a torrent of abuse wash over her. With one part of her mind she was thinking that this woman had been badly served, and with the other she was half listening for . . . ah yes. There was a tap on the door, and in came Ianthe's head.

'Oh, I see you're busy, Mrs Abbot. The password is . . .'

Bea covered the receiver with her free hand. 'Will you write it down for me, please, Ianthe? Here, on my pad. You got my memo about writing down the password for me?'

'Oh, yes. Silly me. There's such a lot happening . . . so busy as we are—'

When had Bea realized Ianthe's fluffy mannerisms hid a brain made of steel?

'Hold on a minute, will you?' Bea put the receiver down on her desk, still quacking away to itself, and tapped the new password into her keyboard. Incorrect password. Well, now; there's a surprise. Bea turned back to Ianthe, who was halfway out of the door by now. 'Ianthe; I think I shall have to set the passwords in future. This one doesn't seem to work.'

'Doesn't it? Oh, how silly of me. Do you think I've given you yesterday's password again? Dear me, so I have. Today we have all the numbers in the middle.'

'Right.' Bea tried that, and it worked. 'Don't go, Ianthe. I understand there's been a spot of bother with work for Maggie—'

'Well, yes. I hate to bring it up, because we all know she's a great favourite of yours, but her handwriting is not at all easy to decipher, and the girls really don't like taking time out to puzzle over her stuff when everything else is piling up around them.'

'If you'll find the handwritten estimate she's prepared – the one that's got to go out this week – and bring it to me, I'll type it up for her.'

Ianthe's hands twisted themselves together and her rings flashed. 'Oh, but Mrs Abbot, are you sure you can spare the time when there's so much else that needs attending to at the moment? We're run off our feet and—'

'We always had time in the past.'

'Yes, but things have moved on, haven't they? I put it down to the agency in the High Street going bust and all their clients transferring to us.'

That might well be. Bea nodded and picked up the still quacking phone. It sounded as if the client had done the threatening-with-solicitors'-letters bit and got to the tearful stage. 'Of course you're upset. I would be, too,' said Bea in her most soothing tone. 'Now, give me the details again so that I can write them down and refund your money. And next time, ask for me and I'll see to it personally that you have someone more satisfactory. Did you say you wanted someone next week as well . . .?'

Two phone calls. An experienced chef located and booked. Client reassured. Problem solved.

Bea put down the phone and went through to the main office. Ianthe was on the phone so Bea asked the nearest girl for the complaints folder and took it back with her to her own office.

The file bulged in ominous fashion. Why hadn't she been told there were so many complaints? In the old days there had been the odd problem client or customer. Sometimes the client had been mismatched with the customer, or there had been some mishap with the paperwork. That happened even in the best regulated of families.

But the current file contained an appallingly high number of complaints which didn't seem to have been dealt with, but left on file. Why hadn't Ianthe brought them to Bea's attention?

The agency might be doing well on paper, but complaints meant clients would be wary of using their services again. Flicking through the letters, again and again Bea noted the words 'inefficient' and 'badly trained'. This was not good news. The Abbot Agency always vetted their staff carefully. Or rather, Miss Brook had always done so. Query: who was vetting them now? Ianthe?

Bea decided to have a word with Ianthe about this when things were quiet.

In the meantime, she would go through the file herself to see how bad the situation might be. It was going to be a massive job. In the past . . . Ah, well, they didn't get through so much business then, did they?

She started to make notes. Where there had been complaints about the behaviour of the staff employed, she found a number of names unfamiliar to her . . . new to the Abbot Agency . . . interviewed for a job by . . .? One of the new members of staff. Previously employed by . . . Mm. Another agency. Now, she knew something about that other agency, didn't she?

She was interrupted in her work half an hour later, when Ianthe popped her head round the door with the news that Maggie's paperwork couldn't be found anywhere. Was Mrs Abbot absolutely certain that the girl had handed it in, because Maggie had been known to mislay things, hadn't she?

Bea said, 'I will enquire,' and went upstairs to find Maggie feeding their refugee's face with a fry up and coffee.

'Maggie, they seem to have lost your paperwork downstairs. Can you rough it out again for me? I'm going out for an hour and will do it when I get back.'

'She's going to help me rescue my clothes from the flat.' Jeremy displayed the confident, hopeful smile of a child looking forward to a treat. 'Then she says we'll have to speak to the police and the letting agency about the damage, because I don't suppose I'm insured though Maggie says I may be. After that we're going to look at some electronic keyboards for me. The Japanese make a good one. I think I've got my gold credit card somewhere. I do hope I didn't drop it in the street. I usually keep it in the back of my Oyster travel-card but I'm not sure I've still got it with me.'

He rummaged through pockets and produced a torn orange plastic folder. 'Triumph! I suppose I'd better get another mobile . . .' And, at that very moment, his mobile phone fell out of his back pocket. He pounced on it with glee. 'Eureka! My lucky day!'

Bea rolled her eyes at Maggie, who rolled hers back.

Bea said, 'Back in an hour or so.' And fled.

'Come!' Piers had left the door to his studio ajar, so Bea walked in. Piers was something of a nomad, who liked a frequent change of scene. He was currently occupying a spacious flat at the top of a red brick terrace near Earls Court. The main room – doubling as sitting room and studio – had a good north light.

Piers never seemed to feel the heat or the cold, and ate out when he felt like it.

Bea would have taken a bet that the oven in the kitchen was pristine, but that his top-of-the-range coffee machine and microwave were in constant use.

He was alone and at his easel. 'Can you manage the coffee machine? If so, help yourself to a cup. There's milk in the fridge, I think. Take a seat. I can do this bit in my sleep.' He was painting a mayoral chain on to the head and shoulders portrait of a fat-faced businessman.

Bea admired his technique as he flecked highlights on to the gold links. 'You've caught a sly look in his eyes.'

'He's so pleased with himself he won't see it. Knighted in the last honour's list, highly esteemed in his home city. This portrait has been commissioned by a grateful council to be hung in the mayoral parlour. Unless, of course, the law catches up with him first. I insisted on money in advance, just in case.'

Piers was tall, dark, slender and not at all handsome; but he had brains, charm and was doing very well for himself as a popular portrait painter. He liked to say he cared little for the fripperies of fashion, but his clothes were always of the finest quality – usually in black, which suited him.

Bea managed to make a cup of coffee for herself though – surprise! – there was no milk in the fridge. She shrugged. She would drink it black. It was good coffee. 'Have you time to listen to my problems?'

Piers stood back to scrutinize what he'd done, nodded, and changed brushes to work some more detail into the collar. 'Max has been round. Says you think it's time you retired and took life more easily.' He flicked at the painting, frowned, and stood well back. 'The trick is to know when to stop.'

Well, yes. Bea had to agree this was true in art as in life.

Piers cleaned the brushes he'd been using and stuck them in an old coffee mug. 'There's no need to do anything in a hurry, is there? Unless you want to up sticks immediately?'

What a relief! Why hadn't she thought of that? 'Good advice.'

He rubbed his chin. He hadn't shaved that morning, but designer stubble was fashionable at the moment; and if anyone understood fashion, it was Piers. 'Max got me thinking. I wouldn't like to lose you. I know I was a spectacular failure as a husband, but we're good friends now, aren't we?'

'That's why I wanted your advice, not only about Max but—'

He lifted his hand. 'Don't say anything till you've had time to think over what I'm about to say. Will you promise me that? Not one word, right?'

What absurdity was he going to come up with now? 'Well, yes; I suppose so.'

'I'm not suggesting that we get married again. It didn't work first time round and I'm not sure I could promise fidelity. But, the lease on this flat is up in a couple of months, and I've always liked that big house of yours. Suppose I move in with you, separate bedrooms if you wish, and I could work from the top of the house in the loft conversion Max has been telling me about.'

Bea gaped at him. Was he really proposing . . .? Without benefit of clergy, so to speak? What was she supposed to get out of such an arrangement? His company, when he felt like it?

From his point of view, it would be a good move. It would save him renting another flat; he'd have a housekeeper and cook on site; and yes, he probably meant to share her bed when he felt randy.

It was true that every now and then she'd wondered what would happen if he made a move on her, as he did on so many other women. He was undoubtedly one of the most charismatic men she'd ever met, but . . . no, No, NO! She wasn't even going to think about going down that road.

She closed her eyes and clenched her fists. Should she hit him or kiss him?

He put his arm around her and pressed his cheek to hers. 'Take your time. Till the end of next week, perhaps?'

She didn't want to kiss him. But she definitely wanted to hit him.

He kissed her ear. 'I know I've a reputation as a randy old so and so, and I can't promise never again to chase a pretty pair of legs, but you and me – it's different, isn't it? More loving friend-ship than lust. I think it might work now we're both older and have learned tolerance. Besides, you need someone to look after you.'

He looked at his watch. 'How about a spot of lunch? I've got someone coming at three.' He picked up a black jacket and checked for keys and wallet.

Bea felt distinctly shaky. With rage. What would happen if she boxed his ears, or kicked him where it would hurt most? Not that she'd ever done that to anyone, and she wasn't sure her fashionably slim skirt would allow her leg to swing up so far, but that's what she wanted to do, all right. How dare he! HOW DARE HE!

He took the portrait of the mayor off his easel and replaced it with an almost finished one of a fiftyish, heavy-set blonde, who even at this early stage of the painting had a steely look in her eye. His next sitter?

Bea told herself to calm down. Act normal. 'Piers, you're not thinking of retiring yet, are you? Well, I don't want to retire, either.'

'I know it's difficult to let go, but there comes a time when—'

'I am far from that time. In fact, I seem to have taken on another of what you once called my 'dirty' crimes. Have you ever come across a composer called Jeremy Waite?'

'I wouldn't have, would I? Unless he wanted his portrait painted. Come along. Time for lunch.' He held the door open for her to precede him.

'Or a woman called Eunice Barrow? A high-paid barrister.'

'Not my line. What have they done?'

'I'm not sure. Piers, have you ever been put in a compromising position by a woman you've been to bed with?'

'What would I have to lose? My reputation as a lady's man? Besides, I don't pay for sex. Why should I? I get offered more than I can reasonably cope with.' He took her arm. 'There's a decent enough restaurant round the corner here, vegetarian. Are you talking about the Badger Game? A married man with a lot to lose is discovered in bed with the wrong woman and pays up rather than owns up?'

'With a twist. The girl says she's under age – but doesn't intend to go to the police.'

'Nasty. I can't say I'm attracted to very young girls. I never was, and I've noticed that nowadays they have a regrettable tendency to call me "Daddy".'

'As in sugar daddy?'

He held the door of the restaurant open for her. 'As if. To my mind a woman is only interesting after she's been around a bit, though I can't say I fancy plastic breasts and puffy Botoxed skin.'

Bea couldn't help but be gratified. At least she hadn't gone down either of those roads. They ordered; pasta and a bottle of good wine.

He looked at Bea and through her. 'I wonder . . .' Shook his head at himself. 'The Badger Game? They say your hairdresser is better than a father confessor; that he sees all, hears all, never judges. My sitters usually want to talk, too. At first they tell me what wonderful people they are, how much they're loved, admired, revered. Etcetera. I don't really listen. Most of it's pie in the sky, anyway. After a while they tell me their worries about their health and their families and so on and so forth. But sometimes . . . Now you've said . . . But I see so many . . .'

'You think one of your sitters may have been caught that way?'

'You tell me your story, and I'll see if it reminds me of anything.'

So Bea related Jeremy Waite's history, giving full weight to the little man's oddities.

'He refused to pay up, and he confessed to his wife and his boss? Brave of him.'

'To tell the truth, I don't think it seemed real to him. He thinks about music all the time; and I mean, All The Time. Except when he's thinking about food. And he's undersexed, definitely.'

'He's missing a lot.'

Bea shot him a look in which fury was nicely blended with frustration. Unfortunately, he was finishing off his glass of wine and failed to see it.

He looked into the distance. 'Henry . . . Something. Another fat cat, honoured by the Queen for services rendered to some obscure charity or other. Three sittings; no, four because he changed his mind halfway through. Started solo but changed to a joint portrait with his wife. I thought at the time he was paying conscience money for some peccadillo or other by including her. A sour piece, but she'd inherited money. Henry . . . who? What was his name, now?'

'You keep records. Can't you find out?'

'True. I photograph all the portraits before they leave the studio, keep them in an album, and of course there's a card index for the years before I got a computer. But there's someone else. Asian. A doctor? No, not him. He was into boys, not girls.'

Bea pulled a face. 'Ugh.'

'Be realistic, my dove. I couldn't afford to pick and choose in those days. But you want someone recent?' He tapped the table, reminding Bea of Jeremy's five-finger exercises. How was Maggie getting on with the little man? And what about the work Bea had promised to do for the girl?

Piers covered the bill with his gold card, which also reminded Bea of Jeremy and his problems. She looked at her watch. 'I must be going.'

'Mm. So must I. Tell you what, I'll have a look through the album when I've finished this afternoon, see if anything jogs my memory. I have a mental picture of a small man with a bald head, tubby as all get out . . . but who he was and why . . .? No, it's gone. I'll ring you if I turn anything up, shall I?'

He held the restaurant door open for her to leave ahead of him. 'Take it easy, won't you, Bea? I don't like to think of you getting mixed up with the seedy side of society.'

She felt a rush of affection for him and accepted a kiss on her cheek without demur. Even though he had his own agenda, he did seem to care what happened to her.

Friday afternoon

There were no taxis in sight, but it wasn't that far to walk home, and she could do with some time to herself.

She knew exactly what to do about Piers' proposition. The very thought of it made her bubble up with indignation. The nerve of the man!

She supposed some women might have fallen on his neck and settled for the occasional bout of fun and games as the price of having him move into the house.

How dare he!

Well, she wasn't playing. Come to think of it; in the past she'd probably had more fun and games with him than he'd had with any of the other women he'd favoured over the years.

The thought made her smile.

She checked her mobile. No messages. Good. Which meant that Maggie was dealing satisfactorily with Jeremy and . . . she

began to laugh. What would Max say when he learned that his
mother had taken yet another orphan of the storm into her house?
She could just imagine it. 'Mother, you do realize you can't sell
the house with a sitting tenant!'

Mm. Well, Jeremy might well like to move in for good – as did
Piers – but she wasn't playing landlady to either of them. No way.

She swung into her road and went straight down into the
agency rooms. The women all stopped working and turned to
look at her.

Why?

'Oh, Mrs Abbot; I'm afraid he couldn't wait any longer.' Ianthe,
fluting away.

'I did try to ring you, to remind you, but you must have
switched your phone off.'

She hadn't. So, what was going on? The back of her neck
prickled. She went through into her office and Ianthe followed.
Something nasty was stirring in the woodshed. So, what was it
this time?

Ianthe closed the door behind her and dropped her voice to a
whisper. 'He wasn't best pleased, I'm afraid. I told him you must
have got held up somewhere—'

'I don't remember making any appointment for this
afternoon.'

Ianthe put both her hands over her mouth. 'Oh, but you must
remember . . . Mr Jackson, from the agency in the High Street?
He wrote suggesting . . . I know I put the letter in your folder,
and you said I should deal with it, so I suggested a suitable time.
I know I put a memo on your desk about it this morning. He
was very upset that you'd forgotten.'

And there was the memo. And, of course, the letter from Mr
Jackson would be in her folder. Neither had been there earlier
that day.

Bea recalled a film called *Gaslight*, in which the heroine had
been driven to the edge of sanity by her husband trying to make
out that she was going mad. A black and white film.

Bea, however, was not a black and white person. She was more
of a 3D, full Technicolor type, and she was beginning to wonder
if Ianthe was playing some kind of double game, trying to ease
her employer out of the agency. Though why . . .? Could Ianthe
have got wind of Max's plans for Bea to sell up and move out?

This needed to be thought through, but not at this minute. 'Never mind, Ianthe. Let's check that you have the right mobile number for me, shall we? Because I didn't receive any call from you this afternoon.'

Ianthe recited it.

Bea shook her head. 'Out by one digit. There's not an eight at the end, but a nine. Would you like to alter your records so that we don't have this mix-up again? Now, have you found Maggie's draft estimate for me? I promised to get it off today.'

'Oh, but . . . I don't think . . .!'

'Then I suggest you go and look for it, now. And if you've changed the password since this morning, I'd like you to write the new one down and give it to me straight away.'

Ianthe faded away, looking distressed. Looking as if she were about to cry. Humph. Had she really expected Bea to dissolve into tears and beg Ianthe's pardon for making so many mistakes? And pigs might fly.

Bea pushed her chair back and put her feet up on her desk, which was something she had never, ever, done in her life before. But this was a crisis. For some reason Ianthe was trying to make out that Bea had become too inefficient to run the agency.

Once she'd got that straight in her mind, Bea realized that she really, really did not want to go. And why should she, for heaven's sake?

Bea came to a decision. 'I'm going to find out exactly what's going on here – and then put a stop to it!'

SIX

First, Bea considered what she knew of Ianthe. The woman had been manageress at a small domestic agency which had collapsed that spring, leaving her without a job.

The Abbot Agency had been looking for someone with managerial skills; Ianthe had applied and been taken on.

Since arriving at the Abbot Agency, Ianthe had managed to clear out all the trusted old staff, and she had replaced them with others of her own choosing. The volume of work had shot

up, and to meet the demand . . . Ah, yes. That was it! To meet
the demand Ianthe had called on the services of men and
women who had previously been employed by the agency
which had gone bust – but, to judge by the letters in the
complaints file, those particular people had not been up to
standard. Result: the Abbot Agency's reputation for solving
their clients' domestic problems had gone down, while their
turnover had increased.

Unacceptable.

Bea had a horrid feeling that it was going to be next to impossible to turn the clock back. If she told Ianthe not to use any of
the incompetent people from the failed agency, there would be
a shortfall of trained staff to meet an increase in demand.

It seemed Ianthe was happy enough to take on all comers at
the moment, which brought her judgement into question. She
was definitely not the best person to vet new staff. Besides, she
had more than enough to do as it was.

Suppose . . . suppose Bea persuaded Miss Brook and Celia to
rejoin . . .? No, no; they wouldn't be happy to work under Ianthe,
would they?

Bea took her feet off the desk because the backs of her legs
were killing her. She rubbed her calf muscles. No wonder women
didn't usually put their feet up on their desks.

Next: Mr Jackson. Bea had met him a couple of times on
semi-social occasions. He ran a big employment agency nearby.
He was not noted for discretion or for supplying exactly what
his customers requested. Gossip said that he had eyes bigger than
his stomach, and that he wanted to be King of the domestic
scene. Twice over the past few years he'd approached Bea with
offers to amalgamate – which she'd refused.

Now Ianthe was pushing his advances forward again. Or was
she? She'd certainly succeeded in making her staff think that
Bea had 'forgotten' an appointment with the man.

What did Ianthe have to gain by making out that Bea was
losing her grip? If the agency closed or was sold, surely Ianthe
would lose her job and have to start looking for another?

Unless . . . unless Ianthe was working on behalf of Mr Jackson?
Unless Mr Jackson had promised Ianthe something substantial
for bringing the Abbot Agency down?

Which sounded fine until you remembered that Ianthe wasn't

working to destroy the agency, but to build it up. Or so it seemed. The figures were all good. If a balance sheet were produced tomorrow, it would place the agency in an excellent position for sale to the highest bidder.

Could Ianthe be working for another, different agency? A larger one, perhaps, who had plans to take over Bea? Well, no; because if that were the case, surely she'd be trying to drive *down* business so that the agency could be sold at an advantageous price to the buyer?

Speculation. Not a single fact in sight.

Time was creeping along, and Bea still hadn't typed out Maggie's estimate.

She went into the main office, to find the staff closing up for the day.

'That estimate!' Ianthe was distractedly flitting around. 'Has anyone seen poor Maggie's estimate? Oh, Mrs Abbot, I don't know what to say, I really don't, because we can't find it anywhere, and we're going to be too late to catch the post if we're not quick.'

'Is this it?' The newest recruit to the office retrieved some papers from her waste-paper bin. 'This is her writing, isn't it?'

'Oh, my goodness!' Ianthe overdid the thankfulness. The newest recruit hadn't realized she was meant to lose the papers, not find them, had she? 'Well, of all things!'

'Thank you.' Bea took charge of the papers. 'I'll see to it right away, so leave the power on, won't you, Ianthe? And –' to the new girl – 'your name is Anna, isn't it? Can you write down the current password again for me? Oh, thank you. That's excellent. Have a good weekend, and see you all on Monday.'

Ianthe pressed her hands together. 'Oh, but Mrs Abbot, what shall I say to Mr Jackson when he calls back, which he said he'd do before we went home this evening?'

'Make sure the phone's switched through to my office and leave it all to me.'

Bea watched them all leave. She didn't give Ianthe a chance to reboot her computer in order to change the password again. Or to turn off the power.

She wondered at herself for being so suspicious. Ianthe didn't really mean any harm, did she? Or did she?

The office looked desolate when they'd gone. Bea checked

that the door was locked to the outside world and went back through into her office with a sense of satisfaction. She liked being on her own. She liked being the one who made things happen. She tested the password Anna had given her to see if it was different from the one she'd been given that morning. It was different, yes. And it worked. Good.

She looked in vain for an email from Oliver. There was none. Oh well, if he didn't care to contact her, she wouldn't bother to contact him. He would be getting all the news from Maggie and CJ, anyway.

Quickly and efficiently she typed up Maggie's estimate, put it in an envelope and called up a courier service to have it delivered that evening.

Mr Jackson didn't ring. Hm. Well, she certainly wasn't going to chase him up.

But Maggie, now. What was the girl up to?

On the heels of that thought came the sound of the front door opening above, with a lot of puffing and panting.

'We're back!' cried Maggie. 'Just unloading from the taxi.'

Friday early evening

'Listen, Nance; the man who runs the coffee shop, name of Jason, says the little man didn't come back last night, but turned up with a tall, skinny girl this morning and piled a whole load of his stuff into a taxi.

'So I scooted round there, only to miss them by a couple of minutes. Jason says the landlord's livid at the damage to the flat and is threatening to sue the little man for everything he's got. Well, I helped Jason to nail a big sheet of ply over the door to the flat, and he promised to let me know the moment anything else happens. Where do you think he's gone? To the Abbot woman?'

'I don't want you stirring up any more trouble—'

'I might drop by there, see if he's around. Or I could get their telephone number and ring them, ask for him by name . . .'

Friday early evening

When Maggie had said they were unloading the taxi, she hadn't exaggerated.

First she dumped a couple of plastic bags in the hall. 'The burglars didn't touch the bedroom, and this is about half of his clothing.'

Jeremy heaved a suitcase through the door and sat on it, panting with the effort. 'Books weigh a ton.' He wiped his brow and staggered back down the steps for another load.

Maggie threw up her hands. 'He had two suitcases. He's put all his books and papers in them, and I had to put everything else into black plastic bags.'

Bea went out to help. Two plastic bags plus another suitcase, plus a laptop which didn't look as if it would ever boot up again, judging by the dent in it . . . plus a dozen or so shopping bags . . .

Breathless, Jeremy staggered past Bea into the hall with a pile of CDs, topped off with an orchid in a plant pot. 'Do you think you could pay the taxi? I'm right out of change.'

Maggie brought in some bulging carrier bags with the name of John Lewis blazoned on them. 'He couldn't find any pyjamas so we went to buy some on the way back but then he thought of other things he needed . . . whoops, mind that stereo system, it's boxed up, but we'd best not drop it . . . and last of all, but not least, there's this . . .'

'This' was a set of large cardboard boxes. For 'large', think 'enormous'. The taxi driver had to help get them out of his cab and carry them in.

'What on earth . . .?' Bea looked for her handbag to pay the cab driver.

'Mind his new keyboard.' Maggie picked up some of the bags. 'I'll start toting these upstairs. I didn't mean to take the day off work, but I couldn't stop him, once he'd started. He was like a child in a sweet shop, wanting everything he set eyes on, wouldn't even stop to eat.'

Bea paid the cab driver and saw him off before picking up some of the black dustbin bags and following Maggie up the stairs. 'I got your estimate off in the post.'

'Oh, good. If we just dump everything in Oliver's room, he can sort it out later.'

Bea lowered her load to the floor and gave Maggie an old-fashioned look.

'On the other hand,' said Maggie, 'I don't suppose he'll bother, so perhaps we'd better sort it for him. I'll bring the stereo up next.'

'I'll fetch another load. But not the books. They can stay downstairs.'

They toiled up and down the stairs until, when most things were stowed away and they were on their way back downstairs, they heard music.

Jeremy had put his new keyboard together in the sitting room and was sitting there, playing something sweet and melancholy which Bea didn't recognize. He didn't look up when they entered, but continued to play, his eyes unfocused.

He had set up his keyboard by the French windows which overlooked the garden, pushing aside the table which Bea occupied when she played patience in the evenings, and using her chair.

What was he playing? Something you could dance to; something by Mozart?

Bea sank on to the settee. Maggie folded herself into an armchair.

He was playing as if he were in a dream. The tune was there, and then it was gone, swept away by a new theme. It lifted you up and drifted you around like the petals from a cherry tree, floating here and there. A rare talent.

Bea listened and remembered going to concerts with Hamilton before he became ill. Maggie listened . . . and remembered . . . what? She was smiling, not looking at anything in particular.

Bea found her own lips had curved into a smile.

He stopped. His hands rested on the keys, his head bent over them.

Maggie shook herself. Bea's first coherent thought was that the little man would say he was hungry in a minute.

'Any chance of a bacon sandwich?'

Maggie uncurled herself, stood and stretched. 'Coming up.' She left her shoes behind her and went out to the kitchen.

Bea sighed. 'Was that one of your own compositions, Jeremy?'

'You liked it? Sometimes I just need to play. This is a beautiful room. I wish . . . I wish.' He pulled the cover down over the keys. There were silver trails on his cheeks, sliding down into his beard. 'I wanted to play something for her, for Josie. She didn't deserve to die for what she did.'

'I know.'

He turned to face her, not bothering to wipe away his tears. 'Will you find out what happened to her? And . . . perhaps . . . get me my home back?'

'I'll do my best.' She got to her feet, too. 'Would you like tea or coffee with your sandwich?'

He didn't answer.

She went out to the kitchen. 'I seem to have promised to solve his murder.'

Maggie blew her nose on a tissue. 'Poor little man. He needs a minder.' She took the sandwich and a cup of tea into the sitting room.

And came back to Bea in the kitchen. 'He's not there. He hasn't gone out, has he?'

'We'd have heard the front door. Wouldn't we?'

'Perhaps he's gone upstairs. He must be wiped out, with all that he's gone through.' Maggie traipsed up the stairs to the top floor. And then called down, 'He's not here, either.'

The front doorbell rang, and Bea answered it. CJ stood there, immaculately tailored, bearing a bouquet of flowers which had definitely not been bought from the stall at the bottom of the road, or plucked from a bucket inside the nearest convenience store. 'Ready?'

'Um.' Bea had forgotten she was meant to be going out for a meal with him. 'Sorry, we've had a bit of a . . . Jeremy's gone missing.'

'Found him!' Maggie sang out from the first floor. 'Sleeping like a babe in the guest room.'

Bea ran halfway up the stairs then – feeling her age – slowed down for the last bit. Maggie held the door open for her to see the little man had shucked off his shoes and curled up under the duvet. And yes, he was fast asleep.

Maggie said, 'Tired out, poor love. Probably forgot that he was supposed to be using Oliver's room up top.'

CJ appeared in the doorway. '"Who's been sleeping in my bed, said Daddy Bear?"'

Bea closed the door. 'This is all your fault, CJ. You wished him on me.'

'The police still fancy him for Josie's murder. They think he paid someone to kill her for him.'

'Nonsense,' said Bea.

Maggie said, 'No way!'

'Agreed.' A wolfish smile. 'So, Bea; are you ready? I have a car waiting.'

She checked on what she was wearing. Heavens! A business suit, which was not at all appropriate for an evening out. And her hair . . . and she was sure her lipstick had long since vanished. 'Five minutes.'

'Ten,' said CJ, handing the bouquet to Maggie, who was still burdened with the tray holding Jeremy's snack. 'Not a minute more.'

Bea's mobile phone rang. As she ran down the stairs to find it in her handbag, CJ followed her, saying, 'Tell them to ring back later.'

Bea fished it out of her handbag, feeling irritated. It was her first husband, Piers. 'Look, Piers; I'm just about to go out. Can I ring you—?'

'This is urgent, Bea. I've found someone, you'd never guess, but you'll have to hear it for yourself. Can you get to the studio about ten tomorrow?'

'Well, I . . .' There was so much going on at the moment, she couldn't think how she was fixed for tomorrow morning. And Ianthe—

'It really ought to be tonight; the shock may have worn off if we leave it—'

'What are you talking about?'

CJ strolled into sight, gesturing to his watch.

'The Badger Game,' said Piers.

'Oh,' said Bea. 'Right. I'll be there.' She clicked off her phone.

CJ said, 'Haven't you a copy of today's *Times*? I've nearly finished the crossword, but . . . I did say ten minutes, didn't I?'

Bea nodded and made her way to the door. What should she change into? How much time did she have?

And then she stopped in her tracks. CJ had asked her out for the evening, but not given her a time at which she should be ready. How like a man to assume you can drop everything and fall in with his timetable!

Bea could see Maggie in the kitchen, finding a vase in which to put CJ's bouquet of flowers. Maggie was not coping well with what was happening. Maggie had been in tears earlier that week, and Bea hadn't stopped to talk to her about it.

Well, she'd talk to Maggie tomorrow . . . after she'd been to see Piers.

Bea put her foot on the first step of the stairs and hesitated. *Dear Lord above, surely it won't hurt to leave it another day?*

Yes, it would.

Which was more important: trying to sort Maggie out, or falling in line with CJ's idea of punctuality?

Bea took her foot off the step and went into the kitchen. 'Maggie, I hate seeing you so miserable. I'm miserable, too. Can't we talk about it?'

Maggie gave a little sob, but continued to slot the flowers one by one into the vase. 'It's all right, honest. I've always known I'd have to move on sometime.'

'I don't want you to go.'

'Yes, but that's the way it's got to be, isn't it? I'll manage. You don't have to worry about me at all. Or Oliver.'

'Is Oliver angry with me? He hasn't been in touch, and I desperately need his advice.'

Maggie twisted round to look at Bea. 'But he said . . . He tried for days but you never replied to his emails.'

Bea blinked. 'What? But . . . Maggie, I've looked every day for emails from him, and . . . do you think that the new computer system is deleting his emails?'

'But he tried texting you and ringing your new mobile number—'

'What new mobile number? I haven't changed . . . On the other hand, Ianthe seems to have been dialling a wrong number and—'

CJ's voice cut her off. 'Ten minutes, Bea?'

'This is important, CJ. Maggie . . .?'

'You mean . . .?'

Bea could hear her voice rise. 'Maggie, if you really want to move out, I'll understand and help all I can. But I don't want to lose you, too.'

'But—'

'I did say ten minutes, didn't I?' CJ was getting sharp.

Maggie abandoned the flowers to wring her hands. 'Max said you were selling up and giving me some money for a deposit on a flat of my own.'

'Ah,' said Bea. 'And you didn't think to check with me?'

Maggie reddened. 'Nor you with me.'

Bea didn't quite know how to explain. 'Max gets ideas occasionally; not always practical. Or desirable. You don't want to
go, do you? I mean, I don't want you to.'

'I give up!' CJ announced. 'I'd better ring the restaurant and
cancel the booking.'

Maggie tried to smile. 'Yes, but I'm grown up now and
capable of earning my own living – sort of. Maybe I ought
to go.'

Bea smiled back. '*I* don't want you to go. *You* don't want to
go. We'd better sit down and talk about it properly, don't you
think?'

Maggie sniffed and reached for a tissue. 'Tomorrow, after I
finish up at number fourteen? The tiler said he'd redo one corner
of the new wet-room, but he's a slippery so and so, and I'll need
to lean on him to make sure he does it.'

'It's a date. Do you think it's safe to leave Jeremy alone for
five minutes tomorrow?'

CJ was not amused. 'Bea, the restaurant will hold the table
for another half hour, but it's in South Kensington, so if we don't
get a move on—'

'I must change. Five minutes.' Bea fled up the stairs.

'Let me help you,' said Maggie. 'You have a shower, while
I act as lady's maid.' She thundered up after Bea, overtaking
her.

Fifteen minutes later Bea descended the stairs, fresh and cool,
her make-up at a minimum but perfectly acceptable, her hair
shining. Maggie had selected a short-sleeved lacy top in apple
green for Bea to wear, over a silvery skirt. At the last minute
Bea had snatched up a russet-coloured pashmina shawl to go
over her shoulders while Maggie stuffed items from Bea's
everyday handbag into an evening clutch. Silver sandals with a
small heel completed the outfit.

CJ ushered Bea out of the house and into the waiting cab
without comment. He was miffed that she hadn't been ready
when he called, and he was making it clear he wasn't going to
make polite conversation until she apologized for keeping him
waiting . . . which she was not prepared to do.

She, on the other hand, felt much better for having talked to
Maggie. At least now they were in this together. Whatever 'this'
might turn out to be. A mystery to be solved, perhaps?

Friday evening

Maggie answered the door, munching on Jeremy's bacon sandwich, while talking on the phone to Oliver.

A well-dressed stranger, holding a pizza box. Not a delivery boy. He had a puzzled look on his face. 'Is this Mrs Abbot's place?'

'That's us.' Maggie said into the phone, 'Hold on a mo, Oliver. Someone at the door.'

The man said, 'I can't believe this is happening. I was just walking along, minding my own business, and a pizza delivery boy got off his bike and pushed this box into my hands. Said he'd been ringing your doorbell for ever and couldn't get a response, and he was late back. He said it was for a Mr Waite at Mrs Abbot's house. And drove off. Do you have a Mr Waite at your house? Has he just phoned for a pizza?'

'I didn't hear the bell. It's not very likely, but I suppose . . . if he woke up and felt peckish . . . Except, would he know where to call?'

The stranger shook his head at the mystery, handed Maggie the pizza, and made off down the road.

Maggie watched him go and returned to her phone conversation. 'Oliver, something rather odd has just happened . . .'

Friday evening

The restaurant was one of those exclusive ones which have a few too many waiting staff for the number of customers being served. CJ opened the enormous menu. Bea looked inside her evening bag for her reading glasses. Oh. No glasses.

She smiled brightly at CJ. 'What a day! Suppose you choose something light for me to eat?' Men liked to feel superior that way. And yes, CJ's rigid stance actually thawed a trifle. She threw in a couple of compliments about the restaurant, which wasn't really her style, but seemed to press the right buttons for him.

'Ah well,' he said. 'I'd forgotten that women can never be ready on time.'

Bea smiled through her teeth, wondering if his long-dead wife had been a poor timekeeper.

The meal was much as she'd expected: tiny portions which

were over-decorated and over-spiced. Also, she suspected, over-priced. The wines were good, though. She exerted herself to draw him out. Why not? It cost her little, and she didn't think he led much of a social life.

On finishing his third glass, CJ actually unbent enough to pat her hand. 'My dear Bea, may I say what a pleasure it is for me to dine with such an intelligent and amusing companion.'

Men always think you're intelligent if you get them to talk about themselves. Apparently, he'd forgiven her for keeping him waiting.

'I trust,' he said, 'that this is only the first of many pleasant evenings that we can spend together, now that you're planning to have more time to yourself.'

Alarm bells rang in her head. 'Oh, I like to keep busy, you know.'

'Yes, but . . .' He pressed her hand again. 'All work and no play . . . you know?'

Play. What did he mean by 'play'? What sort of 'play' did he have in mind?

'Which reminds me,' she said, smiling at the absurdity of it, 'that I had an offer you wouldn't believe this morning. The lease of my ex-husband's flat is up, and he suggested moving in with me.'

'What?' He removed his hand and slid smoothly into mandarin mode. 'Ah, the portrait painter with the golden touch. A favourite with the ladies, I believe.'

'Indeed. As it happens, Jeremy seems to have taken up residence with me so I don't have a spare room to offer anyone. And speaking of Jeremy—'

'I can't discuss him, as I may be called to give evidence on his behalf if the case ever comes to trial.'

Bea raised her eyebrows. What nonsense! CJ had been happy enough to give her chapter and verse the previous day. What was going on here? 'The poor little man has asked me to get his house back for him, and in a weak moment I said I'd try. Surely his wife will hang on to it, even if he's as innocent as a newborn babe.'

'I'm afraid I can't comment, other than to say that the world moves on, whether we move with it or not. We can never bring back our yesterdays, no matter how attractive they might seem in retrospect. Shall we make a move?' With an air of closing the discussion he summoned the waiter to pay with a gold card.

What he said was true. Bea considered her own situation.

Whatever she did with the agency, she didn't see how she could return it to the way it had been run in the old days. Her present success had killed off the past. The agency now had too many clients for her to run it with a couple of women and a part-time accountant. And what about the buyers who were reported to be sniffing at her heels?

Her computer . . . the password . . . her mobile phone number . . . Maggie's work put in the bin . . . Ianthe's motives . . .

It was enough to make her want to retire to the Outer Hebrides and take up weaving, or folk singing. Only, she'd heard that broadband wasn't readily available in those parts. A pity, but perhaps it would be some day soon? Well, that was something to look forward to in her dotage, wasn't it?

SEVEN

Friday evening

'If you'll take my advice,' said CJ, holding the door of the restaurant open for Bea, 'you'll distance yourself from Jeremy Waite. I agree with you that he's probably innocent of killing the girl himself, but if the tabloids get news of your taking him in, you might find yourself in the middle of a crowd of paparazzi, all wanting murky details about your past life.'

'There aren't any murky details in my past life.'

'It's surprising the twist they can put on the most innocent detail. Your charitable impulse to take in Oliver and Maggie could be misinterpreted, as could your continuing relationship with your first husband, whose peccadilloes are well known. The newspapers will make some lies up and defy you to sue them – which it would be folly to do. And what about Max? Suppose they start looking into his life? Is he as squeaky clean as he claims about his expenses?'

'Of course.' Bea flushed, because she couldn't be entirely sure that he was. And he'd dallied with an extramarital blonde or two in the past, hadn't he?

CJ didn't labour the point, but summoned a taxi with a flick of his fingers. An admirable trait in a man, to be able to summon a taxi just like that.

Bea said, 'Whatever happened to justice?'

A saintly tone. 'My reputation depends upon my being an impartial witness.'

Through her teeth, she said, 'Understood. But *I'm* not bound by your need to be whiter than white.'

Except, perhaps, that if the agency were targeted by the press, she might well lose most, if not all, of her clients.

She got into the cab beside him. 'So now you've pointed out that there may be hidden dangers in the situation, where does that leave me? You drew me into this affair, remember. Did you foresee this conversation, when you invited me to have tea with you at the Ritz? One moment you ask me to look after the little man, and in the next you warn me off.'

A condescending smile. 'It is always a pleasure to take an intelligent woman out to dine. I trust you enjoyed the evening and that it is only the forerunner of many more to come.'

Four letter words hovered on the tip of her tongue, but she restrained herself from spitting them out. With an effort.

When they drew up outside her house, she said, 'Thank you for the evening. Most enjoyable. If I turn up any information which is relevant to Jeremy's case, do I tell you about it? Or would you prefer me to contact someone else?'

'A Detective Inspector Durrell is in charge of the case. He gave me his card, which you can have. Yes, here it is. He seems competent enough.' A smile, a wave. He held the door open for her to leave the cab, got back in and told the driver to carry on.

Bea almost stamped her foot. But desisted. Her sandals were too fragile for rough treatment.

Saturday morning

Bea overslept. Maggie had disappeared by the time Bea got downstairs, but had left a note for her. 'Winston's been fed. Back for lunch, with luck. Oliver rang, sends his love.'

Good. Winston was acting as if he hadn't been fed for a fortnight, so Bea gave him some scraps of the bacon she was frying for breakfast. Unlike some cats, he preferred human food.

A soft footfall. Bea jumped. It was Jeremy Waite, barefoot, hair all over the place, still half asleep. 'Breakfast?'

She fed him, asked what he intended to do with himself that day. He didn't reply. She shrugged, gave up on him. 'If you go out, take a front door key with you.' She showed him where the spare hung in a cupboard by the back door. He nodded, though she wasn't sure he'd understood what she'd said. Well, Maggie would be back at lunchtime, and so would she.

She went down to the agency rooms. It was Saturday, and only two girls were on this morning. One was Anna, the girl who'd retrieved Maggie's paperwork from her bin. Both girls smiled and nodded at Bea as she passed through to her office, collecting the mail as she went. Before she went into her own room, she paused to look into Maggie's office. Hm. Just as she'd expected; everything had been cleared off the desk, and Maggie's papers had been neatly placed into a large cardboard box. Maggie was being moved out.

Frowning, Bea went through into her own office, sorting the post out as she went. Bills, mostly. She switched on her own computer. Was asked for the password. Yesterday's didn't work; surprise! Bea got through to Anna on the internal phone and was relayed the new password. Now how had Ianthe got the password changed from last night? Had she instructed Anna or the other girl to change it early this morning?

Bea wished Oliver were due home. He'd know how to disentangle this business of Ianthe's changing of the password every five minutes.

She dealt with the mail with one eye on the clock. Piers had asked her to be at his studio at ten, so she hadn't much time to deal with agency affairs.

She was tempted to shut the computer down for the day, but after considering the problem of the passwords, left it running on a screen saver.

She fluffed up her hair, checked that her short-sleeved blouse and skirt looked presentable, and flagged down a taxi. It wasn't worth taking the car round to Piers', as there was no possibility of parking there. The taxi was held up in traffic and, as she toiled up the stairs to Piers' place, she realized she was going to be a few minutes late.

'Come!' Piers was at work already. This time he was putting

the finishing touches to the background of the gimlet-eyed woman's portrait, the one he'd planned to work on the previous afternoon.

There was another man in the room; a youngish, fattish, hair-receding business type, trying to look comfortable in casual clothes, whereas Bea thought he'd only look right in a three-piece suit. An accountant? Someone in the banking system?

'Come in, Bea. You know where the coffee is. I've actually remembered to get some milk in. Meet "Basil", whose real name I am forbidden to give you.'

'Mummy said it wouldn't be necessary.' Indeed, he bore a distinct resemblance to the iron maiden in the portrait, though somewhat watered down. Son? A man in his mid-thirties who still called his mother 'Mummy'?

'Basil' shook her hand. His was slightly damp. 'It's a pleasure to meet you, Mrs Abbot. Mummy thought about what Piers said overnight, about your husband having a similar experience to poor Daddy's, and she decided that I should give you the facts without mentioning any names. Mummy is sympathy itself for you in your loss, but you must promise me never, ever, to reveal, well, anything, because we don't want the paparazzi . . . You understand? And of course we would deny, if . . . Absolutely.'

Bea treated him to a reassuring smile. 'Absolutely.' So Bea's husband was supposed to have had a problem with another young girl? Which husband would that have been? Hamilton, or Piers? Or some fictional creature thought up by Piers? She shot a glance at Piers, who was looking amused.

Bea made coffee for herself and 'Basil', and fixed an enquiring, sympathetic expression on her face.

It wasn't that warm a day, but 'Basil' patted his forehead with a clean, folded handkerchief. 'I can't really see any advantage in disclosing . . . And indeed, this is all supposition on Mummy's part, you understand? I personally don't agree at all with her conclusions, and there is absolutely no proof. But Mummy . . . She was distraught when it happened. We had to get the doctor in for her. But now . . . Well, everything's worked out brilliantly, because she's a wonder, she really is, and the business has taken a leap forward under her direction. Daddy had always said she would have taken to it like a duck to water if she'd stirred herself.

But then, she never had to bother her head with it while he was alive, did she?'

'Indeed,' said Piers, managing to keep a grave look on his face. 'A pillar of industry, your mother. Going to the top of the honours list, I wouldn't wonder.'

'Well, I don't know about that.' But he obviously hoped for it, oh yes. 'It's true she has risen above what might easily have been, well, a total disaster in terms of . . . nearly three thousand employees, you know? It was such a shock! Her losing all that weight as she did in the months after it happened must have helped her physically, and I do try to make allowances when she . . .'

'Flips?' suggested Piers.

Basil stared. 'No, no. Of course not. Mummy never loses her temper. When she misunderstands, if that's the right word . . . No, when she imagines the worst about a totally innocent friendship which Daddy had with an unfortunate girl who was just like a daughter to him. I'm an only child, you understand? No sister, no brother. Mummy takes against people sometimes, and there's no arguing with her, although anyone else could see that Angie was the last person to . . .

'Daddy knocked her off her bike, you know, not seeing her as he drove out on to the road. So of course he was worried about her. Who wouldn't be? And she was so sweet, and wouldn't take anything from him at first even to get her bike repaired, and she was off work for weeks with her wrist. But she left her address, so naturally he went round there a couple of times—'

Naturally. For 'Angie', read 'Josie'?

'But there was absolutely nothing in it. He swore there wasn't, and I believed him. Mummy says now that he had some sort of mid-life crisis. She says he fancied Angie; well, who wouldn't? Pretty little thing, all dark curls and . . . don't get me wrong. I only caught a glimpse of her that once when I had to drop a note round to her to say Daddy couldn't make it, he was supposed to be taking her to the circus or something, that's how innocent it all was, though you could say it was unwise, but—'

'Where did you take the note?' Bea was interested.

'A back street house, Hammersmith Way. First on the left past St Peter's church – or was it St Matthew's? One or the other. Mid terrace. I could take you straight there, but she's not there now. No, no. It was a mid-life crisis. But when the money went missing from that old account that Mummy had almost forgotten about till she got the annual statement, and Daddy couldn't account for it, because he wasn't thinking straight, his sciatica playing up something chronic, and in so much pain . . . Well, it wasn't surprising that he got his pills muddled up, was it?'

Piers shook his head in sympathy. 'A shocking, unforeseeable accident.'

Basil looked relieved to find Piers so understanding. 'A genuine mistake, an overdose. Mummy was desolated, but she's recovered very well, very well indeed. In fact, everyone says she looks twenty years younger.'

He looked at his watch. 'Now, have you quite finished? I promised I'd take the portrait down to her at the house in the country this afternoon, as she wants to show it to some friends. I asked the chauffeur to bring the car round about now.'

Bea said, 'Did you see Angie, to tell her about your father dying?'

'I went there, yes. But she'd moved.'

Basil left, carrying his mother's portrait with him. Bea watched from above as he loaded it carefully into a chauffeur-driven car below. She made a note of the licence number, just in case.

Piers joined her at the window, to hand over a slip of paper. 'Daddy and Mummy's name and address. In an idle moment yesterday I asked her if she'd ever heard of anyone being caught by a pretty young thing, and her expression told it all. She wasn't prepared to talk then; said she'd think it over. She rang me back later to say her son would give me any details I needed if it would help you to overcome your grief at your husband's death.'

'I don't know whether I'm appalled or amused at your taking my name in vain.'

'It worked, didn't it? In my opinion she's still spitting tacks about Daddy's affair with young Angie.'

'You agree with me that Angie set him up? The trap was sprung. Blackmail was demanded, so he fiddled the books to pay her off. Mummy found out, and he took an overdose.'

'Angie might not be your Josie.'

'Agreed. "Basil" was keen on her too, wasn't he? I wonder if it would be possible to track down her address?'

'If it wasn't a "front".'

'She had to live somewhere. Had to meet her sugar daddy somewhere. Mummy wouldn't have taken kindly to his meeting Angie at their house – or at the workplace.'

Although . . . Bea frowned. 'Basil's' Angie might well not be Jeremy's Josie.

Piers said, '"Basil" will deny everything, remember. If the police were interested, perhaps they could track the place down, but as she's no longer there I don't see the point of our trying to find it. Try these other leads instead. I don't *know* that either of them has been the victim of a Badger Game, but they're both rumoured to have had affairs on the side.' He handed her two more slips of paper.

'Sir Thomas, aiming for the House of Lords. I did his portrait a couple of years back. A man with a face like a squeezed turnip, made his millions in the City and got out just before the boom went bust. He hinted he enjoyed a bit on the side but reckoned it was worth it, put it down to expenses. It kept him young, or so he said. Married into the aristocracy and enjoys the high life. The only thing is that if he'd got involved with your Angie or Josie, he'd have paid up with a smile.'

'The trick being for the Badgers not to ask for more than their victims can afford to pay?'

'Probably. The other man who might or might not be of interest is one Sir Charles, a big brute of a man, smokes cigars. He's been an unsuccessful Tory candidate at two of the last couple of by-elections and proposes to stand again as soon as there's another opening. A generous donor to the party. Ask Max. He might have come across him.'

'He boasted to you about having a bit on the side?'

'No, he's not sat for me, but . . .' Piers rubbed his ear. 'Bea, I'm not sure I want you tangling with this man, because it's not supposed to be safe to cross him. I've seen him around, but never spoken to him. The thing is, I was painting a politician of a different persuasion recently, who said he'd been up against Sir Charles in a by-election and that there'd been allegations of nasty tricks . . . on both sides, I shouldn't wonder. My sitter had wondered about using an item of scandal he'd heard about Sir Charles, but eventually decided it wasn't worth it.

'Apparently Sir Charles believes that women enjoy being "roughed up". He boasts of saving a "juicy little bit" from a mugger, who'd been appropriately grateful afterwards . . . until her pimp had tried to get some money out of him, whereupon Sir Charles had beaten him up so badly he'd ended in hospital. Also there'd been some talk of a cab driver who'd tried to overcharge Sir Charles; he'd ended up in hospital, too.'

'You think he might have been another of Josie's victims?'

'Hardly a victim. In a way you can't blame him as his wife is an anorexic clothes horse who's got a stranglehold on him, since she's the daughter of a big mover and shaker at Central Office.'

Bea was restless. 'Supposition, hearsay and gossip. Did your informant beat him in the polls?'

'Yes, but I doubt if he'd talk to you about Sir Charles. That's it. You asked me to gather some gossip for you, and I have.'

'I'm not sure what I'm looking for. Something which might help Jeremy, I suppose. Apparently, the police still fancy him for Josie's murder, think he paid someone to do the job. Most unlikely. Somehow or other I need to get the police off his back, without involving CJ. No, I don't think you know CJ; he's something in one of the ministries, was drawn into providing an alibi for Jeremy by accident and doesn't want anything more to do with him.'

'What a pleasant man.'

'Well, at least he doesn't tell lies in order to get people to talk to him.'

'Me, tell lies? I've had a dozen women offering to leave their husbands in order to languish in my arms.'

'I dare say. But you haven't been stupid enough to fall for a girl young enough to be your granddaughter. In any case, we can't assume it's the same girl every time.'

'All right. Let's look at it another way. There's a brain behind the girl or girls. How do these girls know which men might fall for their charms? Are they picking out vulnerable but moneyed men by accident?'

Bea could see where this was leading. 'You think there must be an older, worldly-wise person behind the scenes, selecting the men and teaming the girls up with them.'

'In the only case about which we know anything for certain, a photographer was involved. Could he be the brains behind the scam? Is this a two-person venture?'

'From what Jeremy said about the photographer in his case, it doesn't sound likely. I'll have to ask him. Mind you, the most unlikely people can be found studying the *Financial Times* at breakfast. But it takes a certain cast of mind to think up the means by which the girls make contact with these older men. A bicycle accident. A mistaken address. Saving a pretty young thing from a mugger. It seems to me that these are carefully thought up, even orchestrated, events. It looks like a three or even four person group to me.'

She struck her hands together. 'Oh, this is nonsense. These are probably isolated instances in which vulnerable men are taken for a ride by a number of bright young things.'

Piers put his arm around Bea's shoulders. 'You don't believe that, do you?'

She shook her head. She didn't remove his arm, either. It was a comfort, even if her wiser self knew that in ten minutes' time he might be putting his arm around another woman, who would possibly be younger and prettier than Bea. Still. For the moment, she accepted it.

He nuzzled her ear. 'And you've been thinking about my proposition?'

She nodded. It didn't seem quite as outrageous now as it had done at first.

'Good. The light at the top of your house should be fine for painting.'

'No, you don't.' She eased herself out from under his arm. 'That's Maggie and Oliver's home.' And she could just imagine the chaos Piers would create in her household, demanding attention at all hours of the day and night. And suppose he wanted to bring a woman in . . . No!

'But you said—'

'I'm not saying anything, or promising anything. There's a lot to consider and I'll let you know when I've thought it all through.'

'Worth a try.' He looked at his watch, and picked out another canvas to put on his easel. This one was blank. He selected some photographs from a clutch of papers on the table and pinned one up above the canvas. 'I'm not sure how this one is going to turn out. I've had two attempts at this man already and abandoned both. Third time lucky.'

'I can take a hint.' Bea finished off her coffee and departed.

Saturday noon

'Calm down, Phil. You're wearing the carpet out.'

'How can you make jokes when—'

'My job is to do the thinking for all of you, and not to let you fly off like a Catherine Wheel.'

'I want to get Jeremy where—'

'And bring the police down on us? Don't be an idiot. We can't touch him. So let's move on with our next—'

'We know where he is. I can winkle him out of there and—'

'You said there's at least two other women living in that house. So how do you propose to get him away without anyone noticing?'

'I'll tell them I'm the police, and he's wanted for more questioning. Plain clothes police. No problem. Get him in the car, get going. Jonno can drive the car, and once we have him at the garage at the back of the flats, say . . . or anywhere quiet . . . it's the weekend, plenty of places we can dump him afterwards. Come on! You don't like the idea of his getting away with it, either. Am I right, or am I right?'

'I don't like the odds. What about the women? They'll remember you, and when he turns up dead, they'll be able to describe you. We can't risk that.'

'I'll wear heavy-framed glasses and a hairpiece. They won't need to see Jonno, he'll be sitting in the car outside. Look, I promise I'll be back before you know it. It's just a spot of unfinished business, that's all. And then we can concentrate on the next one, right?'

EIGHT

Bea put her key in the door and walked in on Bedlam. At least, she wasn't old enough to remember what an eighteenth-century madhouse looked like, but she assumed that what she was seeing might be close enough.

A large man in a brown suit was standing with his back to her, pointing at his watch and yelling that someone should get a move on, or else!

The garden gnome, clad this time in grey silk pyjamas, was dancing up and down, shouting that it wasn't his fault.

Maggie, in an emerald green top with hair to match, was screaming at someone to get out of her way. So at least Maggie was back to her usual appearance.

A gentle tide of water washed over the hall carpet towards Bea, causing her to dodge sideways into the sitting room . . . which was littered with books, dirty plates and mugs, cardboard boxes and papers. Someone had opened the French windows and a breeze was shifting papers around. Winston, the cat, was chasing the papers up and down the room. What was going on here?

Bea shut the door to the sitting room, in the hope it would keep the water out of there, and advanced on the kitchen . . . which was in a similar state of disarray, with dirty cooking pans everywhere and water sloshing about on the tiled floor.

The large stranger stood in her way. He was red in the face and yelling that he hadn't got time to waste.

Bea used her most authoritarian tones. '*What* is going on?'

A babble of voices answered her. Jeremy first: 'I'm so sorry, I was just trying to wash—'

Maggie looked furious 'He overloaded the washing machine, and—'

The stranger whirled round on Bea with the baffled, angry look of a cornered animal. 'Police! I've been asked to take Mr Waite in for questioning and—'

'It's a different machine, you see, from the one I—'

Maggie screamed at Jeremy. 'Shut up, shut up! Will you just shut up for a minute! Bea, he's pulled the hose off the wall. I've got it back on but—'

'I tried to call an engineer, but I can't find my—'

The stranger's glasses flashed. He made a grab for Jeremy and missed. 'You, come with me, now!'

Bea put ice into her voice. 'That's enough, sergeant . . . er . . . detective inspector, or whatever you are. Now. Everyone. Calm. Down.'

'I told him!' muttered Maggie, furiously using a dustpan and brush to scoop water up from the floor and empty it into the sink.

Jeremy apologized. 'I'm so sorry! Let me help!'

'No!' said Maggie and Bea with one voice.

The stranger said, 'Now, can we please get on? Mr Waite, you are required down at the station—'

Bea seized a mop and began to push the water on the floor back towards Maggie and away from the carpeted hall. 'Well, he's not going anywhere, barefoot and wearing pyjamas.'

Jeremy said, 'I was trying to explain to the sergeant here, that I put all my jeans into the washing machine by mistake, and I rather think my mobile phone may be in there as well, and my credit cards—'

'You need a minder,' said Bea, brushing past the policeman to wring out her mop in the sink. 'Sergeant – or is it detective inspector? – would you kindly move your feet so that I can get at that corner?'

He didn't seem to know where to move, so she grasped his upper arm and pushed him back towards the hall.

'These old houses,' said Jeremy, hopping from one bare foot to the other. 'The floors do slope. It might help to sweep the water out of the kitchen door?'

Maggie said, 'Gotcha!' She opened the back door and began to swoosh water out on to the iron staircase with her dustpan.

'Enough chat,' said the stranger, making another grab for Jeremy and again failing to connect. 'I've a car waiting outside—'

'He can't go like that,' said Bea, moving him out of her way to get working on the floor by the hall. 'You'll have to come back for him when he's dressed.'

'I don't care what he's wearing. I want him now!' There was a rough note in his voice. Panic?

Bea paused in her sweeping operations. 'What did you say your name was? May I see your ID, please?'

Jeremy said, 'Look, I don't mind coming with you if I can just get a pair of jeans out of the machine, but I can't open the door—'

Maggie snapped at him. 'You put too much in, idiot! There's a trick to it.' She re-set the programme, clicked 'on' and let the drum rotate twice – and then stopped it. 'There!' She clicked the door open and started pulling out a wodge of sodden clothing.

Jeremy tried to help her. 'Can you see my mobile phone? Will it still work?'

The stranger looked at his watch again. 'However wet they are, give him his jeans and let's go. They'll dry on him, won't they?'

'Certainly not,' said Bea. 'He'd catch his death of cold. Look, I'll ring your boss and tell him what's happened. Say I'll bring him to the station later on today.'

'We need him *now*!' He made another grab for Jeremy and this time got hold of the little man's upper arm, practically lifting him off his feet.

'Put that man down this instant!' Bea flourished the mop at the stranger's head. He ducked, swearing. And let go of Jeremy.

Someone behind them laughed in genuine amusement. 'Well, well. What have we here?'

Maggie abandoned the pile of washing and threw up her arms with a scream of delight. 'Ollie, my love!' And to Jeremy, 'Out of my way, clot!'

Bea rushed at the newcomer. 'Oliver! Oh, my dear boy!' She hugged him, hard. And then realized she still had hold of the mop.

Oliver put one arm around her, mop and all. And reached out his free arm to hug Maggie, too. 'Home, sweet home! Always chaotic. Mrs Abbot; were you really going to poke that man's eyes out with the mop?'

'What?'

They heard the front door slam. The stranger had disappeared, but Jeremy was still with them. He bobbed up and down in front of Oliver. 'Is it your bed I'm sleeping in at the moment?'

'I can doss down anywhere,' said Oliver, who seemed to have grown another inch or two since they'd last seen him at Easter. Slender and swarthy; handsome in his own way; Oliver had been adopted as a baby but never fitted in. He'd been thrown out by his adoptive father when he was eighteen, only to be dragged home to Bea by Maggie, rather as you'd take home a stray dog. Oliver had made himself useful at the agency until he'd gone up to university; he was brilliant at anything to do with advanced maths and/or computers.

'Welcome home, geek!' said Maggie, tugging at the rucksack on his shoulder. 'We need you. Is this all your luggage?'

'Welcome home, Oliver,' said Bea. 'Did Maggie tell you we were in trouble?'

'So did CJ, who drove over to fetch me this morning. He thinks you need a man about the house this weekend for some reason.'

'Oh, we do,' said Bea. 'Always.'

'I'm afraid I'm more trouble than I'm worth,' said Jeremy, looking forlorn. 'I didn't mean to cause any extra work.'

'You need a nursemaid,' said Maggie, going back to sort out his clothes. 'Now, here's your mobile phone and this looks like your wallet. Both sodden, but the cards should be all right. Oliver, can you get his mobile working for him while I put his clothes in the drier?'

'I can but try.'

Bea mopped up the last of the water. 'Judging by the number of dirty pans and plates hanging around, it looks as though Jeremy's already eaten. Perhaps we should get a takeaway for lunch?'

'I was hungry and didn't know when Maggie would be back,' said Jeremy. 'I wouldn't mind a little something more to eat now, though.'

'Leave lunch to me,' said Maggie, whirling around the kitchen like a dervish, throwing dirty pans into the sink, plates into the dishwasher, and retrieving packages of food from the fridge. 'But get Jeremy out from under my feet first.'

Laughing, Oliver urged Jeremy and Bea back to the sitting room. 'Now, suppose someone brings me up to date. Maggie and CJ both seemed to think I was needed back here. So, what's going on?'

Saturday afternoon

'You blew it! You didn't retrieve Waite, and you've let three more people get a look at you! When I think how careful we've been never to let ourselves be seen . . .!'

'I tell you, it was a chance in a million. Waite let me in, no problem, but he wasn't dressed, looked like he'd only just got up, and he'd been trying to do something in the kitchen and there was water everywhere, and then this girl storms in and yells at us both, and then the madam arrived. Well, I tried to yank him out of there but she went for me! Then, blow me down but a youth arrives, mixed blood looked like, and well – I got out of there, quick.'

A shriek. 'You . . . idiot! If you've put us all in danger—'

'Josie was my niece, for heaven's sake!'

'My niece, too! A niece we hadn't seen since she was born, and who was already on the game when we found her. How long do you think she'd have lasted if we hadn't taken her off the streets? We fed her and clothed her and found her a nice place to live—'

'Waite killed her, and I'm not letting him get away with it!'

'You're on your own, then.'

'You don't mean that. Nance, you wouldn't—'

'You try my patience to the limit. No, Phil. I didn't mean it. Or I did, but . . . we've been together a long time, haven't we? Let's sit down and work something out.'

Saturday afternoon

'You ask what's going on, Oliver?' Bea started to clear up in the sitting room. 'I wish I knew. I can't think straight about anything. One minute I think Ianthe – that's the new manageress – is trying to . . . No, that's not the most important thing that's happening, is it?'

'I really am most terribly sorry,' said Jeremy, picking up papers and putting them down on the table, from which the breeze promptly shifted them again.

Bea slammed the French windows shut and scooped up Winston, who'd been licking out a dirty plate on the floor. 'Take the cat, will you, Oliver?'

Oliver did, the huge black furry animal overflowing his arms. Oliver rubbed the cat's chin. Winston responded by half closing his eyes in bliss.

Bea collapsed on to the settee, first removing a sheaf of papers. 'The most important thing, Oliver—'

'I'm afraid it's me,' said Jeremy. 'Getting mixed up with a murder, though I never meant to.'

Bea slapped papers at him. 'No, even more important than you, Jeremy. But we need Maggie in for this.'

'Soup up,' cried Maggie, bearing a tray of mugs in from the kitchen. 'Mind out; it's hot.'

Bea took a mug and said, 'Maggie, I don't know what else you've got on, but what I've got to say is more important than anything. Please, sit down for a minute. Oliver, sit on the other side of me, but don't let go of Winston or he'll start licking dirty plates again.'

Oliver was smiling. 'We're all ears.'

Bea said, 'My dears; the most important thing is what's been happening – or not happening – between us three. Max has been meddling, hasn't he? With the very best of intentions, of course. He didn't ask me what I wanted, and now I'm in such a state that I don't know what I ought to do. Except that I don't want our family to break up.'

Jeremy sat cross-legged on a chair. 'Mother hen.'

Bea nodded. 'Mother hen; and these two are my almost-grown-up chicks.'

'Some chick,' said Maggie, blowing on her soup.

Oliver said, 'I've been an idiot, haven't I? When I got that text saying you were rather busy but would get back to me—'

'I didn't send you any such text. I've been worrying for days, not understanding why you haven't been in touch. I suppose you also got a text saying my mobile phone number had been changed?'

'Yes,' said Oliver and Maggie together.

'I ought to have used my head.' Oliver reddened. 'You don't like texting, because you prefer to hear people's voices. Come to think of it, anyone can send a text, signing it with your name. I never thought to check whose phone it came from. I was too busy. No; I was hurt and upset and I should have thought. Stupid!'

'Idiot!' Maggie tossed him an affectionate look. 'I didn't make that mistake – exactly. But I must admit that when Max told me the agency was to be sold . . .'

'Is it?' Oliver asked. 'Not that it's any business of mine. And before you start on about having to pay my fees at university, I have to inform you that I've been granted a bursary which will almost completely cover my costs for the next couple of years. By which time I hope to be self-supporting.'

'Bless you, my love,' said Bea, 'but it isn't the money that's worrying me. Something's gone very wrong at the agency, and for the life of me I can't see how to put it right. I don't like the way Maggie has been pushed out into the cold. I hate the way Miss Brook and Celia have been made to resign. I went away for a fortnight's holiday and on my return I find I've lost control of the computer system, my address book has been vandalized . . . and I haven't a clue why.'

Oliver looked alert. 'I suppose that's why CJ wanted me back here; to put the computer systems right for you?'

'I don't think so,' said Bea, in a grim tone. 'I rather think he's got something else on his mind. Wouldn't you agree, Jeremy?'

'I didn't mean to—'

'You never do mean to,' said Maggie, standing up. 'Sandwiches all round?'

'Before you go, Maggie,' said Bea, 'and before we discuss anything else, I want you and Oliver to understand that your home is with me, for as long as you want to stay. I mean that. If I have to leave this house – which I don't want to do, by the way – then I shall buy somewhere that has space for you both.'

Just in time, she remembered that Max had planned she should give Oliver and Maggie something to start up by themselves, and winced. 'Of course, if you'd prefer to take some money from me to get on to the housing ladder—'

'No, we wouldn't,' said Oliver.

Maggie shook her head, too. 'What Oliver means is that we're not grown up enough to leave Mother Hen yet. So yes, please; may we stay?'

'Bless you, my children.' What a relief. 'Phew!' Bea tried to laugh, to lighten the atmosphere. 'My word, how serious we all are!'

Oliver put his arm around her shoulders. 'Did you really think you could push us out of the nest so easily? Wherever you go, we go, too.'

'Amen,' said Maggie returning the empty mugs to the tray. 'Sandwiches coming up.'

Jeremy sighed. 'Mrs Abbot, you remind me of my mother, long gone, may she rest in peace. Oh well. I suppose I ought to ring the police station and tell them I'll be over later. Is my mobile working yet?'

'Give me a chance,' said Oliver.

Jeremy said, 'Sorry. Well, may I use your landline, Mrs Abbot?'

'Try it,' said Bea. 'But I doubt if they'll know what you're talking about.'

'But that policeman—'

'He wasn't. At least, I don't think so. Did he show you his ID when he arrived? Did he give you his name?'

'I'm afraid I wasn't really paying attention . . . The washing machine, you know?'

Bea said, 'The police are supposed to show identification straight off. Maggie, did you see any?'

Maggie shook her head. 'Come to think of it, no. But I was so distracted . . .' And she sent Jeremy the sort of reproving look you'd give a small child who'd spilt his milk all over the table.

Oliver sat up straight. 'Mr Waite, CJ told me he'd supplied an alibi for you when you were suspected of killing a young girl. Is that right? Someone who'd got you into a compromising situation and then tried to blackmail you? So, was our caller part of the same scam? I mean, if he wasn't a policeman, then who was he?'

Bea said, 'That's what I've been wondering. Oliver, will you check while I make us some coffee? I've got a contact name and telephone number for the policeman in charge of the investigation . . . CJ gave it to me and I made a note of it somewhere . . . Yes, here it is. It's Saturday afternoon, maybe he's off duty. But suppose you see if you can find him, ask him if he arranged for Jeremy to go in for further questioning.'

She went out to the kitchen, where Maggie was busy building a pile of sandwiches. Switching on the kettle to make some coffee, Bea tried to think clearly. Their visitor had tried to take Jeremy away with him, even though the little man was hardly dressed for it. The man had said he'd a colleague waiting in a car outside for him. So there were two of them involved.

'I've just thought,' said Maggie, transferring the tower of sandwiches to a large plate. 'If that wasn't a policeman, then what did he want Jeremy for?'

'Great minds think alike.' Bea collected mugs, milk and sugar, ladled coffee grounds into the percolator, and poured on boiling water.

Returning to the living room with the food, they found Oliver replacing the handset on the house phone. 'DI Durrell is off duty but they'll try to get a message to him. As far as they know, no one had been asked to interview Jeremy again. They were keen for us to make a note of what we can remember of the man.'

Jeremy pounced on the sandwiches. 'It's a nightmare. All I want to do is work, and all this –' he waved his arms – 'interferes.'

'We should make some notes while his visit is fresh in our minds.' Oliver popped a sandwich into his mouth and got his laptop out of his rucksack. 'Hold on while I boot up and open a new document.'

Maggie said, 'He looked like a salesman. I think.'

'Hold on, hold on!' cried Oliver. 'Right, now. Height; about five ten. Build; well built, not skinny. Age; about fifty. Hair; he was wearing a chestnut brown toupee—'

'Was he?' said Maggie. 'I would never have guessed.'

'You can tell better from the back,' said Oliver, tapping keys. 'There's a sort of ledge or overhang. Glasses; slightly tinted, heavy frames. Eyes . . . what colour would you say? Mrs Abbot, you're good at noticing these things.'

'My impression is – hazel.' Bea closed her eyes the better to recall what she'd seen. 'Hip-length jacket, waterproof, in a sad green colour. Brownish to khaki trousers, not jeans. Green-and-white checked shirt, open at the neck. Slip-on shoes, brown, polished. No socks. His head was oval-shaped . . . There's probably a technical term for it, but I don't know what it is. Clean shaven. Good teeth but slightly irregular; so probably his own. His watch was a good one; a Rolex with lots of little dials on it. A heavy metal bracelet for it – silver . . . no, steel. No piercings, no tattoos. Naturally pale skin, hardly any suntan, so either he doesn't like being in the sun or maybe he's on some medication or other . . . Perhaps he's been ill?'

'Or in prison?' said Jeremy, reaching for the last-but-one sandwich.

'A slight paunch,' said Maggie, fending Jeremy off to divide the very last sandwich in two and share it with him. 'Not really noticeable, but his shirt bulged ever so slightly over his trousers in the front.'

They thought for a while. Eventually, Oliver said, 'Did I imagine a slight brogue?'

Jeremy looked longingly at the empty sandwich plate. 'Irish. Baritone. Josie was Irish, too, although you could hardly tell. I'd say they'd both been in this country for years. This man was well educated, to judge by his voice. Better educated than Josie, come to think of it.'

Maggie said, 'I wonder . . . I wonder if our visitor could be the man who tried to deliver a pizza to Jeremy last night; only, he wasn't wearing a toupee then, or glasses. Oh, no. How could it be?'

'Why not? What was the colour of his hair?'

'Couldn't see. He wore one of those soft caps with a stiffened brim at the front that older men often wear. No, it can't be the same man, surely, because the pizza man had very heavy, dark eyebrows, almost meeting over his nose. I never gave him a thought. He was just any old passer-by doing a favour for someone else. The sort who walks their dog in the evening, you know?'

'Dressed?'

Maggie shrugged. 'A light-coloured shirt, open at the neck, no tie. Jeans, I think. I was on the phone to Oliver; I hardly looked at him.'

Bea beat off Winston, who was trying to steal the last of her sandwich. 'Jeremy, could our visitor have been the photographer who tried to get money out of you?'

'Oh, no. A very different type. The photographer was tallish, thinnish, lighter in weight, skinnier, shaven-headed. The usual London accent, state school not private, a tenor voice, somewhat rough. Not particularly well educated. He shouted at me. I suppose he thought he could frighten me, being so much taller.'

Maggie collected empty plates. 'Weren't you frightened, then?'

'I couldn't believe it was really happening. And then I got angry. It was only afterwards, when I found that Eunice didn't believe me, or Clarissa . . . That really upset me. But frightened?

I suppose I ought to have been. Now I am, yes. Because . . .
how long is this going to go on? What did they want with me
today?'

No one could answer that question.

The little man wandered over to his keyboard, sat, and let his
fingers explore a melody. A melancholy tune. 'I'd like to write
something for Josie. A goodbye song for her.' He murmured to
himself, rather than to them. 'You promised me . . . a life of
bliss . . . No, a life of ease.' He played a discord, put his hands
in his lap. 'There was a lot of good in her, you know. She used
to talk, sometimes, about her life back home in Ireland. She said
it was a dead end village with no jobs, which is why she came
to London with a friend. Boyfriend, I think. In search of the
bright lights. I don't think she made it up. I took her out one
day into the countryside near Oxford for a birthday treat, and
she loved it. She didn't lie to me all the time, did she?'

Bea collected dirty plates. 'You hired a car?'

'I have a car, a little Toyota, very useful, but most of the time
Clarissa used it because of getting to rehearsals all over the place.
She was out in it the night Eunice told me to leave, or I'd have
used it to cart away my stuff. I didn't bother to go back for it
because there's no parking at the flat I moved into. I suppose my
car's still in the garage at home.'

Add a garage to a house in Kensington and you add noughts
to the price.

'Have you still got the keys to the car – and your house keys?'

'Mm. They're probably in my jeans in the drier.' He started
to pick out a melody again, singing along in a hushed voice,
'You promised me . . . a life of ease. You promised me, our love
would last . . .'

A mobile phone trilled, and Maggie answered it. 'What do
you mean, you can't finish . . .' She wandered out into the kitchen
taking a handful of mugs with her.

Oliver helped Bea take everything else out to the kitchen and
stack the dishwasher.

Maggie disappeared down the stairs, still talking. 'What tiles
are you short of? I thought you'd got . . .'

Oliver went to stand by the kitchen door, looking down at the
shady garden below. 'Jeremy's innocent, isn't he? So why is CJ
getting into such a state about him?'

'If I read him correctly, CJ doesn't like being dragged down to mortal status, having to answer questions from the police and being suspected of aiding or abetting a murderer. He is used to being that rarefied being, an expert whose character is beyond reproach. He finds it upsetting to have his word doubted. It's knocked him off his pedestal, and he wants to shed Jeremy and all his problems and go back to being Mr Perfect.'

Oliver laughed. 'Yes.'

Bea put her arm through his. 'He offered you a place to live, if I threw you out?'

Oliver continued to look down at the garden, and not at her. 'I never knew what the word "home" meant till you took me in. When I thought you wanted to get rid of me, I was too upset to think clearly. I wasted all that time worrying, when I could have rung you and got things straightened out.'

'Except that you thought my mobile number had been changed, so you couldn't have rung me.'

'I could have got to you through Maggie, and I didn't. Or rather, we did talk, but she thought she was on the skids, too. Did you know she was trying to find a place where we could live together? And yes, CJ did offer me a room, but . . . And then Maggie was on the phone to me last night when that man tried to deliver a pizza for Jeremy, though no one should have known he was here. So I rang CJ and he said I'd better come back and deal with things, and he'd fetch me in the morning. Which he did. But he didn't really explain what he wanted me to do.'

'I don't know what we can do.'

'Let's go downstairs, see what's happening there.'

NINE

Oliver said, 'You think this new manageress of yours, Ianthe, sent Maggie and me texts saying you'd changed your mobile number? Why should she do that?'

'I don't know.' Bea was frustrated. 'Sometimes I think I'm imagining things. Sometimes I think she's trying to undermine me, only I can't think why. Let me tell you exactly what's been going on.'

Down in the agency rooms, Oliver booted up one of the office computers, and then moved into Bea's office to do hers. Both asked for a fresh password.

Bea was furious. 'Anna gave me the latest password before she left, and I stayed behind last night to make sure Ianthe couldn't get at her machine to change it, but she has.'

Oliver was amused. 'She's probably set a new password to come into effect at the end of each working day. That way no one can access the system at night or over a weekend. A commendable precaution to take, in one sense.'

'So we can't get into the system?'

'Of course we can.' He wandered back into the big room and sat at Ianthe's work station. He pulled out drawers, checking the contents. 'You say she uses a combination of upper and lower-case letters, mixed with numbers? That's too complicated for anyone to guess, which means it's also too complicated for her to remember from day to day. She must keep a record somewhere. A calendar is the usual place to look . . . No, there's nothing on the office calendar. Her desk diary, perhaps? She must have one.'

'A big black book, a page a day.'

'Top right hand drawer – locked. All the other drawers are open. No keys left around?'

They looked, but there were none. Bea said, 'I saw her lock the drawer and put her keys into her handbag, and didn't realize what she was doing.'

Oliver tried poking a paper knife into the lock. No go. He grinned. 'How much do you want to break her hold on the system? You could leave it till Monday and confront her. Or, would you like to authorize me to break the lock?'

'I've always wanted to see someone do that. Do you need a screwdriver or something?'

'This desk is your property, so breaking the lock is not a crime. Unless – would you rather summon a locksmith?'

'On a Saturday afternoon? He wouldn't come till Monday morning, anyway, unless I paid a tremendous call-out fee.'

'Neither would he. A chisel would be best, I think. Hold on, and I'll get one from the toolbox under the stairs.'

It took him six minutes to find a chisel and hammer, and to break the lock. He opened the drawer and there was the black book.

'It was bought with agency money,' said Bea, 'to record what's happening at the agency every day. So it's my property, not hers, and I can do what I like with it.'

He flicked through the pages. 'Well thought out. She's written down what the password is to be for each day in the month. The changeover time is nineteen-hundred hours, well after everyone's finished in the evening. She has a tidy mind, hasn't she? Now, would you like to invent some more passwords for me to put into the system?'

'No need. Whoever has the book controls the system. The book belongs to the agency, and I have every right to use it as I think fit. Give me the pages out of the book, and I'll keep them safe – and use them myself.'

'She might have another copy somewhere. I think you'd better write down and give me a list of some different passwords, which I'll put in for the rest of the month. And please, keep your own copy somewhere safe.'

She had to agree he was right. 'Very well. Now, while I'm doing that, can you access the firm's Christmas card list and print off a copy for me? My address book seems to have got ruined somehow, and I desperately need some telephone numbers and addresses, particularly Celia's and Miss Brook's.'

She composed a random series of letters and numbers to act as the new passwords, while he pressed keys and printed off the required list.

Oliver put Bea's new passwords into the computer, but didn't look any happier when he'd finished. 'Ianthe's list stopped at the end of this month. I wonder what happens then? Perhaps she just hasn't got round to doing next month's passwords, or perhaps . . . You know her better than I do. Why do you think she's playing games with you?'

'It's driving me insane, trying to work out what she's up to. I thought at first that she was working for Jackson's, another agency, who would like to buy me out. But if so, then surely she'd want to run the agency down so that he could get it at a rock bottom price? Instead, she's building it up. The client list has expanded and we're worth far more now than when she started.'

'So it's not that.'

'Then I wondered if she were trying to take it over herself, by pushing me into early retirement, making out that I'm no longer up to the job. Several odd things have happened which would normally lead me to wonder if I'm losing my marbles—'

'Which you're not.'

'Thanks for the vote of confidence. No, I'm not. But on the other hand, I've come to realize that the agency has changed direction. I'm not exactly sure how or why it's come about, but I don't feel that I'm on top of things as I used to be. Yes, we're thriving, on paper. Our client list looks healthy, but a new problem has arisen; I don't think we're giving value for money any longer. Too many complaints.'

He looked startled.

She nodded. 'They were very rare in the old days, weren't they? But Ianthe is dealing with the increased demand for our services by using half-trained or untrained staff. I suspect some of them may have been let go when that other local agency folded, and we've taken their people on without checking their credentials.'

He gave her an odd look. 'Now I gathered from CJ – don't bite my head off; it's his idea, not mine – that he would like you to finish with the agency and settle down into a gentle retirement, perhaps carrying out the odd bit of detective work for him.'

'Does he, really? Well, that's a ridiculous suggestion.'

'Mm. You're good at it.'

'I suppose an occasional foray into . . . No, no! Doing it every day would be too rich a diet for me. I need to lead a bread and butter life, helping clients out of difficulties, solving people's domestic problems. Besides which, running the agency enables me to stay on in this lovely house, buy my clothes at Harvey Nicholls and have a manicure whenever I want it.'

'Not to mention keeping a home going for your two adopted orphans of the storm. Though Maggie is not technically an orphan, since her terrifying mother is still very much alive . . . and I suppose mine might be, too, if ever I bothered to look for her.'

'Do you want to?'

He shrugged. 'No.'

Bea thought he would look for her, some day. But perhaps not yet.

'The other possibility,' she said, 'is that Max has been stirring the pot. He would very much like me to sell up and retire to the seaside, so that he can move into this house. He said he knew of someone wanting to buy me out. I assumed at first that he meant Jackson's, but that half-baked agency isn't likely to swim in the waters which Max frequents. Perhaps there's another, bigger concern out there pulling his strings – and Ianthe's? Only, I can't quite see what she'd get out of it.'

He yawned. 'Will you confront her on Monday?'

'I'll have to, won't I? Because she won't be able to access the system without me giving her the new password. Thanks for running off the Christmas card list for me; remind me to buy a new address book. My old one seems to have had an encounter with a cup of coffee in Maggie's office. She says she hadn't put it there, and I believe her. Which reminds me . . . she's awfully quiet, isn't she?'

Saturday afternoon

Phil was taking the new girl through her act. 'No, Kath. Put some emotion into it.'

'I'm not one of your poncey actresses.'

'No, dear. You're an extremely pretty young girl, who's about to earn herself a lot of money. Now, let's go through it again. You've been taken into an exclusive hotel bar by a man much older than yourself. You're not interested in him—'

'That's for sure. Especially if it's you.'

'Yes, dear. It'll be me, togged up like a city gent. I find you a seat near the target, whose picture I've showed you. You do remember what he looks like?'

'A slug.'

'Yes, perhaps you might think that at first. But then you'll remember how many millions he's got in the bank, and that makes a difference, doesn't it?'

'All right. Get on with it.'

'I buy you a drink, a large one, and urge you to get it down you. You hardly touch the drink—'

'You keep telling me I can't drink, I can't smoke, I can't swear, and I can't get in touch with my old boyfriend—'

'True; and we won't be beating you up because you've failed

to turn enough tricks on the street, either. Just touch the glass to your lips and put it down again. Act as if you're a little bit frightened . . . All right, skip the acting. We'll work to your strengths. I put my arm around you and fondle your breasts—'

'I can put up with a lot worse than that.'

'I know you can. But this time you push me away. Look really upset. Can you make yourself cry on demand?'

'Don't be daft.'

'All right. Suppose I have a stinky smelling hankie in my top pocket. You'd want to push me away then, wouldn't you?'

'Dead right, I would. That's when I turn to the slug and ask him to rescue me?'

'You've got the idea, at last. Can you make your lower lip tremble . . .? No, perhaps not. We'll just have to rely on your stunning looks and a flash of lacy underwear. Good girl. You've earned yourself a pat on the back.'

'I'd rather have a glass of Red Bull, if it's all the same to you. Now, can I watch the telly?'

Once Kath was installed in front of the television, he got out his mobile phone. 'Nance? Phil here. She'll do, though she's not a patch on Josie. Now, about the little man . . .'

Saturday afternoon

Bea found Maggie in her office, brushing her hands across her cheeks. Had she been crying? Twice in one week? This was so unlike the girl.

'Maggie? You're being very quiet.'

Since Bea last saw it, Maggie's office had been taken apart even more. Her noticeboards were empty. The papers and stacks of catalogues had been moved, in orderly fashion, into a number of cardboard boxes. More boxes held samples of soft furnishings, different woods, and tiles; everything Maggie needed for her work.

Oliver crowded in after Bea. 'What's been happening around here? Where's your computer and your printer? And the landline phone?'

Maggie wasn't looking at them. 'Ianthe's been tidying up. She wants to use this office for herself, and of course she's right. I shouldn't be hogging this space, especially when I'm so horribly incompetent.'

Bea put her arm round Maggie. 'You are not incompetent. You are one of the most efficient project managers I've ever come across.'

Maggie wailed. 'But I ordered the wrong number of tiles! Look!' She thrust a typed copy of an order form at Bea. 'There's not enough to complete the job, and I'm paying the tiler double time to complete the job today and it's all my fault!'

'You don't make that kind of mistake,' said Bea. 'Who typed this?'

A shrug from Maggie. 'I don't know. I asked Celia to . . . but then she left, and Ianthe said she'd try to find someone to do it for me, and as I was short of time, she said she'd see it was put in the post for me.'

Ianthe strikes again?

Bea said, 'Where are your notes on this job?'

Maggie lifted her hands, helplessly. 'I had them there, in my in tray. But it's been emptied. I suppose it's in one of these boxes, but I don't know which one.'

Oliver and Bea exchanged glances. Bea said, 'I'll have a word with Ianthe on Monday morning. This can't go on.'

Oliver took the copy of the order from Maggie. 'How many more tiles do you need?'

'A hundred and fifty. But it's Saturday afternoon, and—'

'If I can borrow the car . . .' He raised his eyebrows at Bea, in an unspoken request, and she nodded. He said, 'Maggie; you and I will go out to the depot, get the rest of the tiles and take them round to the tiler. No, first I'll ring the depot and make sure they've got enough and will keep them on one side for us. What's their phone number?'

Maggie looked wildly around. 'I don't know. Perhaps in this box . . . or that one over there? The catalogue has a black and silver cover.'

Bea and Oliver each took a box to search for it. Maggie did so, too. Bea held up a tile manufacturer's catalogue. 'This it?'

Maggie fell on the book while Oliver got out his mobile phone. 'Read the number out to me.'

While he dealt with the matter of the tiles, Bea sat back on her heels . . . until her knees protested and she hauled herself to her feet.

She went back into her office and threw open the doors to the garden. It was cool and shady out there. She wandered outside, wondering whether to get the garden chairs out or not. The big urns which Maggie had planted up with summer bedding were doing well; red, white and apricot geraniums, mixed with Busy Lizzies and trailing ivies. The high walls surrounding the garden muted the noises of the neighbourhood.

The sycamore tree, too, was quiet this evening. Earlier there'd been a breeze, but now the leaves were still. Bea stood under the tree, with her hand on the bark. A blackbird – or was it a starling? – flew to a branch high overhead. And squawked. No, it was bigger than a blackbird. It must be a pigeon.

All God's children. Pigeons and starlings; Maggie . . . and Ianthe.

Whatever had possessed Ianthe to make out that Maggie was incompetent and oust her from her office? Maggie's skills didn't run to computers but, with proper office backup, she could manage a miscellaneous workforce of plumbers, electricians, tilers and any number of assorted clients, without turning a hair.

So why, Ianthe? Why?

Was she doing this solely because she wanted the kudos of an office of her own? She might think it didn't matter if Maggie worked upstairs in the newly-created loft extension. In a way it did – and in a way it didn't. But Maggie did need secretarial assistance, and it was up to Bea to sort that out for her. Again Bea regretted Celia's departure.

Dear Lord above, whatever is going on here?

Like an echo at the back of her head, she heard a voice say: *All that is necessary for evil to triumph is for good men to do nothing.*

Yes, dear Lord. I understand that, and I'm not going to sit back and let Maggie be sidelined. I have to take action. But is Ianthe really evil? I thought I'd know if I ever met someone who was evil, but I don't feel repulsed by her. I feel . . . I feel that she looks at me . . .

How did Ianthe look at Bea when she wasn't fluttering around pretending to be a dizzy blonde? She looked as if she were a blackbird considering how best to tackle a worm. She looked at Bea as if she were a problem to be dealt with.

Evil can grow from a tiny shoot. Ambition eases the conscience. Inconvenient truths become of no importance. Ambition dictates that the greater good must prevail.

So in Ianthe's eyes, Maggie is expendable? She's undermined Maggie's confidence – a relatively easy thing to do. She's tried to destroy mine – not so easy. But she's tried to cut the links between Oliver and me – and almost succeeded – because . . . because . . . why? Because she thinks he might fight on my side?

But – to what purpose? Why is Ianthe doing this? Is there some connection to Max and his ambitions here?

Silence. Apparently, it was up to her to find out.

Oliver put his head out of the door. 'The sooner Maggie passes her driving test the better! And don't say she'll never make it, because I'm determined she will. I'd better give her some tuition in the summer holidays. Anyway, we're off, now. Oh; car keys?'

'Usual place. Kitchen cupboard.'

He nodded, vanished.

She stood there for a while, with her hand on the tree. She allowed her worries to sink down to the back of her mind. She listened to the song of the birds that nested in the sycamore. She heard the pigeon flap away. Some blue tits swooped down to feed on the nuts which Maggie had hung from a branch of the laburnum near the house.

Maggie had bought Bea a bird bath for her birthday. Bea was standing so still that two sparrows came down to perch on the edge to drink. They rarely got right down into the water . . . but then a blackbird arrived and plunged in, fluttering his wings, sending a shower of fine drops over the sparrows, who chirruped but didn't remove themselves. Perhaps they enjoyed the shower?

I love this house and this garden, said Bea to herself. Would it really be for the greater good if I had to leave?

Who would gain? Max, and his family. But he can afford to buy a house with a garden somewhere in the suburbs, can't he? Somewhere on a tube line which will take him into Westminster quickly. So why should I have to move?

I don't have to.

And Piers? Does my dear ex-husband really want to resume conjugal relations with me? Perhaps he does. Perhaps he's getting to a stage in life when he thinks he might settle down and play at being monogamous.

I couldn't trust him. Not on past form. Do leopards ever change their spots? I don't think so. He'll still be attracting women when he's in his eighties. Besides which, I don't want a man under my feet all the time, needing to be waited on, and considered, and taking charge of the remote control for the television. Wanting to watch sport on television when I want to be quiet. No.

There was a movement on the balcony above, where the outside iron stairs curled up to provide access to the kitchen and sitting room French windows. The birds all flew up in alarm.

Jeremy Waite, still wearing his incongruous grey pyjamas. 'Mrs Abbot, there's someone at the front door, ringing the bell. I can't quite make out who it is, and I don't want to . . . dressed like this. Do you think my jeans might be dry by now?'

'Probably.' She made her way up the outside stairs and through the kitchen to the front door. Oliver had had a spy hole installed some time ago so she inspected their caller, put the chain on the door and opened it a few inches.

'Detective Inspector Durrell.' A stockily-built man, swarthy as Oliver. Short dark hair, a strong face, heavy-lidded eyes. He held up his ID.

She nodded, let him in. 'You heard we had a potential kidnapping?'

Jeremy danced around behind her. 'I am not going down to the police station wearing pyjamas.'

'No, of course not. Inspector, would you mind waiting while I see if my guest's clothes are fit to wear yet?'

Bea hurried Jeremy through to the kitchen, and the DI followed them. 'Who said anything about going down to the station? It's a Saturday afternoon, isn't it? I ought to be taking my sons to watch Fulham play.'

'Fulham, is it?' Jeremy perched on a stool. 'Now I'm all for a good game – but I prefer a smaller ground. Brentford for me.'

Bea started to pull Jeremy's clothing out of the drier, checking to see if any keys or other important articles had been left in them. 'You men and football!'

Jeremy seized on a worn pair of jeans, with an expression of delight. 'These are the most comfortable ones I've ever had. And, oh – here's my house keys, too. Just a mo, and I'll change.'

Bea held up a couple of T-shirts. 'Don't you need one of these?'

He grabbed one from Bea and disappeared into the hall to change.

Bea shouted after him. 'What about socks? And where are your shoes?'

He didn't reply. She sighed and folded the rest of the clothes into a neat pile. 'Inspector, a cuppa while we wait for him?'

'I wouldn't mind.' He took a stool. He had an air of calm, a restful presence. 'You really think it was an attempted kidnapping?'

'What else?' Bea switched the kettle on and shook the biscuit tin, which was, surprisingly, full. Jeremy couldn't have found it yet. Or perhaps Maggie had replenished it behind his back. The cat Winston appeared as if by magic. Naturally. She shoved him off the work surface, knowing he'd be back on again as soon as her back was turned.

Jeremy returned, still barefoot, but now wearing a T-shirt with a hole in it and his jeans. He was smiling. 'I wouldn't mind another cuppa, too.'

Bea made tea in her biggest teapot and put the milk carton on the table for the men to help themselves. What had Maggie planned for them to eat at supper time? She investigated the contents of the fridge. Mm. Not enough sausages to feed four of them, especially as Oliver could eat as much as Jeremy.

There was some half-thawed braising steak, which had probably been intended for tomorrow. Let tomorrow take care of itself. She put it in the microwave to finish thawing and reached for the big Le Creuset stew pot.

Jeremy and the inspector both had their hands in the biscuit tin. Jeremy seemed disposed to like the inspector. He said, 'We can describe the kidnapper to you. But, oh . . . where's Oliver gone? He put our notes on his laptop. He plays the keys like a professional pianist.'

The DI poured them both a cuppa. 'Tell me what you remember.'

Jeremy told him. He was surprisingly good at remembering details.

Bea busied herself sautéing a chopped onion, and she added whatever leftover vegetables she could find at the bottom of the fridge. A stock cube. Bay leaves? Yes, a couple of those. Salt and pepper and a clove of garlic. Water.

'Have you anything to add, Mrs Abbot?'

Bea popped the stew into the oven, thinking hard. 'Well,

Maggie thought he might be the same man who delivered the pizza here last night, but then she said he couldn't be because that man had bushy dark eyebrows, and this man didn't. Only, she didn't seem sure about it. She's out, by the way, and so is Oliver. Business. They'll be back in a couple of hours, maybe.'

The DI seemed to like shortbread, whereas Jeremy was going for the chocolate-covered biscuits. The DI said, 'So the man yesterday was distinguished by thick eyebrows, whereas the man today wore a toupee and thick-rimmed tinted glasses? A good con man adds something distinctive to his appearance, something you'd remember above all else. Heavy eyebrows. Glasses. Toupee. If you took those away, could it be the same man?'

'I don't know. I didn't see the man last night.' Should she make a cake, as well? Oliver would appreciate it, never mind Jeremy.

'I didn't see him, either,' said Jeremy, eyeing the last chocolate biscuit. 'But he asked for me by name, which must mean he knew I was here. But, how ever could he have tracked me down? And why? What does he want with me?'

Bea shivered. 'Leave it to the police. They'll find out.'

TEN

Jeremy's hand hovered over the biscuit tin. 'Inspector, am I officially off the hook for Josie's death?'

'We know you couldn't have killed her. She was a tall girl, wasn't she?'

'Five ten?'

'Near enough. She took a couple of blows to the head, which probably knocked her out, and was then strangled by someone with big hands.'

Jeremy choked on his biscuit. Served him right for taking the last one.

The DI hit Jeremy on his back. 'Your hands are on the small side, aren't they? Is that a problem when playing the piano?'

'Poor Josie.' Jeremy wiped his eyes. 'She was just a little country girl, you know, bemused by the big city.'

Bea felt her eyebrows rise as she took flour, sugar, eggs and corn oil out of the cupboard and started weighing ingredients.

The DI seemed to share her feelings. 'It would help us a lot, Mr Waite, if you could tell us everything you can remember about Josie. You said you were on good terms, right up to the moment she sprung her little, er, surprise on you. Did she say where she came from?'

'A village somewhere in Ireland. I don't think she ever told me where it was. A dead end place, no jobs for a bright girl.'

'How did she come to England?'

'Some boy she met at a dance fell in love with her, promised her marriage, brought her over here under false pretences; the old story, I suppose. Said he'd fix her up with a job and a room to start with – just till he could find somewhere for them to move in together. Then they were to get married. That's what she told me when she first knocked on my door, anyway. I'm not sure I believe that, now.'

The DI had a notebook out. 'What address? Can you remember?'

'Oh yes. It's in the next street to . . . to where I lived. I went round there once to leave a message for her, and it was true that the woman let rooms out, though she said she wasn't supposed to. She denied all knowledge of Josie at first, and then said that yes, the girl had had a room there once, but had moved on.'

'Address?'

Jeremy gave it, wrinkling his brow.

Mm. Bea thought there were similarities here to Angie's story; the pied-à-terre locally, the rooms to let . . .

The inspector peered into the empty biscuit tin. 'Probably about half of that was true. He'd get her over here, seduce her and set her to work for him. If she really did come from a village in Ireland and was cut off from her family and friends, she wouldn't know how to deal with the situation. Can you pinpoint the date she approached you?'

'Sometime early in the spring term. If I could get hold of my diary . . . I seem to have left it at home, or maybe back at the flat? Oh, that's a nuisance. I must find it, as I'm sure there's a meeting I'm supposed to be at next week, or perhaps it was this last week . . . but if I could get hold of it, then I could tell you, because it was just before half term. School half term, I mean.'

Bea separated the eggs, stirred the yolks into the other ingredients, and set the mix aside to line some cake tins with greaseproof paper, all the time wondering how the girl had known Jeremy would be a soft touch. He wasn't an obviously wealthy type, was he? Not at all like the other possible targets she'd heard about.

The DI said, 'I can check when that was. Now, Mr Waite; you may have been surprised not to be asked to identify the girl you knew as Josie—'

Clearly, it had never occurred to Jeremy that he might have been asked to do so. But, 'Knew as? You mean the girl that was killed wasn't Josie?'

'I mean that the fingerprints of the girl we found at the back of the church have been identified as belonging to a girl called Angela Josephine Butt.'

'Angie . . .' said Bea, remembering Piers' story about another girl who'd been on the Badger Game.

Jeremy was puzzled. 'Josie's name was "Butt"? She told me her name was Kelly. Josie Kelly.'

'Hm. Well. She did use other pseudonyms as well.'

'She had a record?' Jeremy was distressed to hear it. 'For . . .?'

'Soliciting. In the King's Cross area. It looks as if a man brought her over from Ireland and put her straight to work. Three convictions, the last one eighteen months ago. Since then, nothing.'

Jeremy hoped for a happy ending, still. 'So, she was off the game when she met me?'

'No recent convictions for soliciting, so yes, it does look as if she was off the streets.'

Bea said, 'On a point of order, do you know how old she was?'

'Nineteen.'

Jeremy sighed. 'I *said* I didn't think she was sixteen. All that about her being under age was made up to frighten me, wasn't it? It lost me my job at school . . . but maybe that was a good thing, because I've moved on, now.'

The inspector asked, 'Did she ever try to get you to kiss her, or suggest you got closer?'

He reddened. 'Well, no. That would have been embarrassing. You see, er, it's not really my thing. Had a bit of an accident, came off a motorbike when I was twenty-one, my own fault entirely, slippery road, didn't listen to warnings, had too much to drink . . . but there it is. All that side of things . . . muted, if you see what I mean? Nothing to be done about it.'

Bea suspended operations with the egg whisk. 'You mean . . . you can't? In bed?' She blushed.

'That's right,' said Jeremy, not perturbed. 'All in the past. They said some feeling might return eventually, but so far it hasn't. Can't be helped. Life goes on.'

'But if Josie never tried . . .' She glanced at the DI, whose mouth, she noted, was also hanging open.

The DI recovered to say, 'She didn't ever suggest anything in that direction?'

Delicately put. Bea shook herself. She began to fold egg whites into the mixture and scoop it into the cake tins.

'No, never. Not until, you know, that last night.' Jeremy's eyes were on Bea. 'Are you making a sponge cake? My first wife used to make it like that.'

'Your first . . .?'

'Didn't last.' He sighed. 'We were newly married when it happened. I thought we might adopt, but she decided to try someone whose equipment was functioning properly, so that was that. And then, when I met Eunice, she said she didn't mind.'

'Eunice knew?' Bea heard her voice squeak as she transferred the stew pot to the bottom of the oven, popped the cake mix in on top, and turned up the gas.

'Oh yes. Of course. She said she wanted a quiet life after the disaster of her first marriage; he beat her up, you know. Well, he only did it the once, because Eunice wasn't one to be put upon. It's only recently that I realized she was perhaps hankering after a little more excitement in that direction.' He sighed. Then brightened. 'How long will the cake be?'

Bea handed him the pile of his clothes. 'Take those upstairs, put them away, and find yourself some shoes to wear. By that time the cake will be done.'

The DI closed the door after Jeremy. 'He doesn't realize, does he?'

'You think Josie must have been told by someone – someone who knew about Jeremy's disability – not to go down that road? You think that's why she never tried anything – before the end?'

'Which didn't matter, because all they needed to do was to get photographs of her naked and clutching him.'

'Only, instead of standing by her man, Eunice turned him out of the house, though she knew he was physically incapable of making love to Josie.'

'Which means she used it as an excuse to get rid of him.'

The DI said, softly. 'Ouch. Poor little man.'

'He's in the clear for Josie's murder?'

'Unless we discover he hired someone to do it for him.'

'Why would he? He'd already lost everything he had: his home, his job – even his car. Oh, I suppose you could say he turned on Josie and killed her in revenge for what she'd done to him. Nah. Doesn't sound like him.'

'We're looking at anyone who might have known Josie in the past, someone who knew her when she was on the streets, someone who might know what happened to her after that.'

Bea started to clear up. 'You might find – I'm not sure that it's the same girl – but I'm told a girl named Angie worked the Badger Game on an elderly businessman, who later committed suicide. Neither he nor his son could believe the girl wasn't as innocent as the newborn day. Elderly man was caught when he fiddled the books – presumably to pay the girl off – by which time the girl had vanished from her lodgings. The problem is that the widow and the son say they'll deny everything if you start asking questions.'

'You think two or three people are doing this as a regular means of income?'

Bea counted on her fingers. 'Josie, who may also have been working as "Angie"; the photographer; and the pseudo policeman who called on us today. Three people. My point is that if they've done it once, perhaps they've done it several times.'

'And maybe will again? There's a nasty thought.' His mobile phone pinged, and he pulled it out with a sigh. 'The wife. Texting to know when I'll be back. I'd better go. You'll keep the little man safe from harm?'

'I'm supposed to keep him safe from would-be kidnappers?

How? With a non-existent baseball bat? Or perhaps with a hockey stick? Except that I've never played hockey. What do they want him for, anyway?'

'I wish I knew. I wish I had unlimited resources and could put a policeman on guard at your door, twenty-four seven. I wish I'd won the lottery and that I didn't have piles. You'll let me know if anything else happens, won't you?'

She showed him to the front door. 'My regards to CJ.'

'To who?' But he smiled. Did he know? Or not? She couldn't decide. He lifted his hand in farewell and trudged off down the street.

As Bea watched him leave, a well-known car drove up, and her son Max got out. 'Glad you're in, Mother. We need to talk.'

Saturday afternoon

'*Listen, Nance. This is foolproof. We can't get at the little man while he's in the Abbot woman's house because there's too many other people there. Now, you remember I'm on good terms with Jason, the man who runs the coffee shop under the flat where the little man used to live? Yes, yes; the flat we trashed.*

'*Well, the landlord is livid about this, right? So I'm just going to pop round to the café – Jason's open all weekend – and tell him I spotted the little man going into a house nearby, and give him the Abbot woman's name and telephone number. I'll suggest the landlord might be pleased to know where his tenant is to be found. Right?*'

'*Without letting on that you were involved with trashing the flat, you mean?*'

'*I'll suggest the landlord might like to get on the phone to the little man and tell him to get over there straight away to talk about paying for the damage. Right? It's a quiet street, and in a little while, at dusk, say, it'll be even quieter.*

'*Jonno and I will be across the way in the van he can borrow; belongs to his brother-in-law or something. So we pick the little man up when he arrives. Foolproof. A shot of mace in his face, he'll be right out of it, we pop a bag over him, shove him in the back of the van, tie him up and get out of there. Jonno will drive us out to the industrial estate, no one much out there of a Saturday evening . . . and Bob's your uncle.*'

'I don't like it. We're all set to go on the next one, so why not forget—'

'I can't forget. Every time I look at Kath, I think how much better Josie did it. We flew high, with her. This Kath, I don't know, not much between the ears, is there? She's as likely to light a cigarette or down a double vodka as smile at the right man. When I think how clever Josie was . . . I could spit. You've got to let me have this, Nance. I can't think straight till we've avenged Josie.'

Saturday afternoon

Bea let Max into the house, wishing he'd leave her alone for a while. He was going to talk about her selling the agency and moving out of the house, and she wasn't prepared for either. 'I've a cake in the oven. Come through to the kitchen.'

'Ah, that takes me back. I must say, you bake a good cake. What sort is it?'

His favourite was chocolate. 'A sponge. I'll see what jam I can find to put in it.'

He seated himself on a stool, hefted the teapot, which was empty. 'Any chance of a cuppa?'

She took the two halves of the cake out of the oven and laid them aside on a rack to cool. She found a clean mug, switched on the kettle again. Smiled at him. This little scene took her back to the long gone days after Piers had upped and left them to fend for themselves. She would come in, dog-tired from cleaning someone's pigsty of a house, and find Max home from school, trying to cope with his maths homework. She'd fry up some fish fingers for their tea, and he'd say, 'Never mind, Mum. One day I'm going to be a millionaire, and I'll look after you so that you'll never need to work again.' He'd meant it, too. The dear boy.

Only, it hadn't turned out like that, because she'd gone to work for Hamilton and soon been running his office . . . and one thing had led to another . . . and that dear man had scooped up mother and son to take them into his heart and his home.

Max probably never would be a millionaire, but he was a steady, honest and loyal member of parliament, who worked hard for his constituency. He'd been a handsome lad, taking after her side of the family, rather than Piers. A pity, really; Piers had enough charm to sink a battleship, and the clean-cut lines of his handsome son were becoming blurred by good living, and by a wife whose idea of cooking was based upon the microwave.

On the other hand, his wife's parents were happy to back Max in a safe parliamentary seat, and provided he didn't blot his copy book by straying in the direction of any young blondes, he was probably set for life as a reliable backbencher.

Bea found a jar of strawberry jam, filled the sandwich, and cut him a big slice.

'Yum,' was all he said.

She made them both some tea, checked the stew, turned the oven down to low, and found some potatoes to peel. She liked cooking, but Maggie usually got there first. She said, 'The family all right?'

'Oh. Yes. Fine. I'll be going up to join them early next week. Meetings to go to, social events, you know? Now, Mother; have you . . . What was that?'

A plaintive melody, being played on Jeremy's keyboard. He must be working on Josie's tune. 'That's my new lodger.'

'What?' He reddened, puffing out his cheeks.

'Jeremy Waite, the composer.'

'Never heard of him. Mother, you can't take on a lodger just when you're about to leave this—'

'I've something surprising to tell you. Your father proposes to move back in with me and use the loft extension as his studio.'

His face! Surprise. Then alarm, as he realized this would be the end of his plan to move back into the house. Then, reflection. What would this mean to him?

Ah, she could see him sift through the possibilities. It was one thing to have a divorced and widowed mother running a domestic agency, and quite another for her to be the partner of a famous portrait painter. And if he did have to give up his dream of moving back, it would be rather pleasant to drop Piers' name into conversations, not as a divorced and distant father, but as a very much present and influential part of the family, a man who knew all the right people.

She sighed. She was afraid Max was becoming something of a snob.

'Ah,' he said. 'Really? He didn't mention . . .' A frown. 'But he did say something about looking for somewhere else to live. Well, that's great news.' He didn't sound entirely sure that it was good news, but he'd come round to it. 'What does he think about this Jeremy fellow?'

'I don't suppose Jeremy will be here for long.' With luck. If she could sort out his domestic problems for him.

'Oh. Well. I'll have to tell my dear wife not to start counting her chickens.'

'Quite. Life's a bowl of cherries, isn't it? Some good, some bad. Which reminds me; you've not been approached by any pretty young things lately, have you? Wanting a snuggle?'

'What?' He was affronted. 'Really, Mother.'

'Well, there seems to be a lot of it going about. Then the demands for money kick in. You're sure?'

'Definitely not. But –' a smothered grin – 'there has been some talk about one of my colleagues who . . .' He shot her a suspicious glance. 'You're having me on. You've heard all about it.'

'No, tell me.' She cut him another piece of cake and returned to peeling potatoes.

'His wife has this toy dog, cost him the earth, he hates walking it, but there . . . the price of peace and quiet, I suppose. Anyway, Tibbles – or whatever the dog's name is – got away from her, in a crowded shop, I think. Went missing. This girl turned up at his place with the dog the following day when his wife was out. Pretty little thing, apparently. Turned his head. Stupid fellow. Ought to have seen it coming. Cocktails for two, hotel room to follow, and snap bang to rights with a camera.'

'It sounds like the same gang who've been targeting one or two other wealthy men. I worry that one day, you might—'

'Nonsense. I'm not that stupid.'

In Bea's book, he was indeed that stupid. But apparently not this time. Good. 'Can you give me a name?'

'No, of course not. I was told in confidence. Besides –' a real belly laugh – 'he was paying in instalments, but then he lost his seat at the last election, his wife divorced him, so he told them to take a running jump when they complained.'

'When who complained?'

A shrug. 'Dunno. Telephone calls, he said. Bags of freshly minted money left in telephone kiosks.'

'There's a good brain behind these scams, don't you think? Someone does their homework before they target their victim. They knew about your friend's dog, and that he was susceptible to advances from a pretty young thing. You don't happen to remember the girl's name, by any chance? Or what she looked like?'

'I never heard.' He turned on his stool, listening to the music coming from the living room. 'This composer person, whatever his name is. Was he a victim, too?'

'Uh-huh. The police are involved this time because the temptress ended up dead.'

'Oh. My ex honourable friend will be glad to hear it.' A pause while this sank in. 'You thought I might be on their list as a target? Well, really, Mother.'

Bea put some double cream into her smile. 'Of course not, darling. You're much too streetwise. But sometimes this gang chooses badly. By the way, do you know someone called Sir Charles something? Bit of a thug, apparently.'

'I see him about. I don't think you should call him a thug. Potential MP.'

'If you ever get an approach, or hear of anyone else being approached . . . would you let me know?'

'If the girl's dead—'

'The brain behind the scam isn't dead.'

'You aren't getting mixed up in another murder case, are you?'

'Only in so far as I'm letting Jeremy sleep here for a few nights.'

'You can't let him stay. What about when Piers wants to move in?'

'Then I'll find him some other place to go. How about your flat? Now you have moved your family up to the Midlands for the long recess—'

'We've rented it out, short let, American tourists. No sense letting it stand empty.'

'Indeed.' She put the last potato into the pan and dried her hands. She said, 'Ianthe.'

'Mm?' Round a mouthful of sponge. Emptied his mouth. 'What's that?'

'Ianthe. Ring a bell?'

He shook his head. Evidently the name meant nothing to him.

Oh well. Strike that idea. He hadn't been responsible for setting Ianthe on to her.

He looked at his watch, compared it with the kitchen clock. 'Must go. What was it I came to see you about?'

'Selling the agency. Though, if Piers moves in . . . he's never been one for paying bills on time. I may need to keep it going for a while. I've had Jackson's sniffing around—'

'Who?' Draining his cup, wiping his mouth.

Neither Ianthe *nor* Jackson's seemed to mean anything to him. 'The other agency who wants to swallow me up?'

'Oh. Them. Double-barrelled name. I'll have them contact you direct, right?'

He was on the move, anxious to get on with his busy life.

Double-barrelled agency? Who on earth could he mean? 'Someone's supposed to be contacting me about selling? Is that going to be before or after you leave London?'

'Mm? Before; I suppose.' He gave her a kiss and left, banging the front door behind him. He'd eaten over half the cake. Did she have the energy to bake another one?

Jeremy appeared, still barefoot. 'Was that someone at the door? Ah, cake.'

Bea cut the remaining cake into three. 'One slice for you, one for Maggie and one for Oliver. I like the tune you're working on.'

He put most of his slice into his mouth. How ever did he manage it?

'It's a lament for Josie. A ballad. Unfashionable, ballads. But I couldn't get it to fit any other form. Can Maggie sing, do you know? She looks as if she might. I've been doing a lot of thinking. About Eunice and my life. And about Josie, trying to remember if she'd ever said anything that would help. She was a bright, happy little thing, you know. Normally, that is. And a good listener.' He licked his finger and went round the table, picking up crumbs and popping them in his mouth.

Winston leaped on to the table. Bea swatted him off and put the remaining two slices of cake high up on a cupboard. The cat could still reach them if he wanted to, but he wasn't that fond of cake so perhaps it would still be there when the others returned.

Jeremy looked wistfully after the cake. 'I don't know what's happened to my shoes. Have you seen them? I may have left them at the flat, but I'm not sure I can face going back there. What they did to the piano . . .' He shuddered. 'The agents took a whacking great deposit off me so they'll not be out of pocket. You know, Josie wasn't happy about setting me up. That last night, when she got off the bed, she gave me a kiss, just a little one on my forehead, just there . . . and she said she was sorry. She'd never kissed me before.'

Bea found Winston's brush and began to groom him. He liked that, mostly. Except when he didn't. Today he lay on his back, with all four paws in the air, and blinked at her. Today he was going to cooperate.

Jeremy leaned over to rub Winston's jaw. 'We never had a cat. Eunice was allergic. A pity. I like cats. Mrs Abbot, if anything happens to me, will you see that Josie's song gets to my publishers?'

'Nothing's going to happen to you.'

'Mm. I'd like to make another will, too. But it's Saturday, isn't it? Or is it Sunday? No, I think it's Saturday. I don't want to wait till Monday. Can you get some information off the Internet about making a will? Then Maggie and Oliver can witness my signature and you can put it in a safe place. Just in case.'

She didn't waste her breath saying it wasn't necessary. He was the oddest mixture of shrewdness and innocence. 'If it will set your mind at rest.'

He nodded. 'Eunice insisted on a prenuptial agreement because she was earning so much and at that time I just had my teacher's salary and the house. She said it wouldn't be fair to split every-thing down the middle, and of course she was right. She worked hard for her money. We both made new wills. I left everything to her then, and she divided everything between me and Clarissa. That was before I started to get such a lot of work for television. I've had several songs published, too, one of which got into the top twenty for a while. I'd like to see Josie's ballad in the top twenty. I understand from CJ that you're a dab hand at solving murders. I want to leave you some money to find out who killed Josie.'

ELEVEN

Bea was taken aback. 'Me? Find out who killed Josie? Oh, but I—'

'I know you'll do your best. Josie brought a lot of happiness into my life. I know she was on the make, but not all the time. She had a great gift – she really listened to what people said. Most people don't really listen, you know. You can see that while someone else is talking they're thinking about what they're going to say next. But Josie really listened. I used to play her some of the music that was running around my head, and she encouraged me to write it down, which I hadn't been doing. She made me talk to people about it, and no one was more thrilled than she was when I began to get commissions. She made me realize I wasn't totally past it.'

Bea blinked. Did he mean that Eunice and Clarissa thought of him as 'past it'?

He shook his head at himself. 'I let things slide, didn't I? I knew things weren't right at home. I knew Eunice was bored with me, and I sort of knew, without admitting it to myself, that she was seeing someone else. I knew Clarissa thought she'd outgrown me, although I could have told her she needed to work hard to improve her technique on . . . But she'd stopped listening to me, about music. About anything.

'Neither of them listened when I tried to tell them about the commissions I was getting, but to be honest, I'm not sure that I listened properly when Eunice told me about her work. In a way, it was understandable, for we were in such different fields. It was like talking another language. You could say that Eunice ought to have made more of an effort to understand what was going on in my life, but I don't think I was any better at listening to her.

'It was such a wonderful release for me, to be able to write music which people actually wanted to hear. For so many years I'd sat on my talent, thinking it wasn't good enough, thinking I had to earn my living as a teacher, thinking that one day perhaps

I'd have the time to write my melodies down and see if anyone might be interested. Then it happened, almost overnight. It was glorious and frightening and I suppose it took over my life.

'I realize now that I ought to have made them stop and listen, made them understand what was happening to me, but I didn't. It's no good saying Eunice was responsible for the breakdown of our marriage, because I was just as blind and deaf to her as she was to me. The only surprise, looking back, is that it took so long for the penny to drop. I just didn't see it coming, did I? It was a bad shock. Knocked me right out for a while.'

Bea wondered if the shock were more to do with Josie's betrayal, than his wife turning him out of the house.

He said, 'I want to finish the song for Josie and to make a will. I'd better find some paper and rough out what I want to say.' He wandered off.

Bea went on grooming Winston, thinking that what Jeremy said clarified Eunice's motives. If Eunice had always known about Jeremy's medical problem – which he said that she had – then she oughtn't to have acted shocked when she heard about him getting snapped with Josie in bed. She'd known it was impossible for him to stray, so why play the tragedy queen and throw him out of the house? Unless she'd been waiting for an opportunity to get rid of him. Which seemed all too likely.

Or . . . carrying that thought one stage further, was it possible that Eunice had actually organized the trap in order to get rid of her husband?

Oh, no. Ridiculous. That would mean Eunice was in league with the Badger Game gang, or knew someone who was. Or, more likely, had passed the word along to her friends and acquaint-ances that she'd be willing to pay a fee if someone would just set him up with a girl and take some pictures of the event.

Mm. A bit extreme. Would a high-stepping, top lady barrister stoop so low?

All right; she might if she had another man in mind whom she wanted to pop into her bed. But, if she wanted to divorce Jeremy, surely there were easier ways of doing it?

Ah, but she loved the house, didn't she? A good house in a good location. Mm. Yes. The house belonged to Jeremy, and by rights it would remain his property after a divorce, because of the prenuptial agreement. But who would know better than she that possession is nine points of the law? Suppose she'd arranged the entrapment so as to push him off balance, thinking that when she ordered him out of the house, he would go without making a fuss? Which he had done.

She hadn't given him time to reflect, had she? Or to consult a solicitor on his own behalf?

Hm. It was a possible scenario, but it all depended what sort of person Eunice Barrow might be.

Winston the cat gave her a pretend bite on her wrist to indicate that he'd had enough of being groomed today, thank you. She let him jump down off the table, and then cleared away all the dirty mugs and plates.

Which reminded her that the little man was still going around without shoes. What had he done with them? Left them in some corner, somewhere?

She went into the living room. Sheets of music were scattered around and over the keyboard he was using. She picked one up. She couldn't read music, unfortunately, and there were so many crossings-out and arrows going in all directions that she wondered how anyone could make sense of it. As far as she could make out, there was a series of verses, some in minor and some in major key. One verse was meant to be sung-spoken – whatever that might mean.

She spoke the words aloud, falling into the rhythm as she did so:

'You promised me – a life of ease.
You promised me – our love would last.
I asked how I'd repay you – for this precious gift of love,
And you answered – "with a kiss".'

Rather sweet. A bit mawkish? This would be Josie's story; the tale of an innocent little Irish girl, swept off her feet by a dashing young man from the big city. Bea sat down to read the next part, which was marked 'to be spoken, while Josie's tune continues in the background'.

'You promised me a kitchen,
With a set of sliding drawers,
A penthouse with an outlook,

And a wedding with a ring.
I asked how I'd repay you,
And you answered – "with a kiss".'

So far, so good. The girl had been seduced in the time-honoured way, with sugared promises. And then what happened? The next bit was marked 'in a different key'. A sadder one, presumably?

'You brought me to this country,
Where the streets are paved with rain . . .'

The words tailed off into a heavily-crossed out section which Bea couldn't read.

Bea shivered. The inspector had told her Josie had been walking the streets for a while. Presumably, she'd left that life in order to become an enthusiastic partner in the Badger Game?

Bea shuffled the sheets together and laid them back on the keyboard. The little man had a talent, didn't he? She wondered how soon the police would be able to find Josie's killer . . . Someone from her seedy past? Perhaps her original pimp? Was 'pimp' the right term for the man who'd seduced her and brought her to this country, or was her pimp the man who'd set her up in the Badger Game? Bea decided she didn't know enough about it.

Now, while everything was quiet, and before the others returned, she'd have time to ring her dear friend from the old agency days, Miss Brook, and see how she was getting on. If that old warhorse was still aching to get back to work, then perhaps . . . Maggie needed someone to keep her accounts straight, didn't she?

Bea also felt the need to contact Celia again. Years ago the woman had been in an abusive relationship, until Hamilton and Bea had rescued her by arranging for her to have a job abroad. Away from her partner and with a demanding job, Celia had regained her confidence to such an extent that, after her return to this country, she had repaid the agency by helping to run it . . . together with the indomitable Miss Brook.

Celia had been a trusted key worker until Bea had taken that fatal holiday.

Bea wondered whether or not Celia could now be induced to look after Jeremy part time? Or, could she perhaps be enticed back to work at the agency, if Ianthe were to leave?

Bea sighed. No, she couldn't rely on Ianthe upping sticks and leaving. Or not of her own accord, anyway.

Perhaps Celia could be enticed back to sort out Maggie's office? Everything depended on whether or not Celia had got another job yet. So, Bea would make some phone calls and find out how the two women were placed.

After that, she must find Jeremy's shoes.

Saturday supper-time

'We're back!' Maggie and Oliver banged the front door shut behind them and thundered along the hall to the kitchen. Or rather, Maggie stampeded along, while Oliver brought up the rear, smiling, noiseless.

'About time, too,' said Bea, lifting the casserole out of the oven. 'I was getting anxious. Hope you're hungry.'

'Ah, food.' Jeremy appeared from nowhere and slid on to a stool. He was wearing bedroom slippers. They weren't even his own bedroom slippers. Bea recognized the bunny rabbit slip-ons which Maggie normally wore; they were far too big for him, but he didn't seem to care. Bea hadn't had time to look for his shoes and was annoyed with herself. Where *had* he left them?

Maggie shucked off her huge tote bag. 'We stood over the tiler till he'd finished—'

Oliver shovelled knives and forks from the drawer on to the table. 'He's made a good job of it, I must say—'

'Sorry I couldn't get back in time to cook. What are we having?'

'Beef stew, with dumplings.'

The landline phone rang. Oliver picked it up, passed the receiver to Jeremy. 'It's for you.'

'Oh, but . . .' Bea was worried. Who might be calling Jeremy here?

'It's all right,' said Jeremy. 'It's my landlord.' The phone quacked at him, and Jeremy rolled his eyes, trying to get a word in edgeways. 'Yes, I know that . . . Yes, the police do . . . Yes, but . . . No, I can't, because I'm just sitting down to supper. Yes, I realize that . . . Well, perhaps after . . . In an hour's time? I suppose so. Yes, yes. But I don't understand why you're not dealing with the agency. I gave them a . . .'

He put the receiver back on its cradle. 'He rang off. Actually, the flat is a wreck and I can't blame him for getting in a state. I'll pop over there after supper, calm him down, and see if I can unearth my diary because I can't find it anywhere.'

Any more than he could find his shoes. Bea considered making a list of things Jeremy had mislaid, and then going through the house looking for them.

'Oliver and I are going to the pub after supper,' said Maggie, who had recovered her usual high spirits. 'He says he hasn't got a girlfriend, but he let it drop that he went to a concert with a girl who's a bit of all right, and I'm going to bully him till he tells me everything.'

Bea felt as if she'd been slapped in the face. She'd hoped – but how silly of her – that she would be the only woman in Oliver's life for some time to come. Ah, stupid, stupid! Of course, he ought to be going out with girls now. It would be all wrong if he weren't. At least . . . she floundered among contradictory thoughts about what one *ought* to feel, and what one actually *did*.

Jeremy held up his plate for a second helping. How could he stow so much away so quickly? 'It's not far, but I'd better take a taxi if I can't find my shoes.'

'We'll find your shoes after supper and then I'll walk you over there,' said Bea. 'It's a lovely evening. Do me good.'

'What's for afters?' Oliver ate almost as fast as Jeremy.

'I made a cake.' Bea lifted the plate down and didn't know whether to smash it over the little man's head, or cry. She'd quite clearly told him the two large pieces left on the plate were for Oliver and Maggie. Now there were two pieces, yes. But they were no longer a decent size. In fact, they were small enough to offer a child. She had no doubt he'd cut each slice in half and eaten the rest, but what good would it do to tax him with it?

She said, 'I'll make some custard to go with them.'

'May I have some, too?' asked Jeremy. 'With a banana in it? I love banana custard. What a treat.'

Saturday evening

By great good fortune, Jonno managed to park the van opposite the coffee bar as it was closing up for the night. They could see Jason inside as he put chairs on tables and turned the 'Open' sign to 'Closed'.

'Good and bad,' said Phil, adjusting his toupee and giving Jonno a baseball cap to cover his shaven crown. 'Good, because it's so close we can hustle the little man across the pavement and into the back of the van without exposing ourselves to prying eyes—'

'And bad,' said Jonno, slipping on some dark aviator glasses, 'because some bad-tempered old lady will probably come along and tell us we haven't any right to park in this road unless we've got a visitor ticket – which we haven't. Well, this usually works.' He put a 'Disabled' parking sticker on the dashboard, where it could be spotted by anyone who passed.

Phil tilted the driving mirror to provide a view of his face as he darkened his eyebrows. 'Haven't you got a "Doctor On Call" notice?'

'I must get Nance to make me one.' He yawned. 'Not many people about. All at the pub or watching the football on telly. He'll come down the road towards us, won't he?'

'Uh-huh. Hah! I think that's the landlord's car, just driven up. Look at him; tub of lard. Bet he never takes any exercise. Probably got asthma *and* diabetes. *Where does he think he's going to park, eh?'*

They watched as Jason opened the café door and yelled to the fat little man to pull over with his wheels up on the pavement.

'The traffic warden will have him for that.'

'It's Saturday night, stupid. They'll all be watching the footie.'

The fat man parked and, wheezing, followed Jason into the shop. His neck bulged over his shirt.

'High blood pressure,' said Phil. 'Ought to take more exercise.'

Jason and the landlord came out of the coffee bar and went round the corner to tackle the door to the upstairs flat. Jason was a big lad. He used a crowbar to tear off the plywood that had been nailed over the door, and then followed the landlord inside and up the stairs. A light went on in the first-floor flat.

Phil slid out of the passenger door. 'I'm going to wait for the

target round the corner from the café.' He took a bundle out of
the back of the van and crossed the road. Jonno returned the
driving mirror to its original position.

Dusk softened the distances and muted the sound of traffic in
the streets nearby.

Saturday evening

Twilight was upon them, and the temperature was dropping. Bea
decided that Jeremy would need something to put on over his
T-shirt as well as change his slippers for some shoes. He seemed
to have left his belongings on every floor, and in almost every
room of the house. He himself hadn't a clue where he'd put
anything, but it didn't seem to bother him, for while Bea played
Hunt the Shoes, he went back to tinkering with Josie's melody on
his keyboard.

Bea tried to work out where he'd left his belongings and why.
On the first night she and Maggie had hauled his belongings up
to the top floor and Jeremy had slept in Oliver's bed. There was
still a lot of Jeremy's stuff strewn around Oliver's room. Oliver
would have to lump it.

Bea pounced on a plastic bag and found two pairs of Jeremy's
shoes: dress shoes and some sandals. In a pile of clothes on the
floor there was a denim jacket which would go with the jeans
he was wearing.

On the second night, he'd crashed out in the spare bedroom,
and Bea found more of his things there, including the pile of
clothes he'd washed, which Bea had asked him to put away. Oh
well. She picked out a clean T-shirt without a hole in it and found
another pair of sandals under the bed.

She sighed. He'd slept in both beds without changing the
sheets. Well, perhaps Oliver wouldn't mind sleeping in the sheets
Jeremy had used once, because Bea didn't have the time to change
them, and she couldn't ask Maggie to help her do this because
she'd gone off with Oliver straight after shoving the supper things
into the dishwasher. As she took Jeremy's things downstairs, Bea
wondered where the little man would try to sleep tonight, and
what Oliver might have to say about it.

'Shoes.' She handed them to him. 'Clean T-shirt. Jacket. Have
you got a cheque book with you?'

'Whatever for?'

'To pay the landlord for the damage.'

'Won't the agent take it out of my deposit?'

'Would it be enough?'

'Three months rent in advance, plus a whacking great deposit? I should hope so.' He shucked off his torn T-shirt.

And the phone rang.

This time it was Piers. 'Bea, my love. Fancy a night on the tiles?'

'You're only asking me out because you want something from me.'

'You wound me deeply. Would I . . .? No, don't answer that. But it's a beautiful evening, and I thought you might be at a loose end.'

'Far from it. I'm babysitting. Someone trashed the flat Jeremy was living in, and his landlord is on the warpath, so I promised to walk him over there to face the music . . . Forgive the mixed metaphors.'

'What? Well, it won't take long, will it? I could pick you up after, and we could—'

Exasperation fought with affection. 'One thing at a time, Piers. Looking after Jeremy is like herding cats.'

Jeremy didn't take offence, which was one of the lovable things about him. He laughed and shook his head at her. 'It's all right. You go out with whoever. I know the way.'

'Hold on, Jeremy. You haven't a key to get back in with.'

He was halfway out of the front door, whistling Josie's tune to himself. And not listening to Bea.

Bea said, 'Look, Piers. I'll ring you back later, if I may. Or . . . no, it's getting late, isn't it?'

'I'm not having you wander the streets at night by yourself, especially now there's a killer loose in your area. Tell me where you're going, and I'll meet you there.'

She told him and rang off. Seizing her handbag, she ran down the steps and into the street after Jeremy. She wouldn't be surprised if he'd set off in the wrong direction. But no, he was trundling along at a cracking pace towards Church Street.

She wished she'd thought to slip into some low-heeled shoes before she set off after him. The lights turned red at the bottom of the hill, the traffic stopped, and he crossed the main road without breaking his stride. The lights turned green, and the traffic moved off as Bea reached the same place. A bus blocked Bea's view of Jeremy. Well, she knew where he was heading, didn't she?

She crossed the street as the lights changed again, but couldn't see him. She followed in his footsteps and turned into the next street – it was little more than a lane, a narrow road with a narrow pavement on one side and no pavement at all on the other. There were parked cars sporting residents' parking tickets down the right-hand side, allowing just enough space for a single lane of traffic to pass through. One way only.

The street was lined with terraced housing which had once been workers' cottages but were now priced out of any work-man's reach. It was something of a surprise to find the road surface was tarmacked instead of cobbled. She'd heard that in some old London streets they'd left the cobbles and tarmacked over them.

There was the café on the corner of the next intersection. Shut. There was a light on inside it, but no one there.

And no Jeremy.

There was a light on in the room above the café. That must be where his flat had been, and he must have gone up there to meet with his landlord. She wished Maggie had come with her, because Maggie would know where the door to his flat might be.

She could hear someone thumping. A dull thump. A van parked in the road outside the café shook in time with the thumps.

What on earth . . .?

There was someone in the driver's seat, probably drunk. How disgusting! The night was closing in and making it hard to see . . .

The driver fell away from her, back across the passenger seat, even as someone big and bulky slipped out of the van through the far door. She only had the fleetest of sightings . . . someone in dark clothing? A man, probably, but she could hardly be sure of that, even. He or she ran away from her down the road, barely making any sound. Wearing trainers?

She looked around. She didn't understand what was happening, but feared . . . she didn't know what. Was that Jeremy sliding down in the driver's seat? No. The driver was a bigger man, wearing a baseball cap.

Probably nothing to do with her, or Jeremy.

The driver was drunk, probably. Too drunk to stay upright.

Another quick glance around. There was no one else in sight.

Absurd to think Jeremy might be in trouble. He'd gone up to his old flat, and if she could only find the door . . .

Despite herself, fear crept down her backbone.

She reached in her handbag for her mobile phone – which she must have left at home. She wished the people inside the van would stop thumping. Were they having sex there, while the driver was . . .? No, it wasn't Jeremy in the front of the van. It couldn't be. Anyway, why would Jeremy be lying down on the front seat of a van in this deserted street?

She rapped on the window of the van. 'Are you all right?'

She was a tall woman, but she had to stand on tiptoe to see inside the van. The driver had fallen down till his head was against the far door, his knees under the wheel. She couldn't make out his face properly.

His mouth moved. Did it?

Could he possibly be dead? No, no. Ridiculous. He was obviously drunk.

Except that someone had killed Josie not a hundred yards from where they were. And someone had left the van by the opposite door in a hurry.

The driver had been wearing a baseball cap, which had ended up over his face. Was his head shaven? Yes, it might be. He was much too big to be Jeremy. Whoever he was, he had fallen into an uncomfortable position and wasn't moving.

Perhaps whoever was banging away in the van could help him. She slapped on the side of the van. 'Help there! Someone, help me!' The thumping stopped, and there was a listening silence. If anyone had heard her, they were not going to interfere.

Suppose the driver had been attacked by his passenger, but was still alive? Suppose he'd had a heart attack and needed medical help? She dithered. Should she ring for an ambulance?

They wouldn't be best pleased to be called out for a drunk sleeping it off in his van, would they? And, she had forgotten her mobile phone.

She set her teeth. She must check before she yelled for help.

She tugged at the handle of the van door, and it opened. The driver never moved, but there was an aroma in the air . . . sweetish. She sniffed. Couldn't place it.

She leaned across him. The man was a stranger. He was warm to touch. Under the shadow of his cap, his eyes looked unnatural. A trick of the light, of course. But it did look as if they were bulging out of his head. His tongue, too.

She tugged on his sleeve, located a hand. It felt floppy. She couldn't feel any pulse. Was she holding his wrist in the right place? She wished she knew some first aid.

Someone or something erupted from the back of the van, shaking it hard. She abandoned her search for the driver's pulse and stood back. 'Your friend . . .'

She recognized him, despite – or perhaps because of – the toupee.

TWELVE

Saturday evening

The man with the toupee recognized her, too. 'What? How . . .?'

Was he going to attack her? Bea took an involuntary step backwards. 'I think the driver may be . . . A man got out of the passenger seat as I came along. He ran off down the road.' She pointed.

'What . . .?' He glanced that way, glanced back. Thrust her aside to lean into the cab. He pushed the driver's cap away, felt for a pulse.

'Strangled, do you think?' Her voice went high on her.

He nodded, his throat working, eyes wide with shock.

The van shook under another assault from inside.

Now she guessed what was making the van shake. 'You've got Jeremy in the back?'

'He killed Josie. He's got to pay for it.' A plea for understanding.

She tried to bring her voice down from panic stations. 'Idiot! Jeremy couldn't have killed her, any more than he could have killed your driver. You were busy in the van with Jeremy when I saw this other man run off.'

He stared at her, in shock. 'Jeremy killed Josie . . . with an accomplice.'

She snapped at him. 'That's ridiculous, and you know it.'

He took a step towards her, and she quailed. Was he going to hit her?

The van shuddered, the back doors flew open, and to a stream of curses, a strangely shaped bundle caterpillared its way over the tail and fell out on to the road, where it rolled over and over. Two denim-clad legs waved in the air.

Jeremy? Well, it was someone about his size with a plastic sack over his head which had been fastened around his hips with heavy-duty tape. Only his legs were showing. He had lost one of his shoes and wasn't wearing socks. By the sound of it, he was having a two-year-old's tantrum. But, thought Bea, who could blame him?

At least he was still alive. And complaining.

She said, 'You've kidnapped the wrong person.'

From somewhere nearby came the sound of a police siren carving its way through traffic. Someone must have seen or heard what was going on and alerted the police.

The man in the toupee heard it, too. He thrust Bea away from the van. She staggered and almost fell, only to see him clamber into the driving seat, pushing his accomplice further over. The keys were still in the ignition. He turned the key and, cool as you please, drove off.

Bea told herself to make a note of the licence number as the van disappeared, but someone had taken the precaution of dirtying the plate. Her hands were shaking too much for her to use a pen, anyway. It was a plain white van, no markings on it.

The police siren came nearer. The bundle that was Jeremy tried to sit up, squawking.

And Piers came strolling along.

'About time, too,' she said, getting down on her hands and knees beside Jeremy and trying to control her shakes. 'Keep still, Jeremy. Let me see how to get this tape off.' She tried to get a fingernail under the tape, which refused to budge. 'Piers, you don't happen to have a penknife on you?'

Jeremy was spluttering and swearing inside his plastic bag. He wasn't going to run out of air and suffocate, was he?

Piers squatted beside her, viewing the wriggling, cursing bundle that was Jeremy. 'Who or what is this? And why is he trussed up in a plastic sack? Of course I don't carry a knife. No one does, nowadays. At least, not if they don't want to be arrested for carrying an offensive weapon. Would a pair of nail scissors do?'

A police car drew to a halt behind them.

Bea tore a fingernail, but still couldn't release Jeremy. 'Oh dear. We're blocking the road. I do hope Jeremy has enough air in there.'

'Hold him as still as you can.' Piers produced his nail scissors and cut a small hole in the top of the plastic bag. 'Careful does it.'

Jeremy continued to thrash around and scream.

'Calm down, Jeremy,' said Bea. 'You're only making matters worse by wriggling.'

'Hello, hello. What's all this, then? Someone had too much to drink? Been playing a prank that went wrong?' A braying laugh. A policeman who fancied himself as a comic. Couldn't he see they were trying to rescue someone tied up in a plastic sack?

Bea asked the policeman, 'Have *you* got a knife?' He was in uniform and equipped with the latest technology, but didn't seem to have the brains to match. His mate – a woman – stayed in the police car, talking to someone on her phone.

'Knife? What would I be doing with . . . Ah, someone's been messing around, here, have they? Kids, was it?'

'Attempted kidnapping and murder,' said Bea, trying to enlarge the tiny hole Piers had made. Unfortunately, Jeremy kept wriggling and mewing, and the plastic was so old and thick that it resisted her efforts. The bag was strong. It reminded her of something. Sacks that were used for garden compost?

The policeman was still laughing as he turned in his report on his walkie-talkie. 'Got it. Disturbance in the street. Man in a body bag. Well, sort of. Neighbours attending. A right pair of jokers here. A prank that's gone wrong, looks like.'

'Let me have a go.' A bass voice. Bea looked up to see a very large man with a ponytail. He must be fifteen stone or thereabouts and bulged with muscle, not fat. He was wearing a sleeveless T-shirt and denims. A long, well-honed knife appeared at Bea's side. 'You sit on his legs, missus, and you, my man, you hold him tight. I'll carve because I'm the chef, right?'

His knife ripped down the side of the bag, and Jeremy's head popped out, eyelids swollen shut, skin a deep scarlet. He was incoherent, spitting with rage and pain.

'Water,' said the big man, producing a large bottle from his back pocket. 'Hold his hands away from his face. Keep his head steady and pour the water on his face, especially his eyes.'

'What?' That was Piers.

'Mace,' said the big man. 'Sprayed into his eyes. Makes them swell up. Needs washing off, sharpish.'

Bea seized the bottle and started pouring, while Piers held Jeremy's body firmly against himself.

The big man continued, 'We was watching from the flat above, the one what used to be the little man's, right? We see him coming along the road, lickety-split, and then this other man steps out in front of him and sprays him in the face with a can of mace. Little chap goes down, screaming. You don't see action like that every day in our street, do you? That's when I rang for the police and an ambulance.'

'We certainly need an ambulance,' said Bea. 'His eyes!'

The policeman was laughing, amused by what he took to be a joke gone wrong. 'If it's mace, he won't be able to see straight for hours.'

The big man ripped away at the bag, trying to free Jeremy. 'The name's Jason. Of Jason's Place. That's my caff. Keep pouring, missus. Slurp, slurp; that's the ticket. Over and over.'

Bea obeyed. Jeremy howled.

The policeman got out his notebook. 'You called for an ambulance, right? Assault, was it? Does he want to press charges? And you; what are you doing, carrying a knife in the street? Don't you know it's illegal?'

'Idiot!' No one could be sure whether Bea meant Jeremy or the policeman, but the knife disappeared.

Jason continued to smile. 'That's it, missus. Keep pouring. It's the only thing that will help. No, officer; you must be mistaken. I haven't any knife. This passer-by must have cut the sack open with his little scissors. Are you going to charge him for that?'

Jason picked Jeremy up under his arms and shook him out of the sack. And laid him down again on the road. 'You haven't seen any knife, have you, missus?'

'Certainly not,' said Bea. 'Now, officer; would you care to take charge of the bag, which may reveal some clues as to the attack on my friend here?'

A large stomach insinuated itself between Bea and the policeman. 'If I can get a word in edgeways. Officer, arrest this man!'

'Which man?' asked the policeman. 'Is this another joke?'

'No joke!' The landlord bent over Jeremy to shout, 'Did you arrange this to get out of paying what you owe me? Because if so; it didn't work!'

Jeremy spluttered and cursed.

The policeman looked amused. 'So who am I to charge with assault, then? What's *your* name, sir?'

Bea said, 'You need the man in the van.'

The policeman looked around. 'What van?'

Indeed, what van!

'There was a van, a white van,' said Bea. 'No markings. Number plate obscured. Two men came in it. The one who jumped our friend here—'

'Popped this sack over him, neat as can be,' said Jason. 'We was watching upstairs, waiting for him. And there he was, being picked up like a roll of carpet and dumped into the van. That's when we called for the police, just as a law-abiding citizen should.'

Was Jason a law-abiding citizen? For some reason Bea doubted it. He'd stowed the knife away somewhere, probably in a back pocket, and was standing with his bare arms crossed, enjoying himself. Tattoos on both arms, and one on his neck. Hearts and serpents and patterned bracelets.

'Better than TV,' he said.

'What I want to know is,' said the Stomach, 'how he's going to pay for what he's done to my flat.'

A paramedic's car drew up behind the police.

'What I think,' said Bea, 'is that we should get Mr Waite to hospital as quickly as possible.'

'Hold on,' said the policeman. 'Is he or is he not responsible for the damage to this man's flat?'

'Yes,' from the Stomach.

'No,' from Bea.

'Well, then. Who's responsible for his condition now? You, missus?'

'Person or persons unknown,' said Piers. 'Let's get Mr Waite the medical attention he needs, and then we'll answer any questions you may have.'

The voice of authority usually carries the day, but in this case the policeman was getting annoyed and so was disinclined to let them go. 'Not so fast. I'm taking all your names and addresses. I'll want statements—'

'Contact Detective Inspector Durrell,' said Bea, beckoning to the paramedics to attend to Jeremy. 'Tell him there was another attempt to kidnap Mr Waite. He can take it from there. Here's my card, if you need to contact me, though the inspector knows where I live.' And to the paramedics, 'A mace attack. We've been pouring water on his eyes.'

'Right,' said the larger of the paramedics. 'Give us some space, will you?'

Piers made to pick up the remains of the sack, but Jason took it off him, holding it by one corner. 'I'll keep that safe for you, if you're going to the hospital with the little man.'

Bea said, 'Thank you. You've been most helpful. Here, take one of my cards, too, in case you need to get in touch.'

The paramedics seemed to know what they were doing. One of them swabbed away at Jeremy's eyes, while the other brought a wheelchair down out of the ambulance.

The police car inched forward, reminding them to move out of the way. The driver leaned out of the window. 'Are we done here? We've got another shout. Ruckus in the High Street.'

The policeman said, 'In a minute.' He turned his attention to the Stomach.

'Now, then; your name and address if you please.'

'It's not me you should be charging . . .!'

Jeremy was strapped into the wheelchair and transferred to the ambulance. Bea and Piers climbed in after him. As the doors shut behind them, Bea spotted Jason disappearing into the coffee shop.

She looked at her watch. 'Piers, have you your mobile on you? I think we ought to let Maggie and Oliver know what's happened.'

*   *   *

Jeremy was discharged soon after midnight. He'd stopped cursing by that time. His eyelids were still inflamed, but he could see, after a fashion, and the nurse in the Accident and Emergency department said his sight wasn't permanently damaged. What the attack had done to his confidence was another matter. The only thing he said in the taxi on the way home was, 'I've got to make a will.'

'Tomorrow,' said Bea, and she tucked him up in bed in the guest room. She checked that Oliver and Maggie were all right – they were having a quiet snack in the kitchen – and absent-mindedly gave Piers a kiss on his cheek when she saw him out of the front door. Then she set the alarm, took off her make-up and, without bothering to have a shower, fell into bed.

Sunday morning

They all slept late. Bea opened her curtains to see a morning haze lifting, hinting at a warm, bright day to come. She heard the bells of the church calling her to worship and wished she had no other calls on her time. It would be pleasant to set aside all her responsibilities, to walk out of the house and attend the service. She was sure she'd feel refreshed, and better able to cope, if she did.

But knew she couldn't.

And then wondered if it was fatigue or inertia that held her in the house.

Dear Lord . . . decisions, decisions! If I go to church, I shall worry about the problems here. Oh yes, I understand that I ought to be able to leave my problems behind when I go to church, in order to concentrate on You. Rightly or wrongly, I feel I ought to try to sort things out here first. Perhaps there'll be an opportunity for me to drop into the church later on today and have a quiet time with You?

She had a bowl of cereal, made a cafetière of coffee and took a cup into the living room, to stand by the open French windows, looking down on to the garden. And there was Jeremy, still dressed in his pyjamas, sitting on a garden chair, staring at nothing.

A rustle of cloth, and Maggie put an arm around Bea. Her

hair was still green, but she was wearing bright red today. 'I offered him breakfast. He refused.'

Bea nodded. The little man was taking it hard.

Oliver put his arm around Bea from the other side. 'He's wearing Maggie's bunny slippers. Regressing to childhood?'

Bea sighed. 'He's got a lot to think about.'

Oliver tightened his arm around her in a hug. 'Mother Hen . . .'

Bea laughed, shook her head.

'I like it,' said Maggie. 'Mother Hen. You are definitely Mother Hen.'

'Idiots!' Bea's tone was affectionate.

'What can we do to help?'

'Ah. Yes. Can you two find a lock and fit it to the door of your office downstairs? Three keys needed; one for you, one for me, and one for your part-time secretary.'

'What? Who?'

Bea nodded. 'I'm going to arrange for you to have a part-time secretary cum assistant, mornings only to start with, and Miss Brook is going to come in every Friday afternoon to keep your accounts straight. As from today it's going to be your office, and that of your part-time office staff.'

'Whoopee!' Maggie threw both arms up in the air, and then sobered. 'That's wonderful. But, can I afford to pay them? Panic, panic! I'm not sure—'

'I am,' said Bea, smiling. 'We're going to set you up in business for yourself. I will rent you office space and two part-time assistants and—'

'I'll do you a website!' Oliver wasn't going to be left out. 'I'll set up all the systems for your secretary and Miss Brook to handle. Can we afford a new computer?'

'Maggie will buy one from the Abbot Agency,' said Bea. 'Second-hand. I'll get Miss Brook to work out the details for us. For the moment you'll have to use your mobile phone for office work, but when you're properly sorted out with a new business name, you can get a landline installed in your name.'

'What name?' Maggie started to dance around. 'What do I call myself?'

'The Mother Hen Agency?' Oliver thought this was hilarious.

'Stupid!' Maggie aimed a blow at him – and missed.

He pretended to be mortally wounded. 'Aaargh! I'm dying. How about Maggie May Transformations?'

Maggie hit out again – and missed a second time. 'That's for wigs, stupid!'

Bea separated them. 'We'll think of the right name in time. When do you go back to uni, Oliver?'

He scowled. 'Don't you dare try to send me back till this is over.'

'But—'

'This is more important. Do you think I'd leave you to face Ianthe alone – never mind trying to keep Jeremy from falling victim to general mayhem? All right, I know I shall have to go back for a few days. Later on. When this is finished, right?'

Bea was touched. In a husky voice, she said, 'Thank you, Oliver.' Then she clapped her hands, returning to normal. 'Well, my dears; you must set about getting a lock put on the office door while I sort out something for lunch and have a chat to Jeremy.'

No sooner were the youngsters out of the house than the doorbell rang. Bea let Detective Inspector Durrell in. He sighed at her. 'Now what have you been up to?'

She shook her head. 'You may well ask. Come through to the kitchen; I'm just checking what food we've got left for the weekend. Coffee?'

He slid on to a stool. 'I got an incoherent message from some plod on the beat. The only bit that made sense was to ring you.'

'Oh yes. That was about an attempted kidnapping, a murder and an illegal removal of a corpse.'

'Is that all?' He stretched, sighed. 'I should be at a family barbecue today. The wife is not amused.'

She set a mug of coffee before him.

'On the other hand –' ladling sugar into his cup – 'my brother-in-law has a habit of criticizing me about the way I bring up my children, my relationship with my in-laws, the type of car I drive, the insurance companies I patronize, and the clothes I wear. So I suppose I'm well out of it.'

Amused, Bea delved into the freezer, bringing out some home-made pizza bases which would do for lunch . . . and a pack of frozen chicken fillets. 'What does your wife say to all this?'

'He criticizes her, too. She wishes she, too, had a job which enabled her to skive off these difficult family occasions. She knows I'll make it up to her, later. She knew I was a hunter when she married me, and that when I'm on the job, nothing else matters. You're something of a hunter yourself, aren't you?'

She was startled. 'Am I? I wouldn't have said . . . Well, I suppose every now and then I get drawn into odd situations where I can do some good. But this time it was Not. My. Fault. An acquaintance asked me to find someone to look after Jeremy, and things just happened from then on.'

'You could have turned the other cheek. Pushed him out into the great wide world.'

She sent him a withering look and requested he pass over a couple of onions from the vegetable stand by the back door.

He drained his mug and said, 'Ah,' in a satisfied voice. 'Now, could you bear to tell me what happened last night? Oh, and you don't mind if I record this, do you? I have a suspicion it's going to take some time, and it would save me taking notes.'

So she told him what had happened while she sautéed onions in some olive oil, thickened the mixture with some cornflour, threw in a couple of tins of tomatoes, salt and pepper, and tasted it. Nodded to herself. She spread the pizza bases out on baking trays, put some of the tomato mixture on each, and rummaged for some hard cheese – preferably Parmesan – in the fridge. And didn't find any.

'Where's the cheese gone? Surely we haven't finished all of it, have we?'

He was staring at his little tape recorder. 'You mean, you really saw this man being murdered?'

'Mm. I assume. His eyes and tongue bulged like this . . .' And she stuck out her tongue and lolled her head. 'Then he fell back across the seat as his killer – I assume it was a man and not a woman, though I can't be sure . . .'

'Describe him. Or her.'

'Can't. Big. Thickset. It was getting dark. There's no street light in that bit of road. He or she – no, I do think it must have been a man – was dressed in dark clothing; sweater and jogging trousers? Probably. Trainers, I think. Not because I saw them, but because he made no sound as he ran away.'

'It wasn't the same man who drove off in the van?'

'No. He's not as big, and I got a good look at him, anyway. He's the man who pretended to be a police officer the other day. You know, the one with the toupee.' She tried the cupboards and found some cheese flakes. Not wonderful, but they'd do. She sprinkled some on each of the bases. 'Do you like anchovies on your pizzas?'

'Mm? Not much. Pepperoni?'

'I'll see what I can find.' She pulled the sliding section of cupboard out to investigate. 'Mr Toupee was one cool hombre. He checked to see if his partner was dead, shoved him further across the seat, got in, and drove out of there just as the police car arrived.'

'Has the world gone mad?'

THIRTEEN

Bea had to agree; they did seem to be living in the middle of a farce.

'Mm. I wonder if Mr Jason of Jason's Place might be able to throw more light on the situation. He says he observed the whole thing from the first floor flat, the one that used to be Jeremy's, which is directly above the café. It was he who rang for the police, and an ambulance, and it was he who cut Jeremy out of the sack and provided the water we used to treat the effects of the mace attack. If mace is what it is.

'Mr Jason seemed to recognize it as such, which makes me wonder exactly what experience he's had with such matters. Isn't it illegal to attack people with mace in this country? So how did he know about it? Has he worked as a security officer, perhaps? Or . . . he was so helpful, but . . . why am I ambivalent about him?'

'Trust your instincts.'

'Mm. Well, however he came by his knowledge of mace, he did us a favour, because he knew that swabbing Jeremy's eyes with water was the thing to do. By the way, he took the sack that Jeremy had been put into.'

'Why on earth did you let him take the sack?'

'What was I supposed to do with it? Take it off to the hospital in the ambulance? Your policeman was no help at all. All he wanted to do was find someone to charge with assault or carrying a knife, or . . . Well, I suppose he'd have liked anything which enlivened Saturday night's patrol. I can't really blame him, as there was I saying that Jeremy had been kidnapped and put into a van – and the van had disappeared by the time he came along. All he saw was Jeremy lying on the ground trying to fight his way out of the sack. He thought it was a prank gone wrong, although . . . I can see his point of view. Reluctantly.

'At the same time the landlord was fulminating – good word, fulminating; don't think I've ever had cause to use it before – while Mr Jason . . . Would you mind turning that tape recorder off for a moment? Thank you. I was going to say something I'd rather you didn't put on tape. You see, Mr Jason used a sharp knife to free Jeremy . . . A knife which I assume he fetched for that purpose from his café, although . . .'

The inspector picked up on that one. 'You think he might normally carry a knife, but in this case you're not prepared to swear to its existence, since he used it to free your friend?'

Bea was pleased with the way the inspector had interpreted the situation. 'That's about it. The policeman wanted to charge Jason with carrying a knife, so we – that is Piers and myself – denied we'd ever seen one, and I expect you would have done so, too, in our shoes. If you visit Mr Jason, I suppose he might not be all that cooperative if you start by asking him about knives. You understand that we couldn't have got Jeremy out of the sack without his help, and the paramedics say that the prompt treatment with water saved Jeremy hours of agony.'

'And if Jason does habitually carry a knife, then that might be another reason why he was so eager to go off with the sack. Getting rid of the evidence, so to speak.'

'Would he go so far as that?' Bea considered the question and shook her head. 'I suppose he might, yes. He gave the impression of finding the whole situation one big laugh. Oh dear. How difficult for you.'

'That's life,' said the inspector, sounding depressed. 'Now, I'm turning the recorder back on again, so be careful what you say. The officer reported that he took a statement from a man called Landis, whoever he may be—'

'The landlord of Jeremy's flat. The place that was trashed by
. . . whoever.'

'You say it wasn't trashed by Jeremy. Who do you think did
it? The men who were trying to kidnap him?'

'Well, it makes sense. They were definitely lying in wait for
Jeremy, who'd been lured there by a phone call from the landlord.
Did you say his name was Landis?'

'Don't rely on the spelling.'

Bea found a tin of anchovies and a packet of pepperoni. 'It
occurs to me, and I'm sure to you, too, to wonder how the gang
knew Jeremy was going to be there.'

'And how do you think they knew it?'

'I have a horrid sinking feeling that it must be through
Mr Jason. I can't see any other point of contact. He's a chatty
soul, Mr Jason. I can see him leaning on his counter, gossiping
away about the man upstairs being accused of killing a girl,
and then relaying the news that his flat had been trashed, and
gracious me! the landlord's coming round this evening to have
it out with him, and won't that be a scene and a half! His
customers would come in for the latest instalment in the soap
opera, treat themselves to coffee and a snack, and a good time
would be had by one and all. There need not be any ulterior
motive in Jason passing on information about what was
happening.'

'Taking that one step further, and presuming that you did
indeed see a third man kill the driver of the van – then how did
the killer know that Jeremy and the two members of the gang
were going to be there? And don't tell me it was an entirely
unrelated coincidence.'

'Mm. What's wrong with both Mr Toupee and the killer
popping into the café for a latte and the latest news? Or even
giving Mr Jason a ring for an update? I suspect that one would
sell news of his granny for a fiver.'

'I like it. Any more coffee in that jug?'

She poured him some. 'Taking it one step further, why does
this other man want to kill the driver of the van?'

Silence. They both frowned into space.

She said, 'I do know why Mr Toupee was after Jeremy, if
that's any help. He said it was because Jeremy had killed Josie.
I pointed out that his colleague was being killed while Mr Toupee

was holding Jeremy down inside the van . . . so he does now realize that Jeremy isn't his only problem . . . which is good news for Jeremy. Presumably, there won't be any more attempts to kidnap and kill him.'

'If you're right – and I suspect you are – it means that there's a third party, or parties unknown, who are also on the warpath. Why?'

'Do you think it's possible that the man who killed the driver also killed Josie?'

The inspector looked into the bottom of his empty mug. 'Well, we know it wasn't Jeremy who killed Josie; he's not tall enough, and he has an alibi.'

'And if you can imagine him working through an accomplice – well, I can't.'

'So who else . . .?'

Bea sat on the nearest stool, still holding the pepperoni and the anchovies. 'I've heard some gossip recently about a gang – though it might not be the same one – that has been playing the Badger Game. They target older, wealthy men with something to lose, using a pretty girl who might well have been Josie. She sets the men up in a compromising situation, the photographer snaps away, and the victims pay up rather than own up. Mostly. Some didn't.'

'Names, addresses?'

She shook her head, thinking how much trouble Piers would be in if she let the names he'd given her, to the police. Besides, she only had first names to go on: Sir Thomas. Sir Charles. Basil. 'Sorry . . . Gossip. No names. Sympathetic grins on the part of the men who told me the stories. I can understand why no one wants to give names. Do you think perhaps one of these men has turned on the blackmailers and is killing them all off, one by one, rather than pay up? Starting with Josie . . . and then the driver of the van . . . though I suppose we really don't know for sure if he was part of the gang.'

'He was in the company of the man with the toupee, who I think we can presume is one of the Badgers.'

'Could there be two sets of people going around dishing out crime and punishment? But if so, how on earth are you going to find out who is killing who – and why?'

'You can get me some names and addresses for a start.'

'I suppose I could try, but whether anyone would be prepared to give me a name . . . I'm not sure that they would.'

'Are you obstructing the police in the performance of their duties?'

Was he serious? Partly.

She shook her head. 'Sorry. I can get back to my sources and ask if they'd be prepared to let you have names and addresses, but that's as far as I can go.'

He lifted his hands in a gesture of submission. 'Don't forget, time's running out. Two dead – so far. How many more?'

'I know.' She felt miserable about it, but wouldn't give in.

He got off his stool. 'Well, this has all been very pleasant, but I suppose I must interview Mr Waite before I finish for the weekend. Where is he? Still in bed?'

Bea looked out through the back door. 'He's in the garden. He's not got dressed yet, or eaten anything. He's in shock, I think.'

The inspector grimaced, stowed away his little tape recorder, and went down the stairs into the garden. Bea finished putting toppings on the pizzas and made some lentil soup. It wasn't really the weather for lentil soup, but needs must when there was nothing else available. Once the chicken fillets had thawed, she'd cook them in a good sauce and serve them with mushrooms and rice for the evening meal.

There was a 'halloo!' from the hall. Maggie and Oliver had returned. Oliver appeared in the doorway. 'We're going down to put a lock on Maggie's office door, now. Unless you need us for anything?'

She didn't. She told herself how pleasant it was to spend time in the kitchen. She enjoyed it; of course she did. But by the time she'd thrown together and baked another sponge cake, she'd had more than enough of domesticity.

The DI came up the stairs from the garden, shaking his head. 'Jeremy says he didn't see anything last night, that he was rushing along to meet his landlord, and this figure stepped out from nowhere and the next thing he knew was a blinding pain in his eyes. I believe him. He says he didn't even see the van you were talking about. Are you sure you didn't imagine it?'

As if drawn by a magnet, his hand reached towards the sponge cake she'd just turned out to cool on a wire tray.

She slapped his hand away. 'What is it with men and sponge cake? Go and join your family barbecue.'

He smiled, treated her to a half salute, and left.

The house was quiet, which meant that Oliver and Maggie had got stuck into something down below. Bea found herself at a loose end.

She took a mug of soup and went down into the garden. Jeremy was sitting on the chair with his hands on his lap, staring at nothing. She put the mug of soup into his hands and was pleased to see he didn't drop it. She got another garden chair out of the shed and sat beside him. He didn't seem to notice.

She put her feet up, leaned back, and closed her eyes.

Presently, she heard him slurp up some soup. Good. She didn't move.

Eventually, he sighed deeply and put the mug down. 'I've been thinking. I've been so naive. Eunice knew all about my embarrassing little problem. She has always known. I never made any secret of it. So, when I told her about Josie jumping on me, Eunice must have known I hadn't encouraged her. She must have known it was a scam.'

'Mm.'

'So why did she throw me out? Only one answer. She was tired of me and wanted to use the evidence to divorce me. She might hope that if I were pushed off balance enough, she could keep the house.'

'Mm.'

'I don't like thinking that she could do such a thing, but there's no other explanation is there? Which leads me to wonder whether . . . it's hard to believe anyone would go to those lengths but . . . do you think she asked someone to set me up?'

Yes, of course she did, you silly man. But Bea didn't want to pour acid on Jeremy's wounds. 'I suppose it's possible.'

'Which means that she knows someone who's in the gang? Someone who knew what Josie did for a living?'

'We can't assume that. I suppose she might have asked around to see if anyone knew someone who might help her. There are rumours circulating about other men who've been targeted by similar scams, and Eunice moves in the sort of circles which might hear about such things.'

'It's unbearable, to think that Eunice – and Clarissa – should . . .'

'Betray you?'

A sigh. 'I knew, and I didn't know. I didn't know before Josie died, but since then I've had to take a good hard look at what's been happening. I don't think Eunice or Clarissa had any hand in Josie's death.'

'No. They had nothing to gain by it.'

'Then who did? The inspector seemed to think it might have been one of her other . . . clients. Would you call them clients?'

'As good a term as any.'

'I didn't pay her for sex. I liked her. I enjoyed her company.'

'I understand that sometimes that may be enough, that men are willing to pay just for company.'

Another deep sigh. 'Poor little Josie.'

'There's one good thing about all this. Since last night's attack on you, the police are pretty sure you had nothing to do with her murder, and I believe that Josie's friends have come to the same conclusion.'

'What I don't understand is, why anyone would want to kill her? She was harmless. She wouldn't have hurt anyone.'

'She was the means they used to threaten other men's reputation. She wasn't without sin.'

'Sin? An ugly word. Wasn't she more sinned against than sinning?'

'And while we're thinking about girls who stray, which of us would want to throw the first stone? Which of us is without sin?'

'What? Oh. That's in the Bible, isn't it? Didn't they used to stone such girls to death? Even knowing what I do now, I wouldn't want to see that happening to her.' He sat up straight, looked around him. 'It's very peaceful here. You have a beautiful home, Mrs Abbot, and you've been more than generous to me. Thank you for giving me sanctuary. I know I've given you a lot of trouble. I apologize and I'll try to make it up to you.'

'Nonsense. Would you like some more soup?'

'No, I'd . . . Do you think you could lend me some black plastic bags? I'll try to get my things together and get out of your house. There's lots of hotels around here. I'm sure one of them can find me a room.'

She patted his hand. 'You're not going anywhere until this is sorted. Do you have a good solicitor, who can help you get your own house back?'

He pulled a face. 'Up against Eunice?'

'Do you want your house back, or not? Think it through. I've got someone in mind who may be able to pop in every afternoon to keep you straight, fill the fridge with food, that sort of thing. If that's what you want.'

He took a deep breath. 'Yes, I would like my house back. You might think it's too big for me all by myself, but I did live there alone before I met Eunice, and it didn't seem too big then. I like space around me. If I get lonely, perhaps I could take in a couple of students, or let part of it to a professional man. That would be sensible, wouldn't it?'

'And it would help to pay the council tax and utility bills. Right. Have you still got your house keys, and the keys to your car?'

'Yes, but—'

'Would you like me to come with you to see Eunice some time – perhaps tomorrow afternoon?'

'You'll think me a poor sort of creature. But, yes; if you could spare the time. One more thing; I may be out of the woods as far as Josie's friends are concerned, but accidents do happen. Oliver's your resident geek, isn't he? Do you think he could get on to the Internet and find me some instructions about making a will, without my having to wait for an appointment with a solicitor?'

'I think the danger to you may be past.'

'Would you risk it, if you were me?'

She was silent. No, she didn't think she would.

He sighed. 'Well, I suppose I'd better get dressed. Did you say there was some more soup going? Or perhaps some bread and cheese?'

Bea collected his mug and took it back upstairs, castigating herself. What on earth have I done now, offering to help Jeremy get Eunice out of his house? Haven't I enough on my plate, what with Ianthe and all? What ever am I going to say to the woman tomorrow? I'm glad Oliver's staying over, though I feel guilty about his giving up his time to help.

Dear Lord, put the right words in my mouth. Be my shield and buckler . . .

What on earth is a buckler, anyway?

Sunday afternoon

It was supposed to be a hot, quiet Sunday afternoon. Sunny, no clouds in the sky. The occasional buzz of a fly, or chirrup of a sparrow, were the only sounds you were supposed to hear. Perhaps the muted hum of traffic might be allowed? Yes, provided one didn't have to ease oneself off the garden chair and do something energetic such as mowing the lawn, or entertaining friends. Bea thought that even going for a walk in Kensington Gardens would be too much trouble.

Jeremy ate two pizzas, a banana and a nectarine, asked Oliver if he could find a will form for him to fill in, and promptly fell asleep on his bed. The one in the spare room.

Oliver went downstairs to help Maggie reorganize her office.

Bea stretched out on a recliner in the shade of the sycamore tree and tried not to think about anything. Supper was organized, sort of. She'd tried to work out what she'd say to Ianthe on the morrow and had come to the conclusion she'd have to wing it. She gave a passing thought to DI Durrell, unwillingly at his family barbecue. It was up to him to sort out the whole horrid mess around Josie's murder.

She drifted off into a doze, only to be awoken by Oliver saying there was a phone call for her. Bother. Couldn't he deal with it?

Apparently not. Someone wanted to meet her by the Round Pond in Kensington Gardens. An elderly woman, said Oliver. By name of Angie Butt. In half an hour, no police, no tape recorder.

'Tell her to get lost. It's Sunday.'

'She rang off.'

Angie. Angela Josephine Butt. Otherwise known as Josie? But Josie was dead. And if Josie were also Angie, which they'd assumed she was . . . Bea squeezed her eyes shut and rubbed her forehead. Who was this new character who called herself 'Angie Butt'? An elderly woman? There'd been no mention of an elderly woman in the case before.

Bea told herself to relax, go back to sleep. After thirty seconds she got up, found herself a sun hat, sun glasses, and checked that her mobile phone, camera and tape recorder were all in her handbag. Before she could leave the house, she went downstairs to alert Maggie and Oliver to what was going on.

Oliver had pinched one of the agency computers and was happily setting it up for Maggie's use.

What could she say to them? Should she warn them to ring the police if she wasn't back within half an hour? Ridiculous. What could happen to her in broad daylight in Kensington Gardens?

She said, 'I'm going out for half an hour. Save me a piece of cake for tea.'

They both said, 'Mm'. She left them to it.

The sun had baked the pavements to scorching point. She wore a loose, cap-sleeved silk top and cool linen trousers in her favourite caramel colour. Sandals, and a large-brimmed hat, which shaded her face nicely from the sun's rays. She walked through the public right of way into the Gardens and turned up the rise towards the Round Pond, where Peter Pan still reigned and where boys of all ages floated toy boats. She took several photos with her little camera.

There were plenty of families around but few elderly women, and only one of these was sitting by herself. This solitary woman was dozing on a bench, with her Zimmer frame before her. An aged panama hat was squashed down over scanty, dyed black hair. Large dark glasses covered much of her face, which was powdered white except for a slash of scarlet lipstick. She wore a long-sleeved blouse of indeterminate colour, with a chiffon scarf around the neck, a long skirt in the sort of beige which always looks as if it needs a wash, and heavy shoes. Wrinkled stockings.

'Miss Angie Butt?' Bea sat down beside the woman, switching on the recording device in her handbag as she did so.

'Mrs Abbot?' A cracked voice. But the ankles above the heavy shoes were slim with no sign of puffiness, and the hands on the Zimmer lacked the freckles of old age.

'You wanted to speak to me?'

'You are not quite what I'd imagined, Mrs Abbot.'

'Or I, you. I assume you are the brains behind the Badger scam?'

'And you are the brains which have kept Jeremy Waite alive?' The voice no longer cracked with age. The disguise was good, at first sight. But the woman was probably no older than Bea – maybe younger.

'I've tried to look after him, yes. You do realize he had nothing to do with Josie's death?'

'So I've been told. I would like to make it clear that I did not approve of the trashing of his flat, but strong feelings were involved.'

'The man in the toupee is on your team?'

'He says that you've earned his respect.'

'I'm honoured. What about the driver of the van? Was he the photographer for your unit?'

'He was.' The hands clutched at the Zimmer frame, then relaxed. 'He's dead. But you know that. You saw it happen. You'd recognize his killer if you saw him again?'

'I wish I could. I saw a vague figure, more of a shadow, leave the van and disappear. A man, I think. Big, well built, clad in dark clothes. Trainers. I think he was wearing gloves. What did you do with the body?'

'We torched the van and left it where it will be found.'

'With the body in it?' Bea winced.

'What else could we do? It will pass as an accident. The wiring was defective – we saw to that. The owner of the van will collect the insurance, and the body will be given a proper burial.'

'You could have informed the police.'

'Hah!' A sufficient reply.

Bea settled herself. 'So, you wanted to see me?'

The woman turned her head to watch Bea. 'Do you have any idea who's doing this to us? First Josie, and then our photographer?'

Bea shook her head. 'You don't know, either?'

'I don't. It's disconcerting.'

'I suppose it must be. Who's next for the chop? Mr Toupee, or you?'

'A good question. Another question would be: how did they know where we'd be last night?'

'I'm beginning to wonder if Mr Jason of Jason's Place may have been supplying information to both sides.'

A sigh. 'Yes. That could well be it. But how did they know where Josie was to be found on the night she died?'

'Someone was following her, perhaps?'

'That was Mr Toupee, as you call him. Josie had received a phone call from a man with a deep voice saying he'd got her in his sights. She was frightened, said she wanted to get out of London for a while. I was out of town or I'd have calmed her down. She was in such a state that she ran out into the street, which was the last thing she should have done. My friend went after her to make sure she was all right. He overheard her ringing Jeremy Waite, asking to meet him. And then he lost her. So we assumed—'

'Jeremy cut the phone call as soon as he realized who was trying to contact him, and before she could tell him where she was.'

'She was fond of him, the silly thing. I suppose she thought he might help her, give her some money to get away.'

'He's a genuinely good man, and he might well have helped her if only she'd managed to get him to listen to her.'

A sigh. 'She didn't want to go through with the scam for him, you know. But we'd arranged—'

'A contract. You'd agreed to set him up, and been paid for it? By his wife, I assume.'

'We won't discuss that, if you please.'

'Very well. But, I think it would be only fair if you got whoever it was to back down. Jeremy's been cleared by the police but has lost his job, been threatened with divorce and forced to leave his house. Tell the person concerned that they can have their divorce, but he wants his house back.'

'I can't do that.'

'Oh, I think you can. You of all people know how rumour can destroy someone's reputation. If a rumour got around that she'd set her husband up, don't you think that would do considerable damage to her earning ability? Try her with that.'

'Hah.' The woman half lifted her Zimmer, then replaced it. 'About Josie's death. Have the police told you anything which might help, such as who frightened her on the phone? If we knew that, we might have some idea who to look out for, and we could take defensive action.'

Bea shook her head. 'I don't know. Why don't you disappear for a while?'

'We have to make a living.'

'By extortion?'

The woman laughed. 'Some men are only too willing to play away, and only too eager to pay up afterwards. What's wrong with that?'

'Arranging for a man to have extramarital sex with a young

girl is entrapment, and demanding money afterwards is blackmail. The last I heard, you can spend time in jail for that.'

A shrug. 'Who's going to complain to the police? You think one of Josie's men has turned on us?'

'Don't you?'

'I suppose so. But who? We've been over and over it, trying to think who's got the guts to fight back. Most of them are mere rabbits, you know.'

'I've heard at least one of your victims committed suicide. How about a son or daughter exacting revenge?'

'Look, they'd go to the police, try to drum us out of business that way. That sort doesn't kill.'

'You're probably right. Well . . .' Bea looked at her watch. 'I've got people to see, supper to cook. I won't say it was nice meeting you—'

'Though it was.' The woman struggled to her feet, leaning on her Zimmer. 'I'll think over what you've said. Maybe it would be best for us to lay off for a while, though it'll put a strain on our finances if we do.'

'You have another girl ready to take Josie's place? Have you picked a suitable man out already?'

'Of course. You'd approve of what we're doing, if you knew the slimeball, too. I'm not going to give you my real name. I'll use Josie's if I have occasion to ring you again.'

So saying, 'Miss Angie Butt' zimmered herself expertly up the rise to the top of the Gardens and out of sight.

FOURTEEN

Sunday afternoon

Bea returned home the way she'd come, wondering whether or not to report the recent conversation to the inspector. She came to the conclusion that she must do so, because somewhere or other there was a burned-out van with a body in it.

She let herself into the house and nearly fell over a couple of bulging black plastic bags. Was Jeremy really taking this business of moving out seriously? From the kitchen came the sound of the radio and Maggie chattering away on her mobile. Normal service had been resumed in that direction. Was Maggie going to be responsible for supper? If so, hurray.

Oliver's head appeared at the top of the stairs leading down to the agency rooms. 'Is that you? Glad you're back. Piers is here, but I've just had a thought . . . something I want to check out.' He disappeared back down the stairs to the agency rooms. Normal service had definitely been resumed.

Piers himself appeared in the doorway to the sitting room, laughing. 'Oliver said you'd gone to meet a dead woman. How like you!'

'Not dead, but using a dead girl's name. I'll tell you all about it when I've had a cuppa.'

Maggie appeared in the kitchen doorway, taking the phone away from her ear long enough to say, 'Tea's up in a minute. I don't know where Jeremy is; up top, I think. He's only just stopped playing some mournful tune or other – for which relief, much thanks.'

Piers held the door open for Bea to pass into the sitting room and shut it after them. 'I'm all ears. I see you've got a house full. Is this your way of saying you don't want me back in your bed?'

He didn't seem too annoyed. Good. 'It just happened. I'm going to try to get Jeremy back into his own house, and Oliver's only here for a few days, but . . . you're right. I don't think it would work.'

'Oliver calls you "Mother Hen". You collect lame ducks, don't you?' A frown. Correction; he was annoyed that his plans had been thwarted, but he wasn't spitting mad.

'Given a fair chance, they're all winners, not losers.'

'So you say.' He let out a long sigh, but relaxed into a smile. And then a laugh. 'Well, I must say I'm disappointed; but if I'm honest I'll admit I've had qualms about it, too.'

'Some new woman turned up in your life?'

'Oh, her. Yes, I suppose you could say . . . But nothing that will last. I don't "do" permanent, you know that. Except for you and Max, who are and always will be permanent in my life, I hope.'

She smiled. 'At a distance.'

'Max told me you were selling up, which started me thinking about the future – yours and mine. But it was never going to work, was it? You don't really want to retire yet, do you?'

'It was his idea, not mine. I think he's come across someone who might want to buy me out. He's encouraged them because he thinks that if I sell up, he can buy this house off me. Once he gets an idea into his head, it sticks, so I've got a fight on my hands there.'

'I'll back you, any day. Let me know if you need any help.'

'Thanks. Stay for supper? And by the way, the police need some help identifying who Josie's clients might have been in the past. May I pass on the tips you gave me? We can disregard the man who called himself Basil, who was collecting his mother's portrait, but what about Sir Thomas, who said he enjoyed a little extramarital flirting now and then, and the cigar-smoking Sir Charles, who is aiming for the House of Commons?'

He hesitated. 'People talk freely when I'm painting them, but there's a tacit understanding that what they tell me goes no further. They could make out a case that I've abused their trust even by passing on various items of gossip to you.'

'Enough said. But if you hear of anything else, do you think you might tell the person concerned that the police are anxious for information and suggest they pass their news items along?'

'I could try.' Clearly, he wasn't hopeful that the strategy would work, and neither, come to think of it, was Bea.

Piers stayed for supper. Bea had to wrench Oliver away from his computer downstairs to join them. Actually, Oliver was using the computer in her office, but that was a minor detail.

Jeremy seemed to have recovered his appetite, but hadn't forgotten about making a will. He asked Oliver if he'd found some information for him.

Oliver hit his forehead. 'Sorry. Forgot. It can't be that urgent, and I'm a bit tied up at the moment. I'll look it up for you in the morning, right?' He took an apple from the bowl on the fridge and disappeared.

Jeremy dropped his fork and looked upset.

'Never mind,' said Piers who, like Maggie, had begun to treat the little man as a somewhat backward if talented child. 'Here . . . write down your intentions on the back of this shopping list . . . Bea usually keeps a pad somewhere . . . Yes, here it is. Have you a pen? . . . Use mine. Now, all you have to do is write down that you leave everything to the National Trust or Battersea Dogs' Home, or whatever, and sign it. Maggie and I will sign below as witnesses, Bea will pin it up on her noticeboard by the door, and Bob's your Uncle.'

'Would that be legal?'

'A notice of intent is legal,' said Piers. 'It will do fine till you can get to a solicitor, who will wrap it up in obscure language and charge you for it.'

Jeremy scribbled away. 'I want to pay for Josie to have a proper burial, too.' Piers and Maggie signed as witnesses, and seconds were eaten by all.

'And now for some music,' said Jeremy, abandoning the supper table, with all its dirty plates, and leading the way to the sitting room.

Oliver didn't reappear. Bea had caught a glimpse of his profile as he left them and she recognized that look. When Oliver was on the trail of something, he became a hunter – just like her, and the inspector.

Jeremy treated them to an impromptu concert of light music, ending with some jaunty little tunes which he said he'd written for a children's television show. He asked, wistfully, if Maggie could sing, as he wanted to hear someone warble Josie's song. Maggie declined the honour, saying she was pretty well tone deaf.

He didn't ask Bea, which annoyed her, even though she didn't think her voice was up to much.

When Jeremy stopped playing and said he needed an early night, the group broke up. Piers said he'd best be on his way, and Maggie went off to join some friends for a drink in the pub. Knowing that the inspector was off duty for the rest of the day, Bea left a message for him to contact her in the morning.

The house lay quiet around her. So where was Oliver? Bea descended the stairs to tell him to pack it in for the night and found him still at the computer in her office.

He looked up with a grin. 'I think I've found the people who might want to buy you out. I was looking in the wrong place. Do you know how many employment agencies there are in this area, any one of whom might cast a greedy eye upon your client list? Dozens. Only a few are specifically for domestic situations, but even then, there are too many to count. Max said it was a double-barrelled name, but it's Someone *and* Someone, which is not double-barrelled.'

'Not Jackson's, then?'

'A different kettle of fish.' He scrutinized the screen, nodded, and printed off a sheet of paper. 'I think this is it.'

'Holland and Butcher? But this isn't a domestic agency, and they're not even in London.'

'Not far out. Grand house. Training for silver service, butlers, etcetera. Honourable mentions wherever you go in society. It's like saying your nanny was Norland-trained. Here's their website. The younger generation – that's Mr Butcher – is aiming for political life. Conservative, of course. Max might very well have come into contact with him as he's standing for some safe seat or other . . . Surrey? Oh, look! He's on Twitter, trying to build a faithful following of fans.'

Bea looked over his shoulder. 'Can you go back to the website? I thought I saw something . . .'

Oliver returned to it. He said, 'They're high class, stylish, and expensive. They've been turning out butlers and other high-earning functionaries since the days of Jeeves and Wooster. The career openings for such people may no longer be in grand country houses, but they're still needed in embassies and by the nouveau riche, Russian millionaires, pop stars and highly paid footballers. Remunerative, very. Ah ha! Is this what you mean? At the bottom it says that all clients who are successful in passing their exams at the end of the training period will be referred to a highly reputable domestic employment agency, who will endeavour to place them in a suitable position. Will you just look at the name of the agency they've been using!'

It was Croxtons, the agency who'd folded earlier that year. Bea let out a long sigh.

Oliver nodded. 'I've got the creeps all up and down my spine. The Holland and Butcher website isn't exactly up to date, is it? You'd expect them by now to have deleted the name of the failed agency and substituted a new one. They desperately need to reassure people that there will be a job for them at the end of the courses they're running. No jobs, no takers for tuition, right?'

'So why haven't they done so?'

'Can you think of another really high class domestic agency who'd fit the bill . . . apart from ours?'

She thought about it. People in the business tended to circulate news and views all the time. Clients report disasters and triumphs. A picture emerges. 'You're right. There are one or two middling good agencies around, but they're not supplying the embassies or Millionaires' Row as we are.'

'What would I do, if I were in H and B's shoes? I'd try out another agency on the sly, without committing myself. The only mystery to me is why they haven't contacted you before now, whether they're interested in buying you out or just coming to a mutually-beneficial agreement.'

'Our reputation hasn't been spotless of late. I've let things slide, and there's been complaints. I suspect we've been trying to place too many badly-trained personnel.'

'If you had well-trained people to offer, you'd be laughing all the way to the bank. An arrangement with Holland and Butcher would suit both parties.'

It made sense. 'Good work, Oliver. I'd never have thought of this, but it feels right. Only, I don't see where Ianthe fits in. Perhaps I'll find out tomorrow.'

He grinned. 'She's going to go spare when she realizes Maggie's back in her own office with one of the agency computers. I wonder if your little tape recorder is good enough to tape your confrontation with her? I'll set you up with something more efficient in case she tries to throw a strop.'

'I think she's more likely to cry. She's the sort of woman who thinks tears will get her what she wants.' Except that every now and then Bea had spotted the iron fist under the velvet glove on Ianthe's hand.

He shuddered. 'Tears? Ugh. Sooner you than me. How many times have you reminded her to give you the password every day?'

'Three. I took the precaution of photocopying each reminder before I put it on her desk, and yes, I know that's grounds to sack her. But she does get through a mountain of work, and if I sack her, how would we cope?'

He shrugged. 'I can stay on for a day or two till you get a replacement.'

She had hoped he'd say that. 'That would be generous of you, and I'd be eternally grateful if you could, even though I know I shouldn't be keeping you from whatever it is you're supposed to be working on at the moment. But before I give her the sack, I want to find out exactly what she thinks she's doing.'

He looked at his watch. 'I said I'd join Maggie and her friends at the pub for a drink before they close for the night. All right by you?'

Monday morning

Some Monday mornings are worse than others. The thought of what she had to do that day filled Bea with dread. Ianthe . . . Jeremy and Eunice . . . Whatever had possessed her to say she'd help the little man get his home back?

She did the power-dressing bit with a white silk blouse over black, tailored trousers. She took care with her make-up and forced herself to eat some breakfast.

If she had to sack Ianthe, how soon could she get a replacement? Advertisements would have to be put in the newspapers, and then time allowed for people to reply . . . and more time before interviews could be arranged . . . and then if the candidate were already employed elsewhere, she would have to give notice at her present job. Say two months in all? Oliver could stay to help for a week, maybe more. But not for two months. No. Out of the question.

Another thing; she must tell the inspector about what had happened to the van with the body in it, and give him the tape-recording of her conversation with 'Miss Butt' and the photo she'd taken of her – not that it would do him much good, as the woman had been heavily disguised.

Jeremy hadn't yet appeared for breakfast. He'd been humming something soft and low in the spare bedroom when she went up to bed. A lullaby? It had certainly rocked her off to sleep.

She took her second cup of coffee down the stairs. The door to Maggie's office was open, and she was inside, talking volubly on her mobile phone while leafing through some papers. Her computer was already up and running. Oliver must have fixed it to respond only to Maggie's new password – whatever that might be. Bea could only hope the girl had written it down somewhere not too easy to find, and also that she could remember where she had put it. Maggie was a wonder in many ways, but remembering pin numbers and passwords was not her forte.

After her down the stairs came Oliver, yawning and carrying his own cup of coffee. He followed Bea into her office and made sure she knew how to start the larger recording device he'd installed in the top drawer of her desk. 'You understand how to start and stop it?'

She gave him a Look. Did he think she was a complete idiot?

He grinned, said, 'Good luck,' and went to join Maggie, closing the door of her office behind him.

Bea booted up her computer and fed in the new password. Some emails had come in over the weekend. Nothing much to worry about there. No complaints; thank goodness.

She shut her eyes and made herself be still. *Dear Lord, grant me wisdom to deal with this.*

She could hear the girls arriving next door. Ianthe would be among the earliest, in order to give out the new day's password to the rest of the staff so that they could access the system.

Ah. Sounds of alarm. Ianthe had discovered the loss of one of her computers, and then the smashed lock of her desk drawer. More sounds of confusion. Cries of 'Ianthe, I can't get on to the computer!'

Surprise, surprise. Bea sighed deeply, switched on the recording device Oliver had installed in her top drawer, and opened the French windows on to the garden. It was a cool, overcast morning, though it would probably warm up later.

'Mrs Abbot? I'm sorry to say there's been a break-in. We'll have to inform the police. My desk drawer has been forced, and one of our computers is missing.'

'No problem, Ianthe. I had to gain access to your drawer yesterday, so I broke it open. I'll get someone in to fix it. And I'm selling one of our computers to Maggie, who needs one.'

'What? But . . .'

Cries from the girls in the big office. 'Ianthe, can you give us the password?'

Ianthe disappeared, saying, 'Just a moment . . .'

Bea waited.

Ianthe returned, looking flushed. 'There's a fault in the system, and we can't get in. Who do we call to get it fixed?'

'No problem. I'll give you the password, and you can get everyone started.'

A hesitation. 'There's a new password?'

'Yes, I put it in. A new one for each day. A splendid idea of yours. Shall I write it down for you, or can you remember it? It's the usual jumble of letters and figures, upper case and lower.'

Another hesitation. 'Perhaps you'd better write it down for me.' Sensible girl.

Bea wrote it down on a Post-it note. 'Oh, and by the way, Maggie's office is out of bounds in future. I'm getting in a part-time secretary for her, and Miss Brook will be coming in to do her accounts every Friday afternoon. You are quite right; Maggie needs to run her own office now.'

Ianthe took the Post-it note, got as far as the door, and stopped. 'How are we to manage? We'll be short of a computer.'

'Get the girls started, and we'll have a chat about it.'

Ianthe left. Bea let out a long breath. That had gone well, hadn't it? Would Ianthe understand that she'd lost control, and accept it? That would be the best scenario, wouldn't it?

No. Back she came. 'I've accessed today's password, but I can't seem to change it.'

'Why should you? I've had the computers reprogrammed so that the only computer that can set the password is this one – and I have to input another password to get into the system. All right?'

Ianthe closed the door and sat, unasked, in the client's chair in front of Bea's desk. So she was going to fight, was she?

Bea sat back in her chair, steepled her fingers, and smiled at Ianthe over them. If the woman wanted a fight, then she should have one.

Ianthe was wearing a white blouse and black skirt. Bea's outfit cost at least twice as much.

Ianthe looked as if she'd come straight from the hairdresser, but Bea's ash-blonde mop had been cut by a master.

No contest. Such apparently small points can sway fortunes in battle. Bea didn't rejoice that she had more money at her disposal than Ianthe, but she did feel it gave her a slight advantage.

Ianthe said, 'I thought you trusted me to run the office for you.'

Bea picked her words with care. 'Perhaps I didn't spend enough time with you when you first came, explaining the way

I like things done. The agency is my baby and my livelihood, after all.'

'But you're going to sell it.'

'What gave you that idea?'

Ianthe reddened. 'But I thought . . . I was told . . .'

'Who told you? What did you think?'

Ianthe fidgeted. 'Well, we could see, we all could, that you weren't . . . that you'd lost interest. There were signs, little mistakes—'

'And it was your job to put the mistakes right? Or to make them seem worse than they were?'

'Of course not!'

'That's what you did with Miss Brook, wasn't it? You arranged things so that she would feel she was losing her grip. When she told me she wanted to resign, I was shocked. It seemed to me that her brain was as sharp as ever, and that if she had made one or two slips, she was still worth her weight in gold to the agency. But, I believed that if she wanted to retire, I had no right to ask her to stay.

'However, time has passed since then, and she's had time to reflect on what happened in the weeks before she left. I spent an hour on the phone to her this past weekend and was delighted to hear that she still misses us. I asked how she'd feel about returning for a few hours each week, and after some persuasion, she said she would . . . but that she didn't feel able to work with you any more.'

'Naturally. She's well past her sell-by date.'

'She says you "forgot" to post her invoices to customers, or sent them out incorrectly addressed.'

'And you believed her?' A light laugh.

'Oh yes. I've never known her to lie about anything, and why should she make up such a story? I also spoke to Celia, to ask why she'd felt it necessary to leave us after so many happy years. Like Miss Brook, she'd felt bruised by the treatment you'd given her, though it seems she suffered a more subtle offensive. There were unkind remarks meant to be overheard, and laughter behind her back. There's a thousand different ways a group of people can make someone in their midst feel unwanted. The question is: why did you want to get rid of Miss Brook and Celia, and all the other girls who'd been working for me for a long time?

I had a good team out there when you arrived, and now there's no one whose face I recognize.'

'They were inefficient and lazy. They had to go.'

'That's for me to judge, not you. You took advantage of me going away on holiday to get rid of the last of them, didn't you? You thought, quite rightly, that I wouldn't make a fuss if you presented me with a fait accompli.'

'Celia was a bad influence. She questioned every change I made.'

'I wonder why. But let's move on to Maggie. When Celia was responsible for Maggie's paperwork, everything went like clockwork. Since Celia left, all kinds of mistakes have been made, haven't they? Errors were made in copying out Maggie's figures, estimates missed their dates. So whose competence are we calling into question now?'

Ianthe's colour was mounting. 'Genuine mistakes, I'm sure.'

'I suppose you'd say that any errors I made were genuine mistakes, too.'

'Of course.' A constricted tone.

'What about the errors that you made? Were those genuine mistakes, too?'

'I . . . what errors?'

Bea sighed. This was like potting sitting ducks. Almost cruel. She pushed back her chair. 'Ianthe, I could ask you to resign right now—'

'On what grounds?'

'Three times I asked you to give me the day's password. That's three warnings.'

'You can't!'

'Give me one good reason why not.'

'Because . . .' She twisted her hands together, and yes, there were tears in her eyes. 'Because I lost my job when Croxtons closed down, and this is a good job. I don't want to lose it. If I've misinterpreted any of your instructions, if I've gone too far in trying to protect your interests, then—'

'If I sold out to Jackson's, would he give you a job?'

'No!'

'If I went into partnership or sold out to Holland and Butcher . . .'

Ianthe drew in her breath and changed colour. 'You've heard from them already?'

Bea said, 'Now we're getting somewhere. I know you were office manageress at Croxtons before they went bust last year, and that they used to handle all the work for Holland and Butcher. When you applied for the job here, you told me your last employers had gone bust because they didn't have an upmarket clientele. I can understand why you wanted a job with us, because we do have a certain reputation, and I suppose we might well be considered a fitting partner for Holland and Butcher.'

'I've only ever had your best interests at heart—'

'Croxtons went bust in the spring. You of all people knew of the link between Croxtons and Holland and Butcher. Did you ask Holland and Butcher for a job when Croxtons failed?'

'I asked around everywhere. There aren't that many good jobs around.'

'So you did try Holland and Butcher? But they turned you down.'

'They didn't have an opening at the time.'

'So you heard about us, applied and were fortunate enough to be taken on. You've been in the business for years. You knew how much Holland and Butcher needed to tie in with a reputable employment agency. You saw – probably before anyone else did – that we could replace Croxtons. And you were right. Did you suggest it to Holland and Butcher, or wait for them to come to that conclusion themselves?'

'I might have suggested it. But they were not interested.'

'I'm surprised.'

'They thought they could go it alone, that they didn't need to tie in with another agency, that their training was so good anyone would snap up their personnel.'

'But over a period of time they realized they did need a guaranteed outlet for their staff. So you watched and waited . . . and made plans. You could see that one day Holland and Butcher were going to come knocking on my door. How could you ensure that, whatever happened, you would come out smelling of roses? Well, you could ensure that all the girls here owed their jobs to you. So you got rid of any older members of staff and recruited new ones whose loyalty was only to you.'

Ianthe's colour remained high. 'I aim for maximum efficiency. You've only to look at our turnover to see how successful I've been.'

'Which reminds me. How exactly have you managed to increase our turnover so quickly? Normally, the odd client or two drifts in as a result of word of mouth approval. But we seem to have acquired a lot of extra clients very quickly, and an equal number of not-always-satisfactory staff.'

'When Croxtons went bust—'

'You took the precaution of making copies of their client and staff lists? Ten minutes with a memory stick, and you had all the relevant information ready for reuse here?'

A shrug. 'Standard practice.'

'Those lists were the property of Croxtons. They could have sold out to another agency, and those lists would then have been a major part of their goodwill.'

Another shrug. 'But they weren't.'

'I don't like it. It's not the sort of behaviour I expect from my staff. Now, you've kept in touch with Holland and Butcher all this time, I take it?'

Hands twisted together. 'Of course. I've known everyone there for years.'

Bea leaned back in her chair. 'Mr Holland?'

'That old stick? Huh.'

'So it's young Mr Butcher who's your contact? The one aspiring to a seat in Parliament? If he's going into politics, how much time can he afford to give to Holland and Butcher nowadays? Was it his idea to run the firm without a tie-in with an agency? Yes, that was it, wasn't it? And now he's finally got round to us. Well, I don't mind talking to him about it. Some kind of partnership would suit me very well.'

Ianthe sniffed. 'But you're going to retire, aren't you?'

Bea sat upright in her chair. 'Ah. Now we're getting there. I don't believe that they want a partnership. I suspect they'd prefer total control. They'd like to buy me out.' She wondered if this whole mess had started when Max had met up with young Mr Butcher, who knew of the connection with the Abbot Agency . . . and Max had seized the idea and run with it because it would be to his advantage to get Bea to move away.

Ianthe's lips tightened. 'It makes sense.'

'You have a good job here, so what difference would it make to you if I sold out? Ah, I get it. You want security, and you like the feeling of power that managing the agency brings. You think they'll leave you in post if they buy me out?'

'I am only safeguarding my interests and those of my girls. They'll be very happy to keep me on. I know their operation so well.'

Bea sighed. 'So there it is. You realized some time ago that I wasn't ready to retire, so you began to sideline me, to make out I was losing my grip on the agency. But I'm a tough old bird and not easily phased out.'

Ianthe's eyes brimmed over. 'I've no idea what you're talking about. I've merely tried to do my duty by you, and you are accusing me . . . Oh, this is dreadful.'

Bea sighed. She stood up, eased her back. 'You've failed, Ianthe. I'm not selling.'

FIFTEEN

I anthe went bright red with rage. 'You stupid old cow! Why pretend that you still care about business any more? Why don't you get out and leave it to someone younger and brighter than you?'

'You've misjudged me, Ianthe. I haven't lost my appetite for work. My big mistake was in leaving too much to you, but that's all over. I'm worried that we've been having so many complaints, and that's the first thing I've got to tackle. If, as I suspect, we've been employing badly trained personnel, then that's going to stop, right now. It may mean turning away some clients for a while. As for Holland and Butcher, I certainly won't be selling the agency, though I may or may not go into partnership with them . . . I'll have to see what they're offering. Either way, the Abbot Agency will continue.'

Ianthe's chin came up. 'You can't do that. You can't turn clients away. I've built this agency up. Our client list has almost doubled, and the agency is worth far more now than it was when I joined.'

'You're a good office manageress, Ianthe, and if only you'd stuck to that, you could have had a career with us. As it is, I think you'd better clear your desk and leave right now. I'll send on any monies due to you.'

'You're as good as accusing me of sharp practice, and I won't put up with it.'

'Now you mention it—'

'If you throw me out now, I'll . . . I'll sue you for wrongful dismissal!' She got to her feet, twanging with rage. 'And what's more, all my girls will leave with me!'

Oliver came in and shut the door behind him. 'I've told the girls in the office that Ianthe is not feeling too well and needs to go home. Here's her handbag, and her jacket.'

'Has she got a memory stick in her bag? I hope she hasn't been copying our records, but she did that when she left Croxtons, so we'd better check.'

Ianthe screeched. 'How dare you! As if I would . . .! I wish now that I'd thought of it, but I'd no idea you were going to throw me out! After all I've done for you!'

Oliver rummaged in Ianthe's bag. 'No memory sticks here. I'll take her out into the garden and up the outside stairs. Then she can go straight out through the house to the front door so that she doesn't need to answer any questions from the rest of the office staff.'

'I've every right to talk to my girls and—'

'Put your point of view?' said Bea. 'Tell them you've been sacked for disloyalty and sharp practice? Why don't you resign and leave quietly? That way what's been said between these four walls will remain that way . . . Unless you try to sue for wrongful dismissal, in which case . . .' Bea pulled the drawer of her desk further out, revealing her tape recorder in action.

Ianthe ground her teeth. 'If you sack me, I'll tell the world all your secrets!'

'What secrets?'

'That you've been harbouring an escaped murderer, who killed an under age girl from his school—'

Bea spurted into laughter. 'What nonsense.'

'I've seen him with my own eyes!'

Bea shook her head. 'The police have cleared my guest of all charges, so I'd be careful what you say, if I were you. Remember that slander can bring a heavy fine.'

Ianthe was sobbing in great gulps. 'Your threats carry no weight with me.'

Bea said, 'If you've left any other personal items in your desk, I'll see they're sent on to you.'

Ianthe screeched, 'You ungrateful, dried up old cow! No wonder both your marriages ended badly, which is no surprise to me, seeing how badly your half breed of a son has turned out!'

Bea gasped.

Oliver's face was set in stone. 'May I show you out?'

Ianthe snatched her handbag and jacket and stormed out into the garden and up the stairs, with Oliver following her.

Bea sank down into her chair, and closed her eyes.

She was shaking. *Phew! Lord, that wasn't very nice. I remember You got shouted at a lot, by all sorts. Well, well. You survived. And so will I. Breathe deeply. In . . . and out. That's it. Don't think of anything at all, except breathing in . . . and out.*

She heard the front door slam far above. After a little while Oliver opened the door from the main office and came in. 'All right?' he said. His self-control was, as always, admirable.

She held up her hands. 'I'm still shaking, but I'll live. How about you?'

He grimaced. 'That woman is poison, isn't she? I seem to remember someone saying once that bricks and stones may break our bones, but hard words never will.'

Yet a pulse beat fast, too fast, on his temple.

She tried to laugh. 'I feel as if I've been ten rounds with a heavyweight boxer.'

'I'm told it does a woman good to have a cry on these occasions.'

She smiled, shook her head. Laughed. Stood up and brushed herself down. 'I'm all right.' She turned off her recording device. 'I'd better see how many of the other girls want to leave now Ianthe's gone.'

'Before you go. Jeremy caught me going through the house. He wanted the name of a solicitor. I told him the name of the one you use and pointed him in the direction of the telephone.'

Bea nodded. 'Good.'

'Oh, and Celia's arrived. She's in with Maggie now, catching up on all the gossip. Is she to work for Maggie, or to take Ianthe's place?'

'I had thought that she'd help Maggie out, but now . . . Do you think she'd agree to stepping into the breach, to help us get the agency back on track? I know she doesn't want the responsibility of the top job, but if she could only run the office till we can advertise for someone else, it would help us out of a hole. After that . . . who knows?'

Bea steadied herself, leaning against her desk. Her own pulse was still too fast. *Calm down, Bea.*

'I'll go and speak to her about it now. I'll have to find at least one more person to work in the office straight away. Perhaps they could do Maggie's work part-time as well? We need someone new, someone who's not been contaminated by working with Ianthe. Would you draft an advertisement for the post of office manageress, Oliver? We must try to get it into the papers today and interview as soon as possible.'

She left Oliver working at her desk and went into Maggie's office to speak to Celia. Twenty minutes later she entered the main office, and every face turned towards her. The phones were ringing, unregarded. Hardly any fingers were on keyboards.

A buzz of speculation died away. The only sound was that of the fans which were working hard in this sultry weather.

Bea spoke directly to the girl who'd joined them most recently, the one who had found Maggie's work in her waste-paper bin. 'Anna, would you switch all calls through to the answer machine for a while, as I have an announcement to make?'

Anna did so, then slid back into her place.

Bea took a deep breath to steady herself. 'Owing to a difference of opinion as to the way I run this agency, Ianthe has resigned her position and left.'

Dead quiet. The odd glances were exchanged. Some lips were thinned.

Bea said, 'There have been rumours that I'm about to retire and sell the agency. They are false. I am not about to retire, nor to sell up. The Abbot Agency has always had a name for discretion and service. It is our aim to arrange for the best personnel, trained to the highest standards, to accommodate our clients' needs. I believe we may have been falling down on this of late.

'With my son's help, I plan in the next few days to go through the complaints files to see if the staff we've sent out to jobs recently are in any way at fault. If they are, then we will not be using them again. What's more, we must be more rigorous in checking the CVs of anyone who applies to us for a job in future. Is that clear?'

Sideways glances. Some reluctant nods. Anna had her eyes down, doodling on a pad. Bea thought that Anna seemed less likely than the others to follow where Ianthe had led.

'Are there any questions?'

Some fidgeting. A lot of frowning. A heavy-set girl spoke up. 'Suppose you do find a single complaint against someone on our books, does that mean we're not to give them any more jobs?'

'A single complaint can be investigated. It may not be substantiated. Bring any such to me. Two strikes: he or she is out, and we don't use them again.'

'But there's never enough well-trained staff to fill all our vacancies.'

'I know. We will have to decline some jobs if we can't fill the vacancies with people we can trust to do the job properly.'

'But –' this was the heavy-set girl again – 'Ianthe set us targets and promised to give us a bonus in September if we've met them. If we're to turn down business, we'll never meet our targets and bang go our bonuses.'

A murmur of approval.

Ianthe had promised them a bonus in September? That was a good way of ensuring their loyalty through a changeover, wasn't it? Ah, but why September? Was Bea supposed to have retired by then?

'Scrap the targets,' said Bea. 'Good work deserves a rise in salary. Yes, we may handle fewer cases in the next few months, but that means we can give better service. In the short term we may not make so much money, but in the long run—'

'Well, I don't think much of that.'

'Nor I.'

'Stuff that for a lark.'

Bea noted the girls who were going to follow Ianthe into the wilderness. Bea thanked God that they were the ones most closely allied to Ianthe, and therefore the ones she least wanted to keep. 'If you wish to leave the agency, then please do so now, this minute. Clear your desks and go. I will send on any wages due.'

She waited. The heavy-set girl and one with a face that would sour cream got up and, with much huffing, extracted their personal effects from their desks and made their way out of the office and up the stairs to the street. From the floor above came the faint sounds of a melody, swelling and fading. Jeremy on his keyboard, of course.

Bea looked around those who remained. There was one more woman she would like to dispense with, but she could work with what was left. 'I take it the rest of you wish to remain. You earn a good wage, and if we can get the agency back on track, the future is rosy. Meanwhile, if you come across someone applying for a job whose credentials look dicey, please refer them to me or to Celia. Yes, Celia – whom I'm sure most of you will remember. For those who don't know her, she used to work for us in the past, and I considered it a sad day when she left. She will be acting manageress for the time being, though—'

'I should be promoted to manageress,' said a woman with a permanently angry expression. 'I've been here the longest and know the ropes.'

This was the last of the women whom Bea wanted to get rid of. Bea nodded. 'We are going to advertise the position, of course. I hope to be able to run interviews early next week, and any of you can then apply for the post. Meanwhile, Celia has kindly offered to step into the breach and will run the office until I can appoint someone on a permanent basis.'

Bea opened the door to Maggie's office and ushered Celia into the room. 'Celia, will you come in, please? I'm sorry the top drawer of your desk is broken, but I'm sure you can get that fixed. Anna, will you turn the phones back on, please?'

Celia was a pretty blonde, a softer version of Ianthe, of about the same age. She looked around the office with a pleasant expression on her face. 'Afternoon, everyone. Most of you I know already, but I'm going to go round to each desk to make sure I know all your names and what you're currently doing.'

Bea continued to stand on guard, watching, while Celia went round each desk, introducing herself and checking that she had all the girls' names correct. The phones came back on.

Anna lifted her hand. 'Call for you, Mrs Abbot. A Detective Inspector Durrell.'

'Thank you, Anna. I'll take it in my office.'

Bea found Oliver there, busying himself at her computer. Well. Fine. She supposed. She tried to shift her brain back from office matters to what it was the inspector might want with her. Something about . . . a body in a van. Yes. She lifted the receiver. 'Inspector? I trust you got to spend some time with your family yesterday.'

'Thank you, yes. And you?'

'I had a call yesterday afternoon from the woman who seems to be the brains behind the Badger Game, suggesting a meeting. She wanted to check my views on recent events, especially the fracas on Saturday night outside Jason's café. She said she'd come to the conclusion that a third party is homing in on the gang, trying to knock them off one by one. She wanted me to confirm that Jeremy is definitely not to blame. Which I did.'

'What does she look like?'

'Middling in age. Middling height. Hard to tell because she was got up like an old lady with a Zimmer frame. I took a shot of her with my camera and made a tape recording of our conversation, though I don't suppose either will be much use. Someone in that lot knows all about disguises. Someone who used to be an actor, perhaps?'

'Interesting. I'll call round later to fetch them.'

'Hold on. There's more. She confirmed that the man I saw being killed was the gang's photographer. He is dead. She said they'd torched the van and left him in it. Do you want to look into that? A white van, no markings.'

'How many of those are there around? A thousand, say? Licence number?'

'Sorry. Dirtied.'

'Large, medium or small?'

'Mother Bear, rather than Baby or Daddy.'

A sound like a sneeze came over the phone. 'Is there anything else you can remember about it?'

'Well . . . one of Jeremy's shoes might be inside it. He lost it in his escape from the van, so it might perhaps still be there. I don't suppose that's much use if the van's been torched.'

A sigh. 'Anything else?'

'I asked my ex-husband if he would break confidence and give you the names of possible victims that he'd heard about. He's doubtful. He says he was told these stories in confidence. From what I've seen and heard of his sources, the names wouldn't help you because the people concerned will deny everything.' Particularly, she thought, in the case of those wanting to get into Parliament or the House of Lords. Sir Thomas. Sir Charles.

'I disagree. It would be helpful even to know the sort of people targeted by the gang. If they're all upper crust, then the gang must have an insider giving them information about who to try.'

'From what I've been able to gather they're not upper crust, necessarily. Manufacturers, moneyed men. Men hungry for power and recognition. I don't know how they're selected. Perhaps Madam Brains is the secretary of an exclusive club, or attends business conferences in some capacity.'

'Ask your ex again, will you? I'll be round later on. Will you be in?'

'Probably. Ring beforehand?'

She put the phone down and remembered she ought to be taking Jeremy to see his wife . . . but surely Eunice would be out of the house and working today, wouldn't she? They could wait till the evening to interview her. Anyway, he was still playing the keyboard upstairs; a march, it sounded like. Didn't he ever give it a rest?

Oliver pushed back his chair. 'I've drafted two advertisements; one for manageress, the other for a part-timer to help Maggie. Have a look, see if they're OK. Meanwhile, I need to get at the filing cabinets next door if we're to review all the recent complaints. Is it safe to enter the lion's den?'

'Celia will tame the lions for us. Yes, go ahead.' She checked the advertisements, shortened them, counted words. Yes, they'd do. She faxed them off to the newspapers.

Celia rang through. 'Mrs Abbot; can you take some phone calls for us? Being short-handed here . . .'

'Of course, Celia. Switch them through.'

Bea dealt with some routine telephone enquiries and interviewed a woman who said she was a cordon bleu cook, but whose references didn't match that description. And then one whose references did.

As soon as she was free, Oliver brought in a sheaf of files, frowning. 'I've been trying to match up the complaints with the personnel files. I've found three youngsters so far who . . . Well, let's put it this way. I don't think Miss Brook would have sent them to any of our clients. Straight out of school. Two of them dropped out early. The handwriting on their application forms leaves a lot to be desired, and I'm not talking dyslexia. Miss Brook was in the habit of taking Polaroid photographs of applicants we've accepted on to our books, but I can only find a photo for one of them. There's none for the other two.'

Bea scanned the files. 'I agree, their CVs are not exactly encouraging. One claims to have done some evening bar work, but only lasted a week. The other two don't seem to have done anything except collect dole money. It's good that they want to work, but they must accept they need training before we can use them.'

'I'll prepare a blacklist of those people we're not going to use again, right?'

'Can you look in our own personnel files, see if you can track down one particular woman . . . the name escapes me, but she was excellent. She had to leave – it's maybe a couple of years ago – because her mother was ill and she wanted to look after her. I seem to remember she sent us a Christmas card which said she was hoping to return to work soon. I wonder if she could be induced to come back to us.'

'If she's in the system, I'll find her. May I use your computer again?'

She moved out of her chair to let him get in, and her phone rang again.

'A call for you, Mrs Abbot. He wouldn't give his name.'

'Put it through.'

She moved behind Oliver to watch as he accessed their records on the computer.

'Mrs Abbot?'

'Yes.' Another complaint? She hoped not.

'Don't interfere.'

What? She looked at the phone. What was that?

'Mm?' said Oliver.

She put the phone down. 'A male voice, deep. "Mrs Abbot. Don't interfere."' Her heartbeat went into overdrive. She dialled 1471, only to be informed that the caller had withheld his number. Of course.

Oh, this was all too much! First Ianthe, and then having to face the office staff, and now . . .

Oliver swivelled round in his chair to look up at her. 'Do you think . . .?'

'I don't know. He didn't give a name.' She got herself to the settee by the window and let herself down on to it. 'Do you know something? I'm fed up with this. I am being threatened with anonymous phone calls, just because I took Jeremy in. I could spit!'

Oliver grinned. 'Not like you. Spitting, I mean. Ah. I think I've found the woman who went off to nurse her mother. Home number, mother's number. Which would you like?'

Her phone rang. 'Mrs Abbot, a call for you from a Mr Butcher.'

Of Holland & Butcher? Had Ianthe got on to them already? No, no. Why should she? Was this the formal approach from the firm which had been hovering for some time? She took the receiver from Oliver. 'Mrs Abbot speaking.'

'My name's Butcher, of Holland and Butcher. You have heard of us, perhaps?'

'Indeed.'

'I believe we have interests in common. May I suggest we meet to discuss how we view the world in general, and our own sector of it in particular? Perhaps you would care to come out here – we could send a car for you if you wish – and we could show you around and give you lunch.'

Nicely put. An educated voice, warm and with a hint of humour. A good choice for a first approach. But.

Bea thought quickly. If there were – or had been – any links between Ianthe and Holland & Butcher, it would be best to make it clear that as far as the Abbot Agency was concerned, Ianthe was now dead meat. 'I'm afraid it's not a good time for me to leave the office as I've just had to sack my manageress. Perhaps we could meet in a week or two when I've appointed someone else?'

'My commiserations. Especially as you have a reputation for running a tight ship.'

She hated people who talked about 'running a tight ship'. What on earth did they mean by it, anyway? That they tied people to the mainmast and gave them forty lashes if they disobeyed orders? Deprived them of food and water for a fortnight?

She said, 'You may know her. She used to work for Croxtons. Her name's Ianthe, and she is extremely efficient, in her own way.'

'Ianthe? No, the name doesn't ring a bell. Should it?'

Yes, it should. Or, perhaps it shouldn't? What, after all, did Mr Butcher have to do with someone who once worked at Croxtons? But – he ought surely to know the manageress of a firm they'd been associated with for a long time? 'Oh? Well, she seemed to know you, though perhaps she was making that bit up.'

'What?' Startled. Annoyed. 'How? Why?'

'Ah,' said Bea, putting honey into her voice. 'My apologies. The lady in question is, perhaps, a little fanciful? You'll have a good laugh when I tell you all about it. Yes, we should meet, but I can't really afford to take a whole morning off to come out to you at the moment. How about you having lunch with me one day this week, here at my place in Kensington. Wednesday, at twelve noon, shall we say? Excellent.'

She put the phone down and made a note in her diary.

Oliver lifted an eyebrow.

'Oliver, Mr Butcher wants to meet us. I'll get a catering firm in to provide a light lunch for three on Wednesday. Can you arrange to stay till then?'

Oliver grimaced. 'So you mean to sell, then?'

'Certainly not. But, if we can clean up our act here, I don't see why we shouldn't go into partnership with them, because, as you said, we can always do with a fresh supply of well-trained people, can't we? Now, let's have a look at some more of those complaints, before the phone rings again. No, first I'd better ring that woman who used to work for us. Where did you put those phone numbers?'

SIXTEEN

Monday afternoon

Bea and Oliver worked steadily through the files, finding more complaints which were justified, and more personnel they would not wish to use again. He carried the names through to Celia, who put up a blacklist and kept it up to date. Bea made excuses to go into the main office every now and then, but everyone seemed to be working well enough . . . apart from one malcontent.

Bea phoned the woman who'd left to nurse her mother. She was out, but returned the call later. She said that her mother had passed away six weeks before, and so she would very much like to return either part or full-time. Oliver managed to come up with the contact number for another girl who'd worked for them in the past. She said she was currently working with a firm that was relocating to the other side of London, so would be glad to hear of a job nearer home. Bea asked both to come in and have a chat on the morrow.

Jeremy continued to provide background muzak, but moved on to playing something soft and soothing. Maggie went out on a job, locking her office behind her.

Bea and Oliver had a scratch lunch of cold meats and a salad down in the office. Celia came in to report that everything was quiet on her front and the remaining girls working well, except for the one who aimed to be manageress, who was tossing her head and acting like a spoilt teenager.

'I'll have a word with her,' said Bea, just as her phone rang yet again. This time it was the inspector, who'd arrived outside the house in his car and wanted a few minutes with her.

'You go. We'll cope,' said Oliver.

Celia asked, 'Who's that playing the piano? It isn't the radio, is it?'

'Someone who needs a minder,' said Bea, turning her mind with difficulty from manpower to mayhem. 'Come up and meet him when you've finished for the day.'

Upstairs, Jeremy hadn't stopped playing to have any lunch. He was tinkering around with Josie's wistful song, again.

Bea let the inspector in.

He cocked his head. 'Nice tune.'

'That's Jeremy, composing something in Josie's memory. Come through into the sitting room, and we'll see if we can get him to stop playing for a while.'

Jeremy was wearing – oh dear! – his grey pyjamas and Maggie's bunny slippers.

His hair was unbrushed. The pile of manuscript paper by his piano had grown since Bea last saw it.

'Hello,' he said, and he smiled at them, unfocused.

Bea sighed. Did he even know who he was taking to? 'We're fine, Jeremy. Don't stop. We'll go into the kitchen.'

Once there, she put on the kettle. 'I need caffeine. Chocolate. Time out. Life is getting just too much. Oh, I forgot to tell you, I've had a threatening phone call. A man, deep voice, telling me not to interfere. No name, of course. And yes, I did dial one-four-seven-one, but the number had been withheld.'

'Valentine Dyall,' said the inspector. 'The Man in Black. The Mystery Man who used to introduce the Saturday night plays on radio.'

'You're too young to remember that.'

'My father used to talk about him and imitate him, too. When he wanted to threaten us kids with dire consequences, he used to put on this special voice, deep down, and we knew we were in trouble.'

Bea hadn't thought she could laugh, but she did, and she felt all the better for it. 'Yes. Well.' She found her handbag and handed over her tape recorder and camera. 'I'll put the shots of the woman on my computer and send them to you, if you like, but as you can see, she's made a good job of hiding what she really looks like.'

'Ah. Mm. Interesting. We found your van, by the way. Once you'd pointed me in the right direction, I only had to ask, and hey presto, up came the report on the burning of your medium-sized white van, reported last night.'

'It's not *my* van.'

'With your body in it.'

'It's not *my* body.'

'True; it belonged to one John O'Dare, late of County Antrim and later still of various addresses in East London. He studied photography but wasn't good enough to launch out on his own, or disciplined enough to work for others. He had a varying career working behind bars and in fast food places. Betted on the horses, drank a little too much, got into the occasional fight. Was arrested in a nightclub for carrying drugs but said they were recreational, and perhaps they were. He's not been in trouble for a couple of years. Rest in Peace.'

'How do you know so much?'

'The torching was amateurishly done. Not enough gasoline was used to make a really good funeral pyre. Also, some passing youths – who were probably up to no good, but we won't quibble about that this time – saw the flames and acted with amazing promptitude and civic responsibility. They called the police, the fire brigade and the ambulance men. They probably also took photos on their mobiles and sent them to the local press as well. Mr O'Dare was still recognizable. Also, his prints were on file. Would you like to see a picture of him?'

She shuddered. 'Not if he's been well roasted.'

'A mug shot. Nothing to alarm, I assure you.' He produced a photograph of a shaven-headed rat-face man.

She nodded. 'Yes, that's him. Yuk. What a way to go. So that's a dead end.'

'Not quite. We have the names of some of his associates. Most are petty criminals, drunk and disorderly, petty theft, indecent exposure. But on that last charge, the one of carrying drugs, he was bailed by a man who gave his name as Philip James, screen-writer and actor.'

'Would this be Mr Toupee?'

'Here's another photograph, this time from *Spotlight*, which is a sort of catalogue of actors.'

She studied the picture. A man in his mid to late thirties, with fair hair receding from his temples. He was resting his chin on his hand and trying to look soulful. A pale skin, pudgy hands. Open-necked shirt, a hint of a gold bracelet on one wrist.

'Failed actor,' said the inspector. 'Repertory. Tried to get into television. Some work as an extra in crowd scenes. He tried writing for the stage, and for radio. Got some one act plays put on, amateur nights only. When he posted bail he gave an address, but he's moved on from there some time ago. No known offences.'

'Not the criminal type.' Bea held the photo up to the light. 'Yes, it might well be Mr Toupee. I'd ask Maggie, but she's out. We'll ask Oliver in a minute. So what's the link between John O'Dare and – what did you say his name was? – Philip some-thing? Why would Philip post bail for O'Dare? Hah! You think they were already working together on their scam? O'Dare got out of line, got caught, and Philip came to his rescue?'

'It sounds possible.'

'Especially when you add the brains behind the Badger Game into the mix. And she is clever, make no mistake. A businesswoman. It takes one to know one. Let me play you the recording I made of our conversation.'

She played it back. Both listened intently.

Bea said, 'How I think it works is this; she picks the target, someone who has a lot to lose if they're found in bed with a totty. Philip devises an apparently innocent meeting between Josie and the prospect. O'Dare snaps them in bed and asks for money. The girl does as she's told. I wonder where they got her from? Ireland?'

'O'Dare has never been named as a pimp but, drifting around as he did, he may well have come across a girl who was ripe for a move off the streets and into a nice flat, with all mod cons and a credit card for clothes.'

'And now they've lost Josie. But the Badger woman, the madam, said they didn't want to stop yet. I wonder if they've found another girl to use.'

'They'll need another photographer, too.'

'Could this Philip do the job?'

'Doubtful. Anyone can point a camera, but are they professional enough to capture what's needed on film? They've got to get a recognizable image of the victim with the girl, while they're both fully active.'

'Nicely put. No, I see what you mean. Probably not. May I show these to Maggie when she comes back? And are there any other known contacts?'

'These prints are for you. And no, there aren't. I don't think Madam has come to our notice before, but we are pursuing other lines of enquiry. I've got men out trying to trace a girl answering to Josie's description who moved off the streets into "something better" some time last year.'

'Tell me, the girls on the streets are "owned" by different men, yes? Wouldn't they object to losing one of their working girls?'

'They wouldn't object if the price were right.'

Bea shivered. Souls for sale. Ugh. Perhaps Jeremy should put that into his song. Which he'd stopped playing for the moment. Hallelujah!

The inspector had concentrated his gaze on the biscuit tin. Well, it was marked 'Biscuits', wasn't it? Bea pushed it in his direction, and he opened the lid. Empty. Jeremy strikes again?

Bea started to laugh. 'It's not funny, I know. It's just that I'll either laugh or cry, and crying is not exactly my scene.' She opened cupboard doors, found some more packets of biscuits, refilled the tin and handed it to him. 'Brain food?'

'Ah. Dark-chocolate covered biscuits. A policeman never knows when his next meal is going to be. May I run a scenario by you? The Badgers have been a successful con gang for some time. All goes well. The money rolls in. Then suddenly the pattern is broken. One of their victims decides to fight back. We don't know whether he paid up to begin with or not, but he warns Josie off.

'First question: how did he warn her off? We know she had a mobile phone with her, because Jeremy received a phone call from her the evening she died. No mobile phone was found on her body. We assume that the Badgers had given her a mobile phone so that she could keep in touch with them at all times, and also so that she could make arrangements during the "grooming" period to meet her victims. I'm thinking the killer took it away with him after he'd killed her.'

'Because his phone number would have been listed on her mobile?'

'It sounds right, doesn't it? Second question: how did he know where to find her the night she died?'

She stared at him. 'The Badgers should have made her lose that phone. A big mistake to keep it. Let me think. Well, I did hear of another victim who used to visit a girl called Angie – who may or may not have been Josie – at a house in Hammersmith where she'd taken a room. He paid the price by fiddling the firm's books and committed suicide. His son called round to tell Angie-cum-Josie about it, but by that time she'd done a flit. No, I can't give you the name, but he exists.

'They didn't go for hotels, probably because it would have been difficult for them to get their photographer in to take pictures at the right moment. So they provided the girl with a suitable background by renting a room for her in someone else's flat or house. Somewhere they knew they could access at any time by copying a front door key. Somewhere they could meet during the day without it being remarked. There's masses of multiple occupancy flats and houses around here because lots of young people work in Central London but can't afford anything better.

'Suppose the killer took some precautions when he was having his wicked way with Josie. If he was technically inclined, he could put a bug into her handbag . . . or simply pretend to leave but hang around till she went out, and then follow her back to her base.

'After that he could keep watch on the flat or house where the gang lives. He could find out the names of who lived in the same house easily enough. Then, when he was ready to make his move, he could ring her mobile and say he had her in his sights. That would have spooked her into running off and trying to phone Jeremy, wouldn't it?'

'I like it. Next question: why Jeremy? He doesn't fit the pattern, and yet he crops up everywhere in this investigation.'

'You're right; he doesn't fit the pattern. I think he was set up by his wife, who was tired of him and has been seeing another man. His wife is Eunice Barrow, the barrister. She probably never met the Badgers, but knew of someone or heard of someone . . . Perhaps passed a request down the line, dangling a nice fat fee before their eyes? So much per incriminating photo. Then she sat back and waited for the proofs of his infidelity to drop through her letter box. Do you think you could spare the time to visit her, make her give up the name of her contact?'

He scrabbled for his notebook. 'I'll put it on my "to do" list. Mind you, she won't be easy to frighten. But if she started this, she deserves to be frightened, and if we can get a name or names from her, it might lead us to the Badgers. Meanwhile, I suppose you'll continue to look after Jeremy?'

They listened. No sound of music. Bea relaxed. 'Peace and quiet. He's been at it since first thing this morning, not even stopping to eat. He'll be demanding food in a minute. I'm trying to fix him up with a minder for a couple of hours a day. You must admit, he's lucky. It was pure chance that he went to that concert and spent the evening with someone who could give him an alibi.'

'Only, the Badgers didn't accept he was innocent, and they went after him . . . somewhat ineffectively, you must admit.'

'Trashing his flat wasn't ineffective. Causing him to lose his job wasn't, either. I'm sure he was a good teacher because he cared about his pupils, and it hurt him to let them down just before they were due to take their exams.'

'He's so wrapped up in his music, it doesn't seem to have upset him for long. Oh, by the way, we found a black dress shoe in the back of the white van. Just the one. I'll bring it along when Forensics have finished with it, and you can see if it's one of Jeremy's. Now, can you explain the coincidence of O'Dare being killed at the very time that Jeremy is being kidnapped?'

'I think you need to look at Mr Jason of Jason's Place for that.'

The inspector hit his forehead. 'I called there earlier. He's got a woman running the place today. She says it's his day off, and she hasn't his mobile number, which I didn't believe, but there you are. Anyway, he was nowhere to be seen. The landlord was very much in evidence, overseeing the fitting of a new front door to the flat above. He wants me to arrest Jeremy for the damage done to his property but I told him to contact the local police, who'd give him a case number to send to his insurance people.'

'I think Mr Jason may have been feeding information both to Philip, the failed actor in the Badger team, and to the killer – or his representative. I can't think . . .'

'You hesitated there. You've remembered something you saw?'

'No. Yes. He moved . . . He moved like an athlete. He eeled his way out of the van and was off into the dark. Heavyset, but light on his feet.'

'He works out?'

'I suppose that's it. No, it was a something and a nothing. When I opened the van door, I smelled something sweet . . . It reminded me of something, but I can't think what.'

A rich alto voice cut the air.

'You promised me – a life of ease,
You promised me – our love would last.
You brought me to this country,
Where the streets are paved with rain.
You took my childhood from me,
And you sold me to your friends.
I asked how could you do this?
And you answered – with a blow.'

Bea shuddered, and the inspector froze with his mug half way to his mouth.

Bea tried to laugh. 'Someone walked over my grave.'

'Did Jeremy think that up?'

She nodded.

'That's extraordinary. I mean, to look at him . . . Who's the voice?'

Bea marched into the sitting room, to find Celia with Jeremy. Celia's waist was no longer as slender as it had been in her teens and twenties, and her short, bubble-cut hair was fairer than it had been in her thirties, but Jeremy was looking at her as if she were a toothsome bundle.

And, looking at him, Celia seemed to be in a golden daze.

Bea said, under her breath, 'What have I done?'

'What?' said the inspector, on her heels.

'Never you mind,' said Bea. 'Jeremy, I see you and Celia have met.'

Celia turned a radiant smile on them. 'Isn't his music wonderful? I came up to have a word with you, and he asked if I could sing, and I used to, in the old days. And he played the tune for me, and . . . Well, I hope it was all right.'

'It was more than all right,' said Jeremy, with an adoring look. 'You picked it up so quickly. You have perfect pitch, don't you?'

'I used to have, but . . . So sorry, Mrs Abbot. I came up just for a moment, really, to say that one of the girls wants to see you before she leaves for the day. I'm afraid she's not happy about me being in charge.'

'I'm sure you know how to deal with that,' said Jeremy.

Bea closed her eyes. Was Jeremy metamorphosing from mouse to man before her very eyes? Beside her, she could sense that the inspector was bubbling with amusement.

Celia blushed. Actually reddened to the roots of her only slightly bleached hair. 'Oh well. You know how it is.'

'I do,' said Jeremy, standing up. 'I don't know about you, Celia, but I could do with a bite to eat. May I treat you to a steak somewhere?'

'Oh, but I . . .'

He looked down at himself. 'If you could give me time to change? Twenty minutes all right with you?'

Celia looked at her watch, but Bea didn't think she really saw it. Celia was floating on cloud nine. Celia had fallen head over heels in love. Oh. Dear. Me.

Jeremy treated Bea and the inspector to a bright smile and scurried past them. Celia followed him, with uncertain footsteps.

Bea closed the door after them and leaned against it.

The inspector had doubled over with laughter. 'Heh, heh . . . hoo, hoo . . .'

'All very well for you,' said Bea, annoyed. 'Here I was thinking of Jeremy as a wayward child, and he turns out to be a spider who's wrapped his victim in a silken cocoon, to be taken off and devoured at his leisure.'

'Hor, hor, hor . . .' He produced a hankie and blew his nose, hard. 'Sorry about that, but . . . heh, heh . . .'

'I was hoping Celia would run the office for me for a while, and maybe put in an extra hour or so here and there to keep Jeremy's affairs straight, but he's going to co-opt her and take her off to his lair . . . Oh well, he hasn't got a lair at the moment, has he? And he's still married to Eunice. Although somehow I don't think that's going to stop him. Or her.'

A jangling noise from the inspector's pocket. 'My phone.' He fished it out, wiping bleary eyes with his other hand. And listened. 'Right, I'm on to it. Meet you there. What did you say the address was . . .?' He shut off his phone, all traces of amusement gone. 'Another body; a woman found in a dumpster.'

'Josie's replacement?'

He shrugged. 'If the murderer knows where they live, he could pick them off one by one.' He started for the front door.

She followed him. The sun had gone behind a cloud. She cradled her arms, feeling chilled. 'I did advise "Miss Angie Butt" to make herself scarce.'

'Keep in touch, right? And don't let any pizza delivery men into the house.' He made his way to a parked car and drove off.

Bea shut the front door with a bang. She considered finding a glass of red wine and a box of chocolates, and taking them off to bed. Unfortunately, she'd still got to deal with a staff problem, and then there was supper to sort out, and what did Oliver think he was doing, still stuck in her office with her computer?

She went down the stairs, making hardly any sound in her light sandals. Celia was in the toilet, no doubt redoing her make-up; not that she wore much.

What was the name of the big, black-haired woman who wanted to be manageress? Dahlia, that was it.

Dahlia was trying the door of Maggie's office, which

fortunately had been locked against intruders. The rest of the staff seemed to have gone for the day.

Bea said, 'Maggie's office is to be kept locked in future. You wanted to speak to me?'

Sitting in a chair beside Dahlia's desk was a big, loose-lipped untidy youth with a big conk, who didn't seem able to breathe through it. Badly bleached hair, which had not been washed recently. Acne. He was wearing overlong jeans, frayed from being trodden under his heels, and a stained T-shirt. He was concentrating on playing some computer game or other.

Bea didn't recognize him. 'Well, Dahlia; come into my office.'

Dahlia displayed aggressive body language. That black hair was dyed. 'He, your supposed son, threw us out, said it was private in your office. He was looking up porn sites, I wouldn't wonder.'

Oliver on porn sites? Bea blinked. 'My adopted son? I doubt it.' Her office was empty, but the doors to the garden stood open. Oliver must have slipped out for a minute. Bea seated herself behind her desk. Her computer had been left on, and the files they'd been dealing with earlier were still piled on to her desk. She pulled out her top drawer and started her voice recorder. 'Now, Dahlia; what is it you wanted to speak to me about?'

'You've no need to advertise for another manageress, or to bring in someone from outside. Save yourself some money and let me have the job. After all, I know what's to be done better than anyone else.'

'It's standard practice to advertise when a responsible job like this becomes vacant. The advertisements have already gone in. As I said earlier, you are welcome to apply.'

'Yes, but . . . the thing is, if we're not getting the bonus we've been promised, it's going to be difficult, so being made up to manageress would be very handy. And I know where the bodies are buried.' And she winked at Bea.

Startled, Bea said, 'What bodies?'

'I'm not blaming you for leaving so much to Ianthe, taking time off when we're rushed off our feet. It's only natural you want to take it easy at your age.'

Bea tried not to grind her teeth. She knew she'd taken time out of the office for this and that over the past few months. There'd been regular visits to play with her grandson, and she'd spent time sorting out a couple of nasty crimes which had drifted her way. But the agency hadn't suffered, had it? She'd worked early and late to keep it on track . . . until she'd made the mistake of appointing Ianthe and letting Miss Brook and Celia go.

Dahlia hadn't finished. 'What I think is that you need someone who you can rely on when you need to take time off. Someone who knows what's what around here.'

Her tone of oily satisfaction was too much for Bea. Almost, she snapped at the woman. 'Thank you for your concern. I'll take it on board. I hope to start interviewing next week. Now, if that's all . . .?'

Dahlia flushed. 'Well, if that's how you're going to take my offer, which was made with your best interests at heart . . .! But no, it's not quite all. My nephew, that's sitting outside at the moment. You've put him on the blacklist. I know he didn't do himself justice at school, what with his parents splitting up, and his getting a depression, and then there was that stupid teacher, who'd never liked him, saying he'd been up to no good with the computers in the lab, which was an outright lie . . .!'

Bea held up a hand to stop her. 'We have a file for him?'

Dahlia pounced on the files and shuffled through them till she found the one she wanted. No photo. No wonder Bea hadn't recognized the lad.

Bea flicked through the file. Zack – save the mark! – had been sent out on three occasions as a waiter on Silver Service events. The results were a disaster. He'd turned up late, improperly dressed, been rude to the others on the team, and walked off the job without clearing up. Three separate times.

'A poor report, three times.'

Dahlia bit her lip. 'It's not his fault. He lacks self-confidence, having always been put down by his father, who never had a good word to say for him, and even threw him out of the house, would you believe? So I took him in, naturally, doing my good deed for the day, and he's like my own, you understand? Not that I ever had any.'

Bea sighed. What could she say to a lad who'd already accumulated a catalogue of disasters? 'Let's have him in, shall we?' Even as she went to the door, she was aware of an altercation taking place in the big office.

Celia was storming at the lad, who'd seated himself at one of the office computers and had accessed . . . oh, no! Some porn?

Celia was trying to turn the computer off, and the lad was battling with her, laughing, thrusting her away.

'That's enough!' Bea didn't normally have to shout to get attention.

'Gerroff me!' The lad flailed at Celia.

Oliver arrived from the garden and dived for the computer, trying to push the lad away from the screen.

'Oi, you!' The lad produced a knife with a wickedly glinting blade.

Celia screamed, trying to get out of range, tripping over her own feet, falling backwards.

Someone hit the lad's wrist with the edge of a ruler.

He dropped the knife, which landed on the floor, and stuck there, upright, quivering. 'You've broken my wrist!'

'Serve you right if I had, but I haven't,' said Jeremy. 'Now, anyone seen my shoes?'

SEVENTEEN

Monday evening

The phone rang. And went on ringing.

Jeremy picked Celia up and dusted her down. 'You all right?'

She nodded. 'Oh, Jeremy!' She might as well have swooned into his arms, like any lovesick Victorian maiden, and said, 'My hero!'

Jeremy knew what to do. He put his arms around her. 'There, there.'

The phone went on ringing.

The lout turned to Dahlia, clutching his wrist, tears in his eyes. 'He hurt me!'

'There, there,' said Dahlia, also crying, but holding out her arms to him.

Oliver picked up the phone and, with his free hand, pressed buttons to exit the porn programme on the computer. He held the phone out to Bea. 'For you. The inspector.'

'Hello?' Bea found it difficult to move. What should she say to the police? Should she charge that stupid young lad with assault? With accessing porn on her computer? With carrying a knife?

'Durrell here. Just to say, the girl they've found is not one of the Badger Game gang. A streetwalker, yes. But a heroin user in her thirties.'

'Oh. Understood. Thank you.'

'Are you all right?'

She wasn't making sense, was she? 'Oh. Yes, I think so. Thanks for letting me know. And if you hear anything more?'

'I'll let you know.' He clicked off.

She put the phone down. Oliver was switching off all the computer systems. Good. She supposed.

Jeremy had his arms round Celia, who was weeping gently into his beard. Surprise! She was no taller than he. He'd managed to get dressed, after a fashion. A clean but wrinkled shirt and jeans. He was still wearing Maggie's bunny slippers, though. Where were his shoes, anyway?

Dahlia had her arms round her nephew, who was wriggling his wrist up and down and moaning with pain. Dahlia shot angry looks at Jeremy. 'You shouldn't have done that. He didn't mean no harm.'

Bea shook her head. 'Dahlia, enough said. I admire your loyalty to your nephew, but if you want to keep him out of trouble, you'd better get him some anger management and proper training. And what are you going to do about him carrying a knife?'

'A knife?' Dahlia focused on the knife, and she turned on her nephew. 'That's my best kitchen knife, you . . .' She set about him, slapping his head this way and that as Bea would never have had the nerve to do. 'You . . . you dare touch my knives again, you ungrateful little turd!'

Oliver hunkered down to rock the knife back and forth till he could ease it out of the floor.

'You give me that!' Dahlia snatched it from Oliver and dropped it into her handbag. She turned on her nephew. 'Here I am trying to do my best by you, and look what happens!'

The phone rang again. Bea put her hands to her head. Shock. She was in shock.

Celia put her hands over her ears. Jeremy stood guard over her.

Dahlia gave her nephew another whack around his shoulders. 'Get going, you! I'll deal with you when we get home.' She turned to Bea with an attempt at a smile. 'Oh, Mrs Abbot, what we do for our families, eh? Er, I don't suppose you can overlook what's happened, can you? Give me another chance?'

'Please, just go. I'll send on what money is due to you.'

Oliver held the phone out to Bea. 'Someone called Jason for you?'

Bea cleared her throat and told herself to snap out of it. 'Hello? Mr Jason of Jason's Place?'

A hearty, healthy, booming voice. A voice seemingly untouched by tragedy. The voice of someone who enjoyed life. 'Mrs A? You gave me your card the other night. Is the wandering minstrel in hospital or with you, or what? A whole stack of mail arrived for him today. Also, his landlord's hired a skip and thrown out everything that was broken from the flat, and some bits and pieces of the little man's as well, which I thought was a shame, seeing as it wasn't his fault, so I've got a bag of his stuff sitting behind the counter here. Would he like to collect them or isn't he interested?'

Bea didn't think quickly enough to be cautious. 'I'm sure he'll be interested; and yes, he's staying here with me. How late are you going to be there?'

'I stay late on Mondays, taking stock, placing orders. I'll be here till nine. That OK by you?'

'Thank you. Yes.' She put the phone down, wondering why it was still ringing. No, it wasn't her landline, and it wasn't the same ring as her mobile, so it must be the front doorbell, upstairs.

Dahlia was sniffing, on the verge of tears as she took various personal items from her desk and pushed her nephew up the stairs and out into the street. Unasked, Oliver went after them to make sure the door to the agency was locked behind them.

The front doorbell above pealed again, then opened to the sound of loud voices. And banged shut.

Maggie shouted out, 'Halloo, I'm back! And Max is here. Where is everybody? Downstairs, are you? Is there anything for supper?'

Celia was regaining her composure, trying to smile. Being the brave little soul. Tucking her hair behind her ears, blowing her nose, undoing the top two buttons of her otherwise prim dress.

And what a difference undoing those top two buttons made to her appearance! She had one of the prettiest busts you could ever wish to see. Would Jeremy notice the signal? Er, yes; he had done. Oh, but . . .?

Bea said, to no one in particular, 'Whatever next?'

Oliver went through to her office, closed and locked the French windows, secured the grille. 'All safe down here.'

Max appeared. 'Hello, hello? Company? Mother; a word?'

'Yes, dear. In a minute. Celia, would you like to stay to supper – if I can find something to eat?'

'Mother!' Max never liked being kept waiting. 'It's important.'

Important to Max might not be important to anyone else, but Bea nodded and shooed everyone up the stairs. Oliver followed, shutting off lights, checking that the door to Maggie's office was locked.

Upstairs, Maggie had turned on the television and the radio. Of course. She was busy throwing stuff on the kitchen table. Cold meats, salad stuffs. 'There's not much, I'm afraid. Baked potatoes with salad for everyone?'

Jeremy had his arm round Celia. 'I'm taking Celia out for a meal, if that's all right with you, Mrs Abbot?'

'Would you hold on a bit, Jeremy? That last phone call was from Mr Jason, who's rescued some of your stuff and has a stack of mail for you. I said we'd collect it this evening, but I'm not at all sure that's wise. I mean, is he playing both sides against the middle or am I imagining it?'

'Mother!' Max's colour was rising.

'Yes, dear; in a minute. Oliver, will you fill Maggie in on what's been happening? Now, Max . . .' She led the way into the sitting room and closed the door. 'Sorry. It's been a difficult day.' And did a double take. Had a new suitcase been added to the jumble of Jeremy's black plastic bags in the hall?

'Really, Mother, you ought to tidy the place up a bit. All that rubbish in the hall; it could give visitors the wrong impression.'

'It'll be gone soon. Are you staying for supper? It's only a scratch meal, I'm afraid.'

'I was hoping you'd find me a bed for the night. Well, for a few days. You see, I've found someone to rent our flat for the summer but he wants to move in straight away. So I thought I could bring some of my stuff over and store it here. The car's outside, full of everything personal that I don't want to leave in the flat. And I'll be up and down to London over the break.'

Bea let herself gently down on to the settee and leaned back, closing her eyes. How was Max to be accommodated? Every bed in the house was already taken.

'Hmhm.' Jeremy was standing in the doorway. 'Sorry to interrupt, couldn't help overhearing, because I was going to ask . . . Well, never mind that. I understand that there's a problem. It's more than time I moved out, Mrs Abbot. You've been absolutely marvellous, but your family comes first, doesn't it? And I'm well and truly back on my feet now.'

'He can come home with me,' said Celia, at his side.

Bea took a deep breath. 'No, he can't, Celia. He can't go anywhere. There's been at least two attempts to kidnap him, and I'm not letting him out of my sight till the villains have been caught.'

'Kidnapping?' From Max. 'What nonsense is this?'

Celia said, 'Jeremy?'

'I'll explain in a minute, Max,' said Bea. 'But for the moment let's all calm down and not make any decisions we might regret later.'

'Supper up for the first sitting,' said Maggie. 'Oh, I nearly forgot. There was a note pushed through the letter box for you.' She held an envelope out to Bea. 'Anyone want grated cheese on their potato?'

'Haven't you anything else?' Max followed her out to the kitchen.

Celia went with them, saying, 'Can I help?'

Bea gestured to Jeremy to stay behind, while she tore open the note. Typed. Ordinary A4 sheet.

Mr Toupee was killed by someone waiting for him in the foyer this morning. Take care. Miss Butt.

Oh. Dear.

Jeremy said, 'Are you all right, Mrs Abbot?'

She patted the seat beside her. 'Jeremy, the Badger Gang is being hunted down and killed, one by one. I've been threatened, too. I think we should all take precautions and not let any strangers into the house till this is over.'

'But you need my room, and Celia has offered—'

'That's another thing. Celia is an old friend and perhaps a little naive about men. You are a charismatic and even glamorous man of the world.' She was surprised to find herself saying this, but realized it was true. 'Is it right for you to take advantage of her?'

He was honest enough to redden. 'As soon as I saw her, I thought . . . I could see . . . there was something between us. It felt right. I could see the sort of person she is, kind and generous and caring. I felt at home in a way that I haven't done for, well, for ever. But you're right, and I mustn't put her in danger. I'll go to a hotel.'

'You'll stay right here. Now, with regard to Celia, I want you to promise me that you'll take things slowly. Take time to get to know her. Tell her . . . Well, tell her everything about yourself, if you know what I mean, so that she doesn't expect more than you can offer.'

He said, eagerly, 'I did go to a therapist and learn how to please a woman when I was going to marry Eunice, only she said she didn't want to know about all that.'

It was Bea who blushed this time. 'Well, that's good. But I don't want either of you to get hurt, so take it gently?'

'Promise.'

'And now . . . supper. Sorry it's not much.'

There was a flash of light.

Lightning? Puzzled, she looked out of the back window. The sky was clear.

Jeremy was shouting something about a fire. A fire? Where? Here?

There was a sheet of flame, a roaring sound, from the front of the house. She dashed to the front window, was held back by Jeremy who was shouting, 'Careful!'

The front of the house was on fire.

No. The steps down to the agency rooms were on fire.

Oliver opened the front door, then dashed back to fetch the fire extinguisher that lived in the cupboard in the hall. Out of the front door he went, banging the nozzle open and directing the foam down the steps.

Max burst into the sitting room. 'Mother, there's a fire! Get away from that window!'

Maggie shot in behind him, with Celia on her heels, asking for Jeremy. Maggie looked excited but acted calmly, getting out her mobile phone, summoning the Fire Brigade.

Oliver had the blaze targeted. The flames lost intensity and collapsed in on themselves. Bea started for the front door, only to be held back by Max. 'No, Mother! I won't allow it!'

Celia said, 'There used to be another extinguisher in the office downstairs. Shall I get it?'

'It'll be too heavy for you,' said Jeremy. 'Show me where and I'll get it. Tackle the blaze from below.'

Oliver retreated into the hall, throwing down the empty extinguisher. 'It's out. I think someone poured petrol down the steps and tossed in a lighted match.'

Various curious neighbours had begun to gather. Bea went out on to the steps and called out, 'Did anyone see anything?'

Heads were shaken.

There hadn't been much damage. Charred steps. The little bay tree which stood at the bottom of the steps in the area had been given the kiss of death. The two that flanked the stairs at the top were charred, but might recover.

Oliver wiped his arm across his forehead. 'I'm a bit worried about the door to the office.'

'Jeremy's on to it from the inside.'

Oliver looked worried. 'Did they want to get at you – or Jeremy?'

'Or both?' She found she was trembling, but put Max's arm aside and went down the stairs to the agency rooms. Jeremy was patting the agency door from the inside. 'Good stout door, only faintly warm. I don't think it's going to burst into flames.'

Bea felt the wood, as he had done. She wanted to lie down and howl, go to bed and pull the duvet over her head and let the world go on its wicked way, but she was Mother Hen and had to be strong. Well, sort of.

Thank you, Lord. Oh, thank you. Thank you for Oliver's quick thinking. Thank you for making sure all the extinguishers were up to date, which was part of Miss Brook's job, come to think of it, so she's saved our bacon . . . again. So thank you for Miss Brook and her foresight and attention to detail. We can easily get the steps cleaned and buy another plant. I suppose the insurance will cover it.

'Thank you, Jeremy. Quick thinking, Celia.'

Max appeared, making a great production of feeling the door up and down. Neeh-nah, neeh-nah. The fire bridge had arrived. Oh. Splendid. Now they'd need an explanation, with cups of tea and biscuits, no doubt.

'Max, could you possibly deal with the firemen for me?'

He patted her shoulder. 'Leave it to me. You go and put your feet up.'

Chance would be a fine thing.

Max climbed the stairs to the hall and could be heard informing the officers that everything was under control.

Bea found someone had put his arm around her. Jeremy was holding her in one arm, and Celia in the other.

'I expect you two could both do with a good cry,' he said.

Celia nodded, wiping her eyes. 'How about a cuppa, with three sugars in it?'

'Trust me for that,' said Bea, trying to smile, too. They went up the stairs to find Max telling the firemen what to do – as if they didn't know far better than him.

Oliver, too, had retreated to the kitchen, now that the danger was past, and was sitting on a stool, resting his head on his hands.

Bea went straight to Oliver and put her arms around him. 'Oh, Oliver. Are you hurt? Are you OK? Thank you for saving us.'

'I'm OK.' But he wasn't. He was shivering. Brave as a lion, quick as a panther in times of danger; now he was having a reaction.

Max said, 'I would have saved you, if I'd been nearer the door.'

Jealous? Oh. Bea held out her hand to Max. 'Of course you would, Max.'

Maggie's voice was wobbly, too. 'Tea, everyone?'

Max seated himself, prepared to be waited on. 'Now, Mother. Who'd want to firebomb your place?'

The chief fireman also wanted to know. He had a strong, lean face with eyes that had seen most things in his time. Bea struggled to put her thoughts in order. She thought of the anonymous phone call warning her not to interfere. She thought of Mr Toupee and John O'Dare in the morgue. Ditto Josie. Well, if this was the killer's way of getting even with Bea, he hadn't made a very good job of it.

She tried to explain. 'I think it's connected to a murder case which is being handled by DI Durrell. We're looking after a witness whom the gang has tried to kidnap a couple of times. That's Jeremy, here; Mr Waite. I was warned not to interfere, and I think this is the result.'

The fireman took notes. 'Inspector . . . who did you say?'

'Really, Mother! Whatever will you get mixed up in next?'

'It's all my fault,' said Jeremy, looking wretched.

'No, no,' said Bea. But even she heard her voice lacked conviction.

'Got a number for this Inspector?' The chief was thorough, she'd grant him that.

She found the number in her handbag and gave it to him. 'He'll be off duty at this time of day, I should think. I'd try him in the morning again.'

The firemen tramped up and down. They checked the door downstairs from the inside and the outside, and made sure the lock was holding fast. They tossed the charred bay tree up to the top of the steps. Max was in his element, overseeing them. They didn't seem to resent it. Perhaps they were used to being bossed by outsiders and knew how to ignore them while calmly getting on with the job in hand?

Finally, they said they didn't think there'd be any more trouble with the door that evening, it was cooling fast and wouldn't burst into flames again. They said they'd inform the police what had happened, and her Inspector Durrell would no doubt be in touch about it.

And then there was supper. Cold meats, salad, microwaved potatoes. None of them felt like eating a cold meal. Even Maggie said she'd really fancy a nice, fattening, filling pizza. Max said he rather thought he'd pop out for something, before settling down for the night.

Oliver still looked drained, but said, 'Jeremy's in the spare room, but there's a brand-new sofa in the sitting room at the top of the house, which is supposed to pull out to make a bed.'

Bea could see that Oliver was going to offer to give Max his room, while he could sleep on the Put-U-Up, but . . .

Max rushed in, too quickly. 'Splendid. And you're going to try it out so that I can have your room?'

'No,' said Oliver, reversing his decision. 'But you can sleep on it, if you wish.'

Jeremy lifted his head. 'It really would be best if I—'

'Yes, Jeremy,' said Bea. 'I was thinking that myself. They may not try again. They may think they've done enough damage. But they're getting too close to you. So just in case, I do think you should go somewhere else, somewhere they don't know about.'

Celia looked up with a smile.

'No, Celia. They know far too much about us for my comfort, and they may know about you. I'm going to ring Piers and see if he'll let Jeremy sleep on his settee tonight.'

'Then I can have the spare room,' said Max, happily. 'I'll start bringing my stuff in, and then I'll go out for a decent meal. Want to join me, Mother?'

'No, thank you, dear. I've got rather a lot to do. Not least . . . Maggie, have we enough clean sheets for the spare room?'

Maggie nodded. Sighed. 'I really fancy a pizza. I think I'll send out for one.'

Bea went into the sitting room to ring Piers, and Max followed her.

'Mother, when is Piers actually moving in?' Was Max worried that Piers, too, might want the spare room over the summer recess?

'Not for some time. He's got a new woman in tow.'

'Oh, well; that's all right, then. I asked Oliver to help me move my stuff in, but he's gone off in a huff.'

Bea half smiled. She wasn't going to step in between those two. Besides, she'd reached Piers on her phone. 'Bea here. Are you tied up tonight, Piers? Can I beg a bed for Jeremy? The settee would do fine. We've had a bit of an incident here. Someone threw petrol down the steps to the agency rooms and tossed a match into it. No, no one's hurt. Oliver put out the flames, and we've had the Fire Brigade round to make sure everything's safe, but I'd feel happier if Jeremy were elsewhere for the night . . . No, he wouldn't be bringing his keyboard, so you'd have some peace and quiet. Yes, just for tonight. We've got to fetch his mail and some of his things from Jason's Place. You remember the corner café? And then I'll bring him straight round to you, if that's all right.'

She put the phone down, feeling her age. It was just one thing after another at the moment.

Max said, 'I'll start bringing in my stuff, shall I?' And banged the front door on his way out. She very much hoped he'd thought to put it on the latch, but he probably hadn't, and someone would have to go and let him in, in a minute.

Jeremy popped his head round the door and, seeing she was alone, came in, with Celia in tow. 'Mrs A, would it be possible for us to drop Celia back to her place first? It's getting late, and I don't think she ought to be out on the streets by herself until this business has been sorted.'

'Agreed. I'll take you on to Piers' afterwards. Get some overnight things together, and we'll be off in, say, twenty minutes.'

'I'll drive you,' said Oliver, materializing behind them. 'No arguments. You know what the parking's like around there.'

Max overheard Oliver's offer as he puffed away, hauling boxes into the hall. How amazing! He'd actually thought to put the door on the latch. Max said, 'I was going to offer to drive you, but there's still a lot of stuff in my car and I don't want to move it now I've got a parking space outside.'

'Thank you both,' said Bea. 'Most thoughtful. Yes, Oliver, I'd be grateful. I'd probably signal left and turn right, if I tried to drive this evening.'

Maggie appeared in the doorway, looking forlorn. 'Anyone else want a pizza? I've packed up some sandwiches for Jeremy to take with him, but it's beyond me to cook tonight.'

This opened up a fresh worry for Bea. 'I don't like the idea of leaving you alone in the house, Maggie. Oliver and I are both going to be out for a couple of hours, maybe. Can you go to a friend's place tonight?'

Max objected. 'Someone has to stay, to man the fort. I'm sure Maggie will be perfectly all right by herself.'

'I'll ring round, see who's free to come and sit with me.' Maggie disappeared.

Oliver held up the car keys. 'We take Celia home first? Then go to Jason's Place, then Piers'. Right?'

Bea thought of telling Oliver that she was feeling a bit tired and would like to stay at home with Maggie, but remembered in time that someone was going to have to show Jeremy the way up to Piers' flat. Piers' present address was at the top of an elderly building, with no lift in sight. Someone would be needed to guide Jeremy up the wearisome flights of stairs, leaving the car unattended down below on a double yellow line, which would make it perfect prey for trawling meter men. Oliver couldn't look after the car and take Jeremy up the steps, so she would have to go. Oh well. On with the fray.

Besides which, she had a lurking suspicion that Mr Jason might be baiting another trap for Jeremy . . . but if she and Oliver were with him, nothing much could happen. Could it?

'I'm off!' cried Max, and he banged the front door behind him. Had he dropped the latch this time?

Celia said, 'I couldn't find any proper shoes for Jeremy, but he says he'll be fine in his sandals.'

'Better than Maggie's bedroom slippers.'

Jeremy looked amused. 'Oh, sorry. Are they hers? She should have said.'

The doorbell rang. And rang again. With urgency.

Oliver let someone into the hall and backed into the sitting room. 'It's . . . I don't know.'

'Let me in,' the stranger said. 'Quickly. And close the front door.'

The woman might have been Bea's identical twin. She was about the same age, of medium height, with short-cut ash-blonde hair, wearing a caramel-coloured two-piece. High heeled shoes, a tan carry-on case, and a pigskin handbag over one shoulder.

Bea gasped. 'That's very clever. Miss . . . Butt?'

'May I prevail upon you to give me sanctuary for a few hours? I'm due to fly out tomorrow, but I need somewhere to stay over-night. I went back to the flat this afternoon to find it had been torn apart. So I packed a bag and left. Only, they'd disabled my car, and when I got a taxi, they followed in another. I think I lost them at Hammersmith station. There are so many exits they didn't have enough men to cover them all, so I hopped on the nearest train, got off at Earls Court and took the next one out, which happened to be coming up in this direction . . . which reminded me of you. I do hope you don't mind.' And she didn't care if Bea did mind.

'I do mind. Very much. Do I take it that you've disbanded your – er – group?'

'You might call it that. There's just me and Kath left, and I've given her some money and told her to make herself scarce. I don't think he'll bother with her.' She looked Jeremy over. 'You must be Mr Waite. A pleasure to meet you at last. And this is . . . your son, Mrs Abbot? And a friend.'

'I'm Celia.' Celia wasn't sure what was going on. Neither was Oliver. Nor Jeremy.

Bea said, 'Miss Butt, you'd do better to ring Inspector Durrell and get yourself locked up. They firebombed this place this evening.'

'Call me Nance, or Annie, if you prefer it. If I can get to Heathrow in the morning without being spotted, I'm out of your hair for good. Why would I want to bring the police in on what is a purely private matter?'

Oliver clicked his fingers. 'You're the brains behind the Badgers? Do you really look like Mrs Abbot?'

Bea snapped. 'Of course not. That's a wig, and she's copied the way I dress in order to confuse the men who are after her. By the way, is it men in the plural? Or just one?'

Unasked, Nance smoothed the back of her skirt and seated herself. 'I seem to have offended quite a few people in my time. At least two, possibly three.'

'Names?'

'Oh, no. I'm so near to disappearing, it would be stupid to give away any secrets.'

Jeremy and Celia were holding hands. How sweet. Though not terribly helpful.

Bea said, 'There's a Put-U-Up bed at the top of the house which is going spare. I'll make a bargain with you. I'll let you stay here tonight, and I won't ring the police till after you've gone in the morning, provided you give me proof that Eunice Barrow set her husband up for your fun and games.'

'You could have asked for more than that. Consider it done.'

EIGHTEEN

Monday evening

Bea felt she'd lost control of events.
   Question: what to do first?
   Answer: take Celia home.

Oh, but before that, check that all the lights were off downstairs; you couldn't trust firemen to see to such details. Show Ms Butt how to turn the television and the side lamps on and warn her not to open the door to anyone – not that she needed any warning. Yell at Maggie that they were on their way. Check that Jeremy had some overnight things with him, chivvy him and Celia out. Check that Oliver had keys to get back in with. Find the car; parked not too far down the street. Everyone in, seat belts on. Phew!

Oliver drove.

Celia lived in a pleasant road, lying quiet in the dusk, the street lights just beginning to flicker on. It was a very warm evening. Perhaps they'd have a thunderstorm later.

'This is me,' said Celia, indicating a red-brick house with a cat sitting on the gatepost. There were lights on in the ground floor, and someone was drawing the curtains on the second floor. 'I'm on the first floor. I would invite you in, but—'

'Not tonight,' said Bea.

'Tomorrow,' said Jeremy, getting out of the car with Celia and making sure she had her keys with her to get in. 'I'll ring you.'

Celia was swallowed up by the house. An upstairs light came on. Jeremy got back into the car with a sigh. 'Jason's Place next? I hope there's a contract for the children's series in the mail.'

Oliver drove again. Bea was beginning to regret the bargain she'd made with Nance, or Annie, or whatever she was called. She was on the verge of asking Oliver if he thought she should ring the police, anyway . . . when he drew up in front of the corner café.

Oliver peered around. 'No sign of an ambush tonight.' So he, too, had had his suspicions about which side Jason was on?

Bea got out of the car with Jeremy. The little man didn't really need her with him, but she didn't want him going anywhere alone. Besides which, she needed to stretch her legs, and to think. She had a horrible feeling that she'd done a stupid thing by allowing Nance to stay the night. She ran her hand round the back of her neck, wishing she'd changed into something cooler before setting out.

There was a dim light on inside the café, though the blinds were down over the windows and the card on the door said 'Closed'.

Jeremy rapped on the door. Big Jason let them in. 'I was just about giving you up.'

'Sorry. There's a lot going on.'

'Not to worry.' Nothing much seemed to disturb Mr Jason. Surely he was as innocent as Jeremy? The big man hefted a black plastic bag over the counter. 'Odds and sods, rescued from the skip. The landlord's got new furniture being delivered tomorrow and reckons to let the place again, double the rent, by the end of the week.'

Jeremy nodded his thanks. 'I was sorry about the piano.'

'Well, he's not replacing that, I can tell you. Says he isn't having any more musicians in his place. Too much trouble. Now, there's a whole slew of mail.' Jason thrust a clutch of letters at Jeremy. 'I threw away most of the junk, but hadn't the time to go through everything properly.'

'Ah.' Jeremy beamed, selecting and opening just one envelope. 'The contract. Celia will be pleased.'

'Who's Celia?' enquired the big man.

'Don't ask,' said Bea, leaning against the counter. For two pins, she'd fall down and never get up again.

Jeremy yelped. 'And another! I must ring her . . . though I suppose it's a bit late tonight to disturb her.'

'Congratulations,' said Bea. And to Mr Jason, 'Did the police collect the big plastic bag the kidnappers used on Jeremy?'

Mr Jason looked blank. 'I haven't seen it recently . . . I wonder where . . .? It's possible the girl who stood in for me today may have . . . I'll have to have a look around for it.' He turned to Jeremy. 'Have you got a place to stay for tonight, because I could maybe get you into a friend's place, runs a B & B out Earls Court way.'

'No, thanks. All fixed up.' Jeremy was leafing through his letters, tearing some open, smiling at some, wincing at the bills.

'We mustn't keep you any longer,' said Bea. 'Thank you, Mr Jason. You've been just great.'

'A friend in need,' said Jeremy, trying and failing to make a tidy bundle of his mail. Bea took them off him and told him to carry the plastic bag containing his belongings instead.

Oliver had drawn up a little way along the road, where it was just possible for another car to squeeze past. 'It's getting dark. Where's Piers living now? The last I heard he was living near the Tower of London.'

'He's in Earls Court now. I'll direct you.'

There was nowhere to park outside Piers' place, either. Oliver said he'd drive around, be back in ten minutes or so. Bea guided Jeremy across the pavement and used the door phone to let Piers know they'd arrived. Up the stairs. Up and up.

Piers met them at the top. He was on his mobile phone, talking to someone, preoccupied. 'Come in, come in. Be with you in a minute. Make yourself at home – but I may have to go out in a while. The settee's quite comfortable, bathroom over there. Turn the telly on if you like. Sorry there's no food.'

Whoever he was talking to snapped off the connection. Piers looked at his phone, laughed, shook his head. 'Well, it seems I'm not seeing her this evening after all. Do you fancy a jar or two before turning in, Jeremy?'

The sitting-room-cum-studio was furnished in minimalist fashion, but the settee and deep armchairs looked comfortable.

Jeremy dropped his things on the floor. 'Don't mind if I do. Nice and quiet here. Thanks, Mrs Abbot.'

'See you in the morning.'

Down the stairs. Her knees protested. She was getting a tension headache. She waited on the pavement, and after a while Oliver drew up in the car. She got in. 'Home, sweet home. I hope. Oliver, I've done something stupid, letting that woman stay, haven't I?'

'Don't know what else you could have done. You have to admire her, in a way . . . Oh, I thought you might like to know, I found out why CJ shoved Jeremy on to you. CJ's scheduled to be an expert witness in a trial in which Eunice is appearing for the defence. He thought there might have been a conflict of interest, so wanted you to get Jeremy off his back.'

'How like him to shove his problem my way. Wretched man. I'll make him treat me to an evening at the theatre when this is over.'

It was getting dark, but no cooler. She felt hot and sticky. How long till she could get under the shower? Oliver turned into their street. There were no parking places left. Max's car was accounting for one, of course.

Oliver double-parked in the road near their house. 'You'd better hop out and I'll drive around, find a place to leave the car. I'll check the agency door downstairs when I get back.'

'I'll do it. I'm not that keen to face our latest visitor.'

'I've a feeling the security lights on the outside stairs may have been knocked out by the fire.'

'Point taken.' She opened the glove compartment on the dashboard and rescued the wind-up torch they kept there. She got out and stretched, wished a breeze might spring up. Sultry was the word for it. Or torrid.

There were lights on in the sitting room. Maggie usually drew the blinds in the dusk. Or Bea did. Ms Butt obviously hadn't thought to do it. Oh well. They'd all had a tiring day.

She made her way round the ruined bay tree in its pot, to the head of the steps leading down to the agency. Ugh, the smell of burned petrol . . .

As she stood there, feeling for her house keys in her handbag, one of the sitting room windows above her was thrown open. She looked up and glimpsed the silhouette of a man. And over-laying the smell of burned petrol, the unmistakable scent of a good cigar.

The scent of a cigar. She remembered . . . two nights ago Jeremy had been kidnapped and shoved into a white van. Bea had opened the door of the van to find out what was the matter with the driver and had smelt . . . the scent of a good cigar. Fresh cigar.

Stale cigar smoke is horrible. It clings to carpets and curtains and . . . clothing.

The man who'd killed Jonno in the van must have been smoking a cigar not long before.

The man at the window was smoking a cigar now. A man with broad shoulders, a man who moved easily, looking out down the road, and then drawing the curtains. He'd looked out, but he hadn't looked down. He hadn't seen her.

No one she knew smoked cigars. No one in her house smoked.

Alarm bells.

There was an intruder in the house with Ms Annie Butt. Friend or foe?

Ouch. Probably foe, because the figure at the window reminded her of the man who'd killed O'Dare, the photographer.

Maggie . . . where was Maggie? Had she gone to stay the night with a friend? Or invited someone in to join her? Bea fervently hoped she was out.

Panic. No, mustn't panic. Keep calm.

Pray.

Dear Lord, dear Lord . . . panic stations here! Help me! Tell me what to do.

When he'd found a parking space for the car, Oliver would walk straight back into the house. And so would Max.

A motorbike puttered to a stop in the street and was hauled on to its rest, parking between two cars at the kerb. Friend or foe?

Oh, nonsense; she was getting paranoid.

Still . . . she felt with her foot for the next step down, and the next. It might be wise to take shelter in the shadows until she knew for certain what was going on. The steps were gritty under her feet. She put out her hand to steady herself. The stone of the wall was gritty, too. The stench of the fire was all around her now, disguising the scent of the cigar.

The front door opened above her, and she held her breath.

She heard heavy footsteps climb the steps to the front door. Which meant . . .

'Well?' A man's voice. Deep.

'She took him off with her. I tried to follow but lost them in traffic.'

Did she know that voice? She rather thought she did, but couldn't place it. The front door shut.

Her heart was going thump-thump.

Miss Butt wouldn't have let the man in. No way.

So, Maggie must have done. Let me think. Maggie had talked

about seeing if a friend would come round, or go out with her. Also, she'd wanted a pizza. It was possible she'd have phoned for one and trustingly opened the door when someone rang the bell – and it might not have been a pizza delivery man who called.

But no: Maggie knew better than that. Or did she?

Suppose Maggie had answered the door and he'd forced his way in? But then, what had he done with Maggie? And/or her friend?

Bea pressed both hands to her head. Think, Bea, think!

There were two of them in her house, with Ms Annie Butt. How had they found the woman? Answer: they must have followed Annie from her flat. She thought she'd shaken them off, but she hadn't. Or perhaps they'd made a lucky guess and decided to check Bea out?

What were they proposing to do with Madam Badger?

That was simple; they were going to kill her, of course. Bea stifled hysteria. She did hope they weren't going to use a knife again. It was so hard to get blood out of the upholstery – or the carpet.

She told herself to keep calm. Think, woman! THINK! No, pray.

Dear Lord above, help! There's Oliver coming back, and Max, and I think I'm next on the list because I know too much. And so does Jeremy – and that's why they've been after him. No, it's not just that he knows too much, is it? He's been elected scape-goat for everything, but that will only work if they can find him and kill him.

If they can rig it that he commits suicide, then everyone will think he committed the murders after all – perhaps with an accomplice – and then committed suicide when the police started to close in on him. And the police investigation will end there.

What am I to do? Time's running out. Help!

I must go up and stand in the street and stop Oliver and Max going back into the house. Yes, I can do that. But, what about Maggie?

Somehow I've got to get her and her friend – if there is one – out.

But first – breathe deeply – I must check that she's not gone out for the evening.

Bea let herself down to the bottom of the steps, to the small area outside the agency door where Maggie's bay tree had once stood. She took out her mobile phone. Thank God for mobile phones.

She switched it on but in her agitation couldn't make out the numbers. Where were her reading glasses? In her handbag. She got them out. Hands trembling.

Mobile phone battery may be running down. Too faint. Don't fade out on me!

Use the torch. Wind up the torch, which needs two hands, so put phone back into handbag while . . .

Ah, in the light of the torch she could read the names she needed.

Maggie's mobile number. The phone rang and rang. No reply.

Maggie always kept her phone switched on, even at night. Nothing short of death or major injury parted Maggie from her phone. So, she was not in a position to answer it, and the only explanation must be that the killer had taken it off her. Which meant that she must still be in the house. Maggie was an innocent bystander, as was her friend, but it would be stupid to hope the killer would spare them once they'd finished off Ms Butt . . . which they might already have done.

Don't panic!

Try Oliver. Oliver would have his phone with him. He might still be driving around looking for a parking place and therefore wouldn't pick up straight away. Oliver, pick up! No. She'd been switched to answerphone. Leave a message. What to say? Keep your voice low, Bea. Remember that the sitting room window above you is open.

'Oliver, don't come back to the house. I'm going to try to get everyone out. The door to the agency rooms is glowing with heat, but I think I can manage to put the fire out if I can only get in and find the other extinguisher.'

Her hands were shaking. She'd promised Ms Butt that she wouldn't call the police, and she hadn't. Maybe it was stupid of her, but she'd given her word and she was stiff-necked that way.

Oliver would surely use his head when he picked up the message. He'd think how stupid it was of Bea to try to fight a fire by herself, and he'd ring the Fire Brigade. Wouldn't he?

Max next. She fumbled the call. Made it. Max was on the phone. She left the same message. Turned the phone off.

Right. She'd done what she could for her two men. What could she do for Maggie?

In a careless moment the torch flew out of her hand and fell on the floor with a clunk!

She froze. Would they hear that, inside the house?

She bent down, trying to find it. Where had it gone? Oh, let it be. She took off her reading glasses and stowed them and her phone away.

Right. Now, to find out where Maggie was and try to get her and her friend out of the house. She fished out her keys and unlocked the door into the agency rooms.

Something was wrong. There were lights on in the main room.

Surely she'd checked that they'd all been turned off that evening before they went out? Yes, she was sure she had. She'd double-checked that all the lights downstairs were off before she left . . . and now the overhead lights were on.

All was quiet. The door leading into the cloakroom was ajar, and there was no light on inside that, but the door into her office was open and there was a light on there. Someone had definitely been in these rooms since she left.

Moving as quietly as she could, she sidled through the main room to her office. It was empty. Her computer was dark. Nothing on her desk looked as if it had been disturbed.

No Maggie; well, that was a relief . . . wasn't it? The curtains at the French windows remained closely drawn, and the grille over the windows was as she'd left it, locked tight against the night outside.

There were faint sounds of movement from above. A man shouting. Not a voice that she recognized. A woman keened.

Maggie? Was Maggie upstairs and being tortured for some reason? The idea sent shivers down Bea's back. She hesitated, her hand going to the phone; she could ring the police.

No, she'd alerted Oliver and Max to a problem; they could do that for her. Meanwhile, her job was to locate Maggie and get her out of there.

Bea stilled her breathing. She needed a weapon and didn't know where to find one. If only Dahlia hadn't taken the knife away with her! It had been a small knife; wickedly sharp. But small. Probably not much good against her current visitors. Two big strong men could easily have taken it off her.

She must rely on native wit . . . and the fact that Oliver and Max would soon be back.

Now, how to find Maggie? She turned off the light in her office, pulled back the curtains and unlocked the grille over the French windows. She didn't want anyone who might be standing near the windows on the first floor to look out and see light streaming on to the garden, because that would alert them to the fact that someone had entered the agency rooms below.

There was plenty of light spilling out from the windows of the kitchen and sitting room above, but in the spot where she stood right up against the house, it was dark. She felt for the first rung of the wrought iron staircase that climbed from the garden to the first floor, set her hand against the brick of the wall at her side, and inched her way up.

At the top of the stairs there was a balcony which gave access to both the kitchen and the sitting room.

She stopped with her eyes at floor level, so that it would be difficult for anyone to see her if they chanced to look out. The kitchen was to her left. She looked into that first.

The kitchen lights were on, but no . . . No one was there. No Maggie. She must be in the sitting room. Bea went down on her hands and knees and crawled across to the other window . . .

And bumped into something. A carry-on case and handbag. Annie Butt's? Why had she put them there? Out of sight. Hidden from view. Bea tried to follow Annie's reasoning.

Annie must have been alerted in some way to the arrival of the intruders – how on earth had they got in? Well, leaving that aside for the present – Annie, fearing the worst, had quickly thrust her belongings out through the French windows on to the staircase, tucking them in against the wall, out of sight of anyone standing inside the room. She was dressed in imitation of Bea. Might she try to pass herself off as Bea to the intruders? The presence of her handbag and case would have given the game away, so she'd thrust them out of sight. Yes. That sounded right.

Loud voices came from the sitting room, and then the unmistakable sound of a slap. Who was the victim; Annie or Maggie?

Why didn't the cavalry come to the rescue?

A nasty thought. Suppose the intruders had double-locked or

even bolted the front door? How would the cavalry be able to get in?

Keep calm, Bea. The most important thing was to make it easy for any possible rescuers to get back into the house, which meant she must make sure the front door was on the latch.

Bea crawled back down the stairs . . . oh, her tights . . . never mind! She slipped back into her office, shutting and locking the grille behind her, and closing the curtains. All must seem to be as it had been before she returned, which meant she must put the overhead light on again. She stumbled across her office and turned it on.

Bright. Too bright. Oh.

She took out her bunch of keys again, went back through the main office, let herself out through the front door of the agency rooms, and with care trod the steps up to street level. She turned her key in the lock of the front door. Good; not double-locked nor bolted.

She let herself into the hall, taking care to leave the door on the latch so that any rescue party could get in easily.

Cigar smoke. How crass to smoke a cigar in someone else's house. When a man smoked a cigar in the same room as you it smelled heavenly, but next day the stink . . . ugh! And it clung to the curtains and the upholstery like nobody's business.

The man she'd seen at the window came out of the sitting room to confront her. 'About time, too. We were wondering if you'd got lost.'

Tall, dark, broad-shouldered; handsome in a fleshy sort of way, and yes, smoking a good cigar. He projected barely contained anger. And excitement.

She didn't know him from Adam, but his silhouette resembled that of the man she seen kill O'Dare.

She put outrage into her voice. 'Who are you?' said Bea. 'And what are you doing in my house?' She darted her eyes around. No Maggie. What did that mean? What had they done with her?

'Ah, but is it your house, that's what I'd like to know?' He grasped her forearm and drew her into the sitting room.

'How dare you!' said Bea, trying to release her arm from his grip. 'And why . . . Well, hello. What's Mr Jason doing here?'

The café owner was standing by the window, wearing leathers. So it was he who had come by motorbike? It fitted his personality. She'd wondered several times if he'd been playing both ends against the middle. His presence here indicated that he'd stopped playing piggy in the middle and was now on the Big Bad Wolf's team.

Bad, bad news.

NINETEEN

The man with the cigar shook her arm. 'Jason, who is this?'

'Let go of me!' Bea cried out, for he was hurting her.

'That's the agency woman that took Jeremy in,' said Mr Jason. 'Mrs Abbot.'

The man with the cigar swung Bea round to face the settee, where Ms Butt sat, composed and serene. Her face looked puffy. Had someone been hitting her? 'Then who is this?'

'I'm Bea Abbot,' said Ms Butt. 'And that woman is an impostor.' Her voice sounded strange. Blood stained a corner of her mouth.

'What!' Bea was startled into a laugh. She darted her eyes around the room but Maggie was nowhere to be seen. Wherever could she be? God forbid; had they already killed her?

No, please God, not that!

She tried to wrench herself free, but the man held on to her. She could feel the power in his fingers. She could feel his anger, too.

He swung her round to sit in a chair opposite Ms Butt. The woman was still pretending to be Bea. Not a bad idea, except that there were now two of them in the room, and one of them was about to be unmasked as an impostor.

Time was running out. Bea risked a glance at the clock. How long since she'd phoned Oliver? How long was it going to take for him to act? Pray God he didn't try to get into the house to deal with the 'fire' himself, because if so they were both going to die tonight.

The man with the cigar snatched Bea's handbag away from her and upended it on the coffee table. House keys. Credit cards, diary, a bank statement; all gave her name.

'Finally, the truth. So this is the famous Mrs Abbot!' He put his cigar down on the edge of the mantelpiece and advanced his face to within six inches of Bea's nose, projecting violence. 'I told you not to interfere, didn't I? But now you have, I'm not inclined to dilly dally. Understood?'

Bea forced herself not to wince. 'What is it you want?' Waste time, Bea. Every second counts.

'First, where have you been? The lady opposite says you went out for a meal. Is that right?'

'Yes, I wanted something hot and all we'd got was cold stuffs.'

He slapped her. 'Tell the truth. You took our friend Jeremy Waite somewhere. Get on the phone. Get him back here, now.'

'Can't. Don't know his new phone number.'

He shook her. 'Where is he?'

'He went home to his wife.'

'Unlikely.' He got out one of the latest phones and pressed buttons. 'Eunice, you there? Has the little man returned to base? No. I didn't think so. He's gone missing, but we'll get him, never fear.'

So Eunice had been in on this all along? The two-faced, lying, humpbacked, crooked toad.

The man switched off his phone and leaned over Bea again. 'If you want to leave this room alive, you're going to have to cooperate. Understand?'

Bea remained silent. Praying. *Please Lord, what next?*

He pulled up another chair and sat knee to knee with Bea. 'My patience is running out. I don't like hitting a woman, but I'm prepared to make an exception where my personal safety is concerned. Where is Jeremy Waite?'

'I've no idea.' This was the exact truth, as Piers had suggested going out for a drink and Jeremy had agreed. They could be anywhere, in any pub or restaurant in the neighbourhood.

'Wrong answer. Jason, hold her still for me.'

Strong hands took hold of Bea's upper arms and held her back against her chair.

The man with the cigar slapped her with his open palm. She felt her neck snap. He hit her again. And again. Again. She tried to fend off his blows. She tried to kick, but he was too close to her knees. She began to pray. *Dear Lord, help! Do I tell them? No, because he's still going to kill me!*

How much of this could she take?

Mr Jason released her all of a sudden. 'What was that?'

The cigar man suspended operations.

Jason looked out of the window. 'Didn't you hear that? The doorbell. You said you were expecting someone else?'

Not Max or Oliver; pray not either of them. Fire Brigade, please!

'Let me see.' The man abandoned his position in front of Bea and strode over to throw up the window and look out. 'Yes, it's the right one. Let him in, will you?'

While Jason went to the front door, the man with the cigar returned to Bea. 'You hoped someone would come to your rescue, did you? I saw you look at the clock. Well, forget it. One of us has been getting very close to you and knows all your secrets. Want to guess who it is?'

Horrors, did he mean . . .? No, he couldn't mean CJ! No, he couldn't. Impossible. Or, who else? She couldn't think. Someone close to her? Maggie, no. Oliver, no. This was ridiculous.

Mr Jason brought the man into the room. A stranger. A total stranger. A well-dressed, willowy man with pale hair and an anxious expression. Bea sagged with relief.

'You recognize him, do you?'

She shook her head.

'Let me introduce you. Howard Butcher, of Holland and Butcher. He's been paying blackmail to Ms Butt for eighteen months. We met at a rather boozy reception and he confided his little problem to me, not realizing that I was in the same boat. He was delighted to hear that something could be done about it, and when he learned that you were poking your nose into our affairs, he helped us by monitoring your movements.'

Through Ianthe? And much good that had done him or her. Except . . . had Ianthe kept the keys to the agency when she left? Bea had a horrible feeling that she had. She remembered Ianthe throwing taunts at her and at Oliver, and Oliver looking in her bag for a memory stick, which she hadn't got . . . and both he and Bea had completely forgotten to ask Ianthe for her keys after she left.

So, Ianthe had given her keys to Mr Cigar, which was how he'd managed to get into the house; not through the front door, but through the agency rooms. He'd switched on all the lights below, so as to find his way to the inside stairs. Ms Butt must have heard him moving around below and thrust her belongings out through the window so that she could pass herself off as lady of the house.

Mr Cigar then had Ms Butt at his mercy while he awaited his accomplices: Mr Butcher for one, and Jason for the other. Jason had been told to bring Jeremy along, but had arrived empty-handed.

Bea thought: memo to self. Must get a lockable door put in at the bottom of the stairs.

Mr Butcher was patting his forehead and neck with a hand-kerchief. He looked as if he spent more time in front of a mirror than working out at a gym. He glanced from one to the other of the two women and did a double-take. 'Which one's which? Why are there two of them? What's going on here?'

'That's what I'm just about to find out,' said the leader of the pack. 'This one is Mrs Abbot, the one you wanted to do business with. That one over there is the cause of all our problems. Want to take a turn at getting the information out of her?'

Mr Butcher was not up for confrontation, and he stayed where he was. It looked to Bea as if he were giving at the knees. His fingers strayed to his mouth. Not a man used to physical violence . . . but none the less dangerous. 'Has she got my file? Where's Waite? You said he'd be here. You said we could use him as a scapegoat, so where is he?'

'That's what I'm about to find out,' said Mr Cigar. 'Want to watch? It won't be pretty, but one of them will tell me in the end.'

Jason shook his ponderous head. 'I went right through every-thing at her flat, including her car. She'd cleaned the place out. No files. She must have everything on her laptop. I watched her leave with it. She had it with her on the tube.'

Mr Butcher approached Ms Butt, making an effort to play the part of a bully. 'What have you done with my file, eh? Tell me, or it will be the worse for you!'

Ms Butt stared straight ahead, ignoring him. The woman had courage.

Bea knew where the woman's handbag and carry-on was, but she hadn't seen the laptop. She had every confidence in Angie's ability. If the woman had dropped it off somewhere – perhaps put it into storage overnight? – it was not going to be found easily.

How long before the cavalry arrived?

Mr Butcher bit his thumbnail, dancing on his toes with impatience. 'Make her tell! Time's running out! I thought we'd be ready to move out by now. It's dark enough, isn't it? Find Waite, fill them all up with gin, take them for a drive in the car and set it alight somewhere . . . then he'll be blamed for everything. But we've got to have those files first.'

Bea repressed a shudder.

Someone opened the front door and cried out, 'Halloo! It's me!'

Bea shivered. Which of her men had walked into the trap?

'Hello, hello.' Max appeared in the doorway, a bottle of wine in his hand. He'd obviously dined well. Perhaps too well. He was flushed and happily smiling. 'I'd recognize the scent of that cigar of yours anywhere, Charles. Didn't realize you knew my mother. How are you?' He stood in the doorway, looking owlishly around. 'You having a party, Mother?'

The three conspirators froze.

At long last, nee-nah, nee-nah. The cavalry had arrived.

The Fire Brigade, to be exact.

They'd have to double-park, which would stall all the traffic.

Jason made for the front window. 'They've stopped right outside. There's no way out back through the garden, is there? What do we do now?'

'Keep calm.' Mr Cigar, aka Sir Charles, was holding on to his temper. Just. 'It won't be for us. They'll go away in a minute.'

Max waved his bottle around. 'Did the fire start up again, Mother?'

Bea said, 'Don't you ever listen to your phone messages?'

The front doorbell pealed and was pushed open. Heavy foot-steps came tramping through the hall. 'Hello, there? In trouble again, I hear?'

'Come in!' cried Bea.

The chief fireman and one of his men filled the doorway with their bulk.

Bea pointed to Sir Charles. 'It was he who set the fire earlier. And his accomplices. No, not the one flourishing a bottle. That's my son.'

Sir Charles gaped at the newcomers. Bea could almost see the thoughts thundering through his head. He'd recognized Max, as

Max had recognized him. He'd attacked Bea, the householder. Jeremy was nowhere to be seen.

The game was up.

She could see his shoulders bunch. He hurled himself at the doorway, in a desperate attempt to get past the firemen and escape.

'Hang about!' The firemen caught him and held him fast.

Mr Butcher sank into a chair. Was he going to burst into tears?

A scrape and a shout. Jason had jumped out of the front window, not realizing or not remembering the drop below.

Aaaargh. A nice, long, juicy scream. He'd hurt himself. What a shame!

Shouts from below as the other members of the fire brigade went to Jason's rescue.

Max was trying to shadow-box. Yes, he'd had far too much to drink, hadn't he? 'Where . . .? Who . . .? What's going on here?'

Freed from constraint, Bea pushed herself to her feet. She was trembling but able to function, after a fashion. Max was more than half seas over, waving his bottle around. She took the bottle off him and pushed him towards the settee. He collapsed, eyes at half mast.

Sir Charles was trying to fight his way out of the firemen's grip. Not that it would do him any good. With Max's identification, he must have realized any possible parliamentary career was over. But he was not the sort to give in easily, and he seemed determined to fight his way out of the situation. He threw himself forwards, and then back, dragging the firemen with him.

Out of the corner of her eye Bea saw a caramel-coloured skirt flick out through the French windows at the back of the room and disappear on to the balcony. Annie could retrieve her belongings but couldn't go any further for there was no back way out of the garden in a terraced house.

A scream. Sir Charles sank his teeth into the fireman's hand on his arm. The man yelled and released his grip. Sir Charles turned on the second fireman and kicked him where it would hurt most.

Sir Charles swayed, mouth bloodied. The way to the door and freedom was clear.

Bea said, 'Oh, really!' She shifted her grip on the bottle of wine in her hand and swung at Sir Charles's jaw with all her might. Thunk!

His eyes rolled up in his head, and he staggered back against the wall, toppling an occasional table on the way. Which smashed. What a pity. It had been her long-dead mother's.

Bea stood over him with the bottle raised for one more strike. 'Just give me an excuse and I'll smash your nose in! For Josie, and Philip James, and John O'Dare.'

As the two firemen gasped, Oliver came through the door, not a hair out of place. 'I see you've managed without me. I rang for an ambulance, as Mr Jason appears to have broken both his legs. Oh, and the police, too. Is that your killer? DI Durrell will be delighted, won't he?'

Bea grinned. *Good for you, Oliver. At least you had the sense to interpret my phone message and act on it. And I didn't break my promise to Ms Butt about calling the police.*

'Hello, hello? What's going on here?'

Jeremy? Whatever was he doing here?

Piers had also arrived and was looking over Jeremy's shoulder. 'Never a dull moment. Bea, are you all right? We were both hungry, and Jeremy remembered Maggie had made him some sandwiches but he'd forgotten to pick them up, so we thought we might pop along and see if they were still going. Do I recognize . . .? Sir Charles?' Piers' voice tailed away. 'Oh, so the rumours about his extra-curricular activities were true, were they? Bea, we'll catch up with you later. Jeremy, we're not needed here. Let's get out to the kitchen and see what we can find to eat.'

This was all TOO MUCH. Bea sagged against the wall, and then shot upright. For where was Maggie? 'Oliver, where's Maggie?'

'Didn't she tell you? She rang a friend while you were showing our visitor how to work the telly and arranged to go out to the cinema with him.'

'But she's turned off her mobile!'

'Her friend insists that she does, whenever they go to the pictures.'

Thank you, God. Thank you.

Mr Butcher sobbed into his hands. He was no help at all, was he! A man of straw, who would give away Sir Charles to the police as soon as pressure was put upon him.

The chief fireman got to his feet with care, panting. His mate was groaning, holding on to his hand, which was dripping blood on to the carpet.

Bea was annoyed. Blood on the carpet . . . she could do without that!

Monday night to Tuesday morning

It was a long night.

Explanations.

Cups of tea. Sandwiches.

DI Durrell arrived, heavy-eyed but sharp of brain. He summoned more police.

Everyone else became heavy-eyed from lack of sleep.

Sir Charles was taken off in an ambulance with a police guard. A different ambulance took Mr Jason and his broken leg away; also under police guard. They fitted the fireman with his bitten hand in with them. Mr Butcher was arrested and removed by the police.

Statements. The rest of the firemen removed themselves.

Maggie returned, bright-eyed, from the cinema, to order pizzas all round. Max snored peacefully on the settee in the sitting room. Bea found a spare duvet and covered him with it.

The police finally departed. Oliver and Maggie went up to bed in their own rooms. Jeremy returned to the spare room. Piers insisted on dossing down on the new Put-U-Up on the top floor.

Finally, the house was quiet. Bea looked at the chaos in the sitting room and decided she would think about all that on the morrow. Max snored peacefully away.

Dawn was breaking, not with a crash, but a sly peep over the horizon. Bea made sure all the windows and doors were shut and locked.

She went down the stairs to the agency rooms, which were grey and full of shadows. She turned off the light in her office, opened the curtains, unlocked and drew back the grille and opened the French windows on to the garden.

It must have been a long, tense wait in the garden for Annie Butt, but she didn't show herself at once.

Bea yawned widely, remarked that she needed to freshen up, and made her way back through her office and the main room to the cloakroom at the street end of the house. There she had a good wash and brush up.

Did she hear someone leave by the agency front door? Perhaps. She certainly wasn't going to look.

She consulted her watch. Too late to go to bed.

She returned to her office and there on her desk were a strange memory stick and a tiny coil from a recording machine.

Somewhere on the journey from her flat to Bea's house, Annie had got rid of her laptop. She'd probably stashed it in a locker at a station somewhere, so that she could retrieve it later. But just in case she lost it, she'd backed up everything on memory sticks, which could be conveniently stowed in her handbag, or tucked into the tip of a shoe in her carry-on case.

So now she'd made Bea a present of the information she needed. Annie Butt paid her dues, didn't she?

Bea started up her computer and fed in the material on the memory stick. Good. Four files: on Sir Charles, Mr Butcher, Jeremy Waite and Eunice Barrow. Photographs of meetings, photographs of lots of crisp fifty pound notes in sequence, fresh from the bank and therefore traceable back to source. Nicely done.

Bea set the printer going and found some plastic folders to put the evidence in.

She played the tape. Recognizable voices, Ms Butt's taking enquiries about framing a woman's husband for divorce. The other woman on the tape must be Eunice Barrow. Good.

DI Durrell would be pleased.

She walked out into the garden. A slight breeze stirred the air. Perhaps it would not be quite so hot tomorrow . . . today.

Five o'clock and the birds were singing their hearts out. Fly away, Nance or Annie or whatever your name may be. Fly away. And hopefully start a new life in another country in some profession which doesn't involve entrapment and blackmail.

At six o'clock Bea left her bedroom, having showered, made herself up and put on clean clothes.

Max was still snoring. She could hear him from the landing. She didn't disturb him. She woke Jeremy and told him to report downstairs in ten minutes.

Oliver, who slept as lightly as a cat, joined them in the kitchen, where Bea was making some strong black coffee. 'What's up?'

She handed Jeremy the folders containing the information Ms Butt had left for him. He looked at its contents and winced.

She said, 'If you can find your house keys, Jeremy, we're going to pay a visit to Eunice now, before breakfast. With any luck we'll catch her off balance. I'm taking my little recorder and a camera along, just in case. I don't suppose she's at her best much before nine in the morning, is she?'

Jeremy was hollow-eyed. 'Neither am I. I'm not sure I can do this.'

'Celia would like to live in your house, wouldn't she?' It was a master stroke, because he knew, and Bea knew, that Celia would love it.

Oliver said, 'I'll drive.'

At seven o'clock Oliver turned the car into the driveway of a spacious, five-bedroomed house in a quiet, leafy street less than a mile away. Jeremy used his keys to let them into a large, square hall.

A clock ticked. A man's jacket hung over the newel post at the bottom of the stairs. An alarm clock went off upstairs. A radio came on. A man who looked to be in his late thirties – someone who worked out a lot to judge by his physique – came out of a bedroom on the first floor, yawning. Bea turned her little recorder on and got her camera ready. Goodie, goodie. She hadn't expected the lover to be on the premises, so this was a bonus.

'Good morning,' said Jeremy. 'Remember me?'

The man gaped. 'What . . .? How did you . . .?'

A dishevelled fortyish blonde wearing a hip-length nightie came out on to the landing and drew in her breath. 'But you're supposed to be . . . How come you're not . . .?'

'Dead?' said Jeremy. 'Not everyone's wishes come true. Does your new lover there know what you've been up to?'

Bea gleefully snapped the pair of them with her little camera.

The toy boy – well, he looked too young to be a match for Eunice – didn't know what to make of this. 'What? Who . . . Eunice? What's going on? You told me Jeremy was wanted by the police for murder.'

'Far from it,' said Jeremy. 'I have been helping them solve a couple of murders, though. Eunice is implicated in at least one of them.'

'No!' Eunice wasn't going to cave in without a fight. 'It's not true. He's making it all up. He was sacked by his school for interfering with an under-age girl, here, under my very roof!'

'I've been cleared of all that. And it's under *my* very roof,' said Jeremy. 'Not yours. Remember our prenuptial agreement? You didn't want me making any claims on you, and I'm not going to do so. Likewise you can't make any claims on me. I'm back now, and I'm staying. So take your lover and your daughter, pack what you can and get out. I'll send the rest on.'

'Don't be ridiculous! The law is on my side and—'

'Mr Butcher, Sir Charles and Mr Jason are now in custody and will be charged today with various offences, including murder. Sir Charles is not talking, but Mr Butcher is very vocal, especially about how he met you at a society function and exchanged confidences about this and that. He doesn't want to go down for murder, you see, whereas Sir Charles definitely will. Besides which, Ms Butt recorded all the details of your attempts to frame me for having sex with Josie.'

'Eunice, tell me it's not true!'

'Idiot! Don't you see he's trying to scare you? Well, I don't scare that easily.'

'I suggest you get some clothes on and start packing. Oh, and while you're at it, you'd better wake Clarissa and tell her to start packing, too. And if she's still got the keys to my car, she'd better let me have them. Now!'

Bea was full of admiration. She hadn't thought the little man had so much steel in him. Then she remembered that he'd risen to the occasion surprisingly well on various occasions recently.

She wondered if there was plenty of food in the house, because he'd undoubtedly need feeding when he was through with his display as Master of the House.

She'd better remind him to get a locksmith to change the locks on his doors, too, before Eunice thought of it. And to change the locks at her place, too. A woman's work was never done . . .

TWENTY

Tuesday morning

DI Durrell wandered in, saying, 'I understand you've been collecting criminal cases for me to look at, but I'm not to ask how you came by them?'

'Ask me no questions,' said Bea, beyond exhaustion, 'and I'll tell you no lies. Or rather, I'll tell you in confidence if you like, but I'm not doing so officially.'

'Annie Kelly, I assume?'

'Who? What . . .? Is that the name of the woman who masterminded the Badgers? I've never known what to call her.'

'You told me the actor was killed in the foyer of her flats. Under the circumstances it was easy to find a body which matched. It was the man you called Mr Toupee. Shocked residents identified him as one Philip Kelly, who lived in a flat on the top floor with his sister Annie and their niece Josie. Annie Kelly was supposed to be some kind of businesswoman, as she seems to have kept office hours and held the lease to the flat. Neighbours say she occasionally invited one of her numerous family to live with them for a while. The place has been swept clean, no paperwork, no computers, no cameras. No sign of any pretty young girl, either. Presumably Annie Kelly told their latest protégée to make herself scarce when "uncle" was found dead.'

'Not real relations, were they?'

'It seems Annie and Philip were brother and sister, yes. Josie was their niece, or second cousin, can't be sure which as yet. The other girl . . . probably not.'

'Annie Kelly.' Bea tested the name out. 'It suits her.'

'So what have you got for me?'

'The files Annie left for me. They're downstairs in my office, under lock and key. Care for some coffee? And I think there's still some biscuits in the tin now Jeremy's left us.'

'No, I'm all right for the moment, thank you.'

She led the way down the stairs, past the carpenters who were

even now installing a stout door at the foot of the interior staircase, and into the agency rooms, where Celia presided over a
reduced, and somewhat subdued, team.

Once in her office, she handed over the four files.

'That first one is for Howard Butcher; there's a photocopy of
an article about him in a trade journal, featuring his wife and
four children. Photographs of him in bed with Josie, showing
him enjoying himself. Apparently, he liked to be spanked before
he was able to perform. Here's a photo of him handing over a
packet to Mr Toupee in a pub. Photographs of crisp new fifty-
pound notes with consecutive serial numbers. I think they must
have photographed the notes so that the serial numbers could be
traced back to him. A perfect way of making sure their victim
could be identified. She – Annie – must have had some method
of laundering the cash later.'

The DI grunted. 'Howard Butcher's got himself a good lawyer
and is cooperating with us to avoid a murder charge.'

'I don't think he did actually commit any of the murders, do
you?'

'He says he's as much of a victim as Snow White. Puts everything on Sir Charles, who, according to him, enticed him off the
straight and narrow. Oh, and he was totally led astray, he says,
by your ex-manageress Ianthe who is a snake in woman's clothing.
It seems she approached him when she first got the job with you,
with a scheme to enrich herself. She knew Holland and Butcher
were going to be looking for a partnership with another domestic
employment agency, and she came up with the idea that she'd
persuade you to sell to them, in exchange for her job and a nice
lump sum. He says he thought she was joking, only to find out
Ianthe was serious.'

'And if you believe that . . .'

'Quite. Mr Butcher says Ianthe kept ringing him up with
progress reports on how she was easing your path to leave the
agency. He says he was beginning to take her seriously and
wondering what to do about it, when she rang to say you'd taken
Jeremy Waite in, and wasn't that a terrible thing to do, him being
a murderer and all. She seemed to think that if the police found
out you'd got Jeremy Waite, that they'd arrest you for conspiracy,
which meant you'd sell quickly, and at any price.'

'What nonsense.'

'True. But she seems to have believed it. We've had her in for questioning, and you wouldn't believe the venom that she spat out. She hates you because you found her out. She is not wholly sane, I think. She boasts that she gave her keys to Mr Butcher, so that he could raid your premises to flush Jeremy out.'

Bea shook her head in bewilderment. 'And did Mr Butcher agree to do that?'

'He says not. He says he thought she was off her rocker, and it's true that the keys weren't on him when we arrested him.'

'Because he'd passed them on to Sir Charles?'

'Precisely. I've brought the keys with me, and with your permission I'll test them on your door here, just to make sure.'

'No can do. New locks everywhere. And bolts. But I had the foresight to ask the locksmith to let me keep the locks he took off. I've put them in plastic envelopes and tagged them. I've got them here in the safe.'

She handed them over. The inspector tested the old lock. Nodded. 'That's how Sir Charles managed to get into the house while you were taking Jeremy over to Piers' place.'

'Did he also pour petrol down the steps and set it alight?'

'No, that was Ianthe. She's proud of it, by the way. Exorcizing demons, she says. She says she's only sorry she hadn't still got the keys, or she'd have let herself in and poured petrol all over the desks and floor before dropping a match into it.'

Bea shuddered. 'Well, you'd better have the rest of the evidence. This next one is Jeremy Waite's file. Photos of him in bed with Josie. As you can see, not exactly convincing evidence of adultery. But what *is* convincing is a tape obtained by Ms Kelly of various phone conversations. This bit is of Eunice asking in a roundabout way of Annie – I think it's her, but can't be absolutely sure – if she knew how to obtain evidence for a divorce against someone, not named, but it's obviously Jeremy. Then more photographs of fifty pound notes, which I imagine you will be able to trace back to her. I really don't understand why Eunice didn't just tell Jeremy to get lost. Divorce him on grounds of incompatibility.'

A shrug. 'She saved herself the cost of a divorce. And, she wanted the house.'

'Humph. At least he's got that back, and a housekeeper-cum-third-wife-to-be as well. Are you going to proceed against Eunice?'

'Not sure. The Crown Prosecution people will have to look at the paperwork. My feeling is that even if she never comes to trial, the word will get about and it'll give her reputation a knock or two. And the last file, Mrs Abbot?'

'Sir Charles. A cutting from a trade paper, wife at Central Office, cuttings of newspaper reports on his failed attempts to get into Parliament. Photographs of him with Josie, which are not for the faint-hearted. He appears to have locked the door and enjoyed beating her, so the photos were taken through a window.'

The DI sighed. 'Nasty. He won't talk, you know. We've charged him with assaulting the fireman for a start, and with conspiracy to commit murder. He denies everything.'

'Won't Mr Butcher's testimony send him down?'

'And that of Mr Jason. He's singing sweetly, too. We found he was carrying a knife on him when he was taken to hospital, which is good for starters. He says he was seduced by Sir Charles, with promises of a hefty bribe, to help trace and deliver Jeremy Waite as and when required. He says he thought Sir Charles was only going to rough the little man up – and you can believe that or not as you choose. He's already asking if it would go easier with him if he told everything he knew about Sir Charles' doings.'

'Can you get Sir Charles for Josie's murder? And that of the photographer?'

'Circumstantial evidence only at present. Maybe forensics will come up with something. And if you would like to charge him with assaulting you . . .?'

'If it will help to keep him off the streets, yes.'

'And, looking on the bright side, I don't think his dear wife is going to be very understanding about all this, especially when she sees those photographs.'

'He frightened me. He projects force. A maddened bull, let loose in society. Ugh.'

'Look on the bright side. It's highly unlikely now that he'll ever be elected to Parliament, isn't it?'

In the autumn

It had been a dry summer, and the leaves were beginning to twist and twirl off the sycamore tree, spiralling down to earth. It was still warm.

The firm of Howard & Butcher had collapsed, but a buyer had been found for it, who was interested in discussing some sort of partnership with Bea.

A new manageress had been installed in her front office, Miss Brook and a part-timer were looking after Maggie, Oliver was back at university and Bea had taken some paperwork into the garden.

Maggie came out to join Bea in the garden, carrying her portable radio. 'A new entry into the charts.'

A woman's voice, backed by a group:

'You promised me . . . a life of ease.
You promised me . . . our love would last.
You promised me . . . we'd be together,
Till both our lives were past.
I asked how I'd repay you . . . for this precious gift of
*   love,*
And you answered – "with a kiss".

You promised me a kitchen . . . with a set of sliding
*   drawers.*
A penthouse with an outlook . . . a wedding with a ring.
You promised you would keep me . . . from all danger
*   and all harm.*
I asked how I'd repay you . . . and you answered – "with
*   a kiss".*

You brought me to this country, where the streets are
*   paved with rain.*
You took my childhood from me, and you sold me to your
*   friends.*
I asked how could you do this? And you answered – with
*   a blow.*

You promised me . . . a life of ease.
You promised me . . . our love would last.
Now I walk the streets of London . . . and other cities,
*   too.*
And I know there's no tomorrow . . . for the likes of me
*   or you.'*

The voice died away into a murmur.

'Mother Mary, pray for me.'

Silence. Maggie clicked off her radio and went back into the house.

Bea picked up her papers, but her eyes looked far away, swooping across London to where girls walked the streets, without hope. Like Josie.

She wished she could help them, but she didn't know how.

She could pray for them, though.

Dear Lord, have mercy . . .